On Mason Mountain

On Mason Mountain

Gary Kalter

Copyright © 2013 by Gary Kalter.

Library of Congress Control Number: 2013918537
ISBN: Hardcover 978-1-4931-1177-0
Softcover 978-1-4931-1176-3
Ebook 978-1-4931-1178-7

All rights reserved. No part of this book may be reproduced or transmitted in any form or by any means, electronic or mechanical, including photocopying, recording, or by any information storage and retrieval system, without permission in writing from the copyright owner.

This is a work of fiction. Names, characters, places and incidents either are the product of the author's imagination or are used fictitiously, and any resemblance to any actual persons, living or dead, events, or locales is entirely coincidental.

This book was printed in the United States of America.

Rev. date: 10/12/2013

To order additional copies of this book, contact:
Xlibris LLC
1-888-795-4274
www.Xlibris.com
Orders@Xlibris.com
142016

BOOK I

Chapter 1

2004

Michael Barnum sat on the USC bench. Down by two to UCLA, their biggest rival, the roar of over ten thousand fans rocked the stadium. Jack Diamond, the star point guard, brought the ball down the court for USC. He faked right and went hard left to the basket, soaring over his defender and slamming the ball through the hoop to tie the game. The fans were delirious, the screams were deafening, but wait, the ref was running toward the foul line and signaling a charge. A rain of boos descended upon the court. Not only was the basket no good, but Diamond had picked up his fifth foul and was out of the game.

Michael sat calmly on the bench. At 6'5", with blond hair and blue eyes, he might have gotten work as a sports model. Unfortunately for Michael, this was basketball, and he was the ninth man on a ten-man team. The odds on his getting any significant playing time were akin to hitting the lotto and having a beautiful girl hit on you, all on the same day. Childs would go in now, and if someone broke a leg or was shot by a terrorist, Michael might get in the game. He'd been on the bench for two years now and knew that only a miracle could move him into the starting rotation.

UCLA worked the ball for twenty seconds before draining a three pointer, followed by a USC miss and the buzzer. Michael took his post-game shower with the team, although he rarely broke a sweat at the games. He tossed his gym bag over his shoulder, walked to the back parking lot, got in his car, and drove home. "Same shit. Different day!"

There were two games left in the season, and he just couldn't see himself doing this again next year. He was starting to feel as if he was a part of the bench instead of someone sitting on it! True, he was getting a full scholarship, and he wouldn't be attending any college without it, but this was destroying him.

He went back to his room and called his parents. His father had a civil service job in Fresno, and there was no way he had money for any kind of tuition, but Mike wanted him to know what he was thinking of doing.

"Hey, Dad, how's everything?"

"Everything's fine, Mike. What's going on?"

"Well, there's nothing wrong. I mean, I'm okay. I'm not hurt or anything."

"I watched the game. I thought you had a shot at getting in for a minute or two. Although I will say, the few times they panned the bench, you looked as if you were a million miles away!"

"You noticed that? I hope no one else did! I don't think I want to do this for two more years, Dad. I'll graduate with a degree from USC and look for a job, sitting on the end of a bench, if you know what I mean?"

"I was wondering how long you were going to accept ninth man as your lot in life."

"You knew I couldn't continue here?" Michael said. "That makes it easier. Here's what I'm thinking. Tonight I'm going to find twenty schools. Maybe smaller schools that don't compete in the NCAA and could use a good basketball player on the court instead of the bench. I'll explain that I can only transfer if they are offering a full scholarship and see what kind of response I get."

"Sounds like a good plan to me, Mike. Mom and I are behind you 100 percent, and if you need some money, we'll figure something out."

"I don't need your money, Dad. I just wanted to be sure you guys wouldn't be disappointed that I wasn't staying at USC."

"We're proud of you, Mike, wherever you go. Now get busy. You want to do this before the term ends and coaches start making plans for next year."

"Thanks, Dad. I'll give you guys a call when I have some idea of what's going on. Bye."

"Bye, Mike."

Chapter 2

Mike spent the next week researching schools, calling coaches, and sending out copies of his transcript. He rode out the final games of the season and started packing up to return home for the summer.

This is unbelievable. Two years of busting my ass, coaching drills and practices. Basically having no life at all. Shit, I haven't gone on one date this semester. Even the parties are pathetic. Groupies surround the stars of the team, and I get the same line five times a night. 'He must be on the team. He's 6'5".' I have no idea who he is, but he can't be any good!

Not my type anyway, thought Michael. *Actually, I'm not even sure what my type is. The average girl I meet at a party is 5'2", and after an hour of conversation, I need a chiropractor. I'm not looking for someone my size, but 5'8" would be nice. Anyway, when you spend the whole season at practices and traveling around the country, playing basketball, or in my case watching it, you don't get much of a chance to socialize.*

Mike grabbed his stuff, packed his Honda, and hit the highway.

He was home by 1:30 p.m. Not bad, considering it would have taken at least twice as long had he left in the afternoon. The roads getting out of Los Angeles were the worst in the world. He'd had rides home where after two hours he still wasn't out of the city. His parents were still at work, so Michael spread out on the couch and started reviewing his fallback schools, just in case his original efforts proved fruitless. He pretty much included the entire country. He was no longer particular. He just wanted to play basketball for two years and get his diploma.

Normally he would have savored a few days of relaxation at home with his family, but he was feeling the pressure and was starting to resign himself to being stuck on the USC bench.

Michael was definitely starting to feel the nerves. So far, there were two outright rejections, one under consideration, and three no responses.

Maybe on Monday, he'd take a ride down to the school and ask the coach if he had any connections. Hopefully he'd remember his name!

He spent a few days visiting with friends from home. Most of them had declared majors, premed, economics, whatever. He felt like such a loser!

Let me see. I was on the team for the last two years. No, I didn't actually get into any games that weren't over by the time I touched the ball, but I did have an excellent seat. No, I don't know what I'm doing next year. No, I'm not sure if I'll be returning to USC. No, I haven't seen Patti Dunne since I was a junior in high school. Say, will you excuse me? One

11

more minute of "What are you going to do now" and I think I would have had an anxiety attack!

There were two more rejections on Thursday. Friday, he received a nice letter from St. Johns in New York, informing him that there might be an opening next year and to please stay in touch. On Saturday, no mail at all. It was as if someone was telling him "That's it. You gave it your best shot, and it just wasn't good enough."

On Monday, he went down to the schoolyard to look for a pickup game—anything to take his mind off this hole he was trying to crawl out of. Luckily, he found a pickup game and was on fire. He hit his first five shots in a row. The hoop looked twice as large as normal. At least he could still start on the local courts. He got home around five and actually went into the house before reminding himself to at least take a look in the mailbox. There was one letter. It was from the University of Rhode Island. He wasn't sure why he applied there in the first place. If it were any further away, he'd get jet lag just from commuting! He sat down and opened the letter.

"Dear Michael, after speaking with the coaching staff and looking over your transcripts the last two years, I believe you would make an excellent addition to the University of Rhode Island. We would be able to give you a full scholarship to play basketball. This would, of course, be subject to a workout by our coaching staff, to make sure you are fit to play, and an interview with our dean to make sure you would make an acceptable addition to our student body.

"If you are ready to take this step, I suggest you contact me ASAP so that we can get this transfer started. Looking forward to speaking with you, and congratulations. Yours Truly, Annette Linwood, Dean of Admissions.

"*Yes!* I'm back!" He could still have a two-year college basketball career and get a business degree from a good school and no longer have to worry about splinters in his ass from those old benches. Who was he kidding? There was a smile on his face for the first time in who knows how long. He was actually looking forward to August and working out with his new team and being Michael Barnum again, instead of that guy on the end of the bench.

At dinner, he waited until his mother sat down. He tapped his fork lightly on his plate, cleared his throat, and said, "I have a brief announcement before we begin dinner. I would like you both to know that as of September, I will be attending and playing basketball for the University of Rhode Island."

Five seconds passed, and both his parents sat like statues. Mike was dumbfounded, and then he realized they were waiting for one more sentences.

"I'm sorry, with a full scholarship." Michael could hear his father exhale.

"That's great news. A small school but an excellent one. Well done!"

"Mom, I can tell you want to say something. Whatever it is, let's hear it!"

"You're going to freeze in Rhode Island! You don't even have a winter coat."

She was right. This was going to be the first cold winter of his life. Whatever! He was psyched!

Chapter 3

Summer 2004

Michael had been in Rhode Island since the beginning of August. The team worked out five days a week, and Michael would be one of the starters. The past few weeks had been enjoyable. The campus was practically empty, but after practice, Michael had enjoyed walking the campus and occasionally venturing into the surrounding areas. This was a beautiful country. Now that the semester had begun, the University was swamped with kids. As the basketball season began and the students began to recognize him, he would no longer be the unknown ninth, and that would be a welcome change of pace!

The guys on the team seemed to be a nice bunch of guys. Most had girlfriends and even those that didn't seemed to be pretty tight with each other. They had, after all, been together for the last two years. He wasn't worried. He had a feeling this was going to be a great year.

With that optimism intact, he entered the student center. This was the area where most students killed time between classes or grabbed a cup of coffee or a soft drink. For the most part, it was composed of twenty rectangular tables that sat twenty students each and were normally filled by different fraternities and sororities, plus a handful of smaller round tables for five, utilized by independents and outcasts.

Michael grabbed a coffee, found one of the outcast tables, and sat down with his books. Students occasionally gave him a look. He was tall and probably on the team, but they weren't sure as there had been no games yet, so they politely ignored him.

He was just about finished with his coffee when he noticed a group of girls enter from the opposite side of the room. They were a distance away, but he noticed that one of the girls was considerably taller than the others. He saw her give him a quick look as she sat across from him, separated by four large tables and a handful of people. The second thing he noticed was she seemed to have a great figure for a tall girl; she had to be close to six feet tall. She started to speak, and her face was so expressive that he was mesmerized, but it wasn't until someone said something to her and made her smile that he lost it. She had a smile that absolutely lit up her face, and he couldn't take his eyes off her. He watched her with delight in his eyes and his mouth hanging open.

This must have been obvious, because after saying something to her friends, she stood up and walked across the room, stopping some ten feet in front of him. With her hands on her hips and a significantly pissed-off look on her face, she said, "I walked into this room ten minutes ago and sat down with my friends. You have been blatantly staring at me the entire time and for the last two minutes with your mouth hanging open. If I'm not being too inquisitive, perhaps you could tell me what the hell you think you're doing?"

This would have been difficult enough one-on-one, but with two or three hundred students straining not to miss one word of this annihilation, it was infinitely more difficult. He knew immediately that throwing the bullshit or coming up with a clever line would not make it, and so he threw caution to the wind and tried the truth.

He stood up and immediately saw the quick flicker in her eyes when she realized that he was quite a bit taller than she was. He would take a wild guess and say that looking up at someone was not the norm for this girl.

"Well," he said, "I was sitting here enjoying a cup of coffee and catching up on some reading when I saw you walk in with your friends. I immediately noticed that you were tall, and then when you all spread out to sit down, I noticed that you were in great shape. I was doing my best not to stare, but then you started to engage in conversation, and I noticed how expressive your face became, and then someone said something funny and you smiled. I realized at that time that you were breathtakingly beautiful! And that's when my mouth fell open!"

There wasn't a sound in the room. The girl looked at him for a good fifteen seconds, at which time, as hard as she tried, she could not keep that stern look on her face from dissolving into a total smile. The entire student center rose as one in applause, at which time Michael extended his hand and said, "Michael Barnum."

She gave him her hand and said, "Karen Stillman." He pulled out a chair for her, and the rest, as they say, was history.

CHAPTER 4

"I can't believe you didn't text me!"

"What happened?"

"Who is he? Is he on the basketball team?"

"Are you going to see him again?"

"Did he ask you out?"

Karen put her hands up and shouted, "Quiet! Give me two seconds to sit down and I will tell all."

"Okay. So first let me tell you. I don't believe in love at first sight. He's okay looking, nothing to write home about. He made quite a stand there in the student center, but after an hour of getting to know one another, he was just another guy. His father has a civil service job in Fresno, California, so he's on a basketball scholarship, which translates into hamburgers and fast food. He was a reserve at USC before he transferred here, so he's not going to be playing in the NBA when he graduates. Oh, and don't even start with 'Is there any correlation between a man's size and a man's size?' Because; one, I have no idea, and two, I just met this guy, for God's sake. Okay then, if that's it, I've got to run."

"Where are you running off to? You just got here."

"Well, if you must know. I want to book my flight early. I'm flying to Fresno for Thanksgiving to meet Michael's parents, and then we're meeting at Starbucks to check Craigslist and see if we can find an apartment for next semester."

Amy Winters was Karen's best friend since they met freshman year, and she knew from the minute she walked in that Karen was lying like a rug.

Amy stood up and said, "Karen Stillman, you are a liar and a fraud. You are head over heels in love. You couldn't get that silly grin off your face with a crowbar. Go ahead and deny it!"

Karen looked at her friend as her grin threatened to bruise her cheeks, walked over to her, and gave her a hug that took the breath out of her. She whispered in her ear, "Don't let me go. I'm afraid I'll start giggling."

Chapter 5

Summer 2005

Amy left Rhode Island and took a job with her father's law firm in New York City. Her parents lived on the Upper East Side, and she loved being in New York. She found it a little too competitive in all respects—business, clothing, and social. I mean, if you weren't a stick, you were a little overweight. God forbid your nose was too big, or you had a slight speech impediment. New Yorkers would pick you apart piece by piece. You either flourished or you drowned. There was no middle ground.

She had grown up in New York and understood it all. She was, first of all, extremely cute. She was 5'4"with shoulder-length brown hair and big hazel eyes. She had a nice figure, but more importantly, she knew how to handle herself. As they say in the city, she was street smart.

Having worked for her father for several summers, Amy could help out in just about any area. Today she was reviewing contracts. She'd been reading one contract after another for close to five hours, and her eyes were beginning to burn.

"You can't read straight without taking a break now and then, or you'll go blind," said an intern named Scott, who seemed to be doing the same type of work as Amy.

"Excuse me, what's your name, Scott? I'll have you know that I've been reviewing contracts for three years and I really don't need your help."

"So you think that three years of this makes you an expert. You'll see when you finish high school that it's a lot more complicated than you think."

"First of all, I am entering my senior year at the University of Rhode Island, and secondly, I know the complications involved extremely well."

"Don't go ballistic on me. You look young, that's all. Why don't we go out for dinner tonight and get to know one another?"

"Let me think. Okay, number one, this is my father's law firm, and I do not date his employees or trainees or whatever you are, and secondly, and this outweighs number one, I don't date men with army haircuts, so to sum up, If your hair was down close to your shoulders and you were old enough to have a real job, I would consider it. In the meantime, I think you have quite a pile of contracts to go through before your day is done."

Scott gave her one more look as she left. She really was cute. Ah, well, it was a long summer.

Amy didn't run into Scott again until the day before she was returning to school. She was about to say something when he put his hand up and said, "Please if you insult me any more, I'll be afraid to go outside by myself!"

"Listen, Scott," she laughed, "you caught me on a bad day. I was very rude, and I apologize."

"Hey, no problem. Does that mean you'll have a farewell drink with me after work?"

"No, Scott, everything I said stands. I'm just apologizing for the way I said it. Have a nice life!"

Damn, that girl was cute, Scott thought as Amy walked away.

Chapter 6

Amy returned to school in the fall. Karen was with Michael every minute, so she was pretty much on her own. She met them occasionally for dinner, but that wasn't too often. She had a few secondary friends that she hung with, but mostly life was boring.

In November, she met a boy at one of the basketball games. They went out for a few months on and off, but she wasn't into him, and when she got back from Christmas break, she broke it off.

It was January 20—she always remembered the date, as it was inauguration day—that she received a call on the dorm house phone that she had a visitor. *Probably Karen with one of her come-with-me-immediately games.* "I have to drop something off on the other side of the campus and I need company."

When she got downstairs, there was a man standing in the doorway.

"I'm sorry. Can I help you with something?"

"Well, excuse me if I misunderstood, but according to the conditions set forth in our contract . . ."

"What are you talking about? What contract?" His voice was familiar, but she had no idea what the hell was he talking about.

"I am now working full time for a law firm in New York, other than your father's, and you will notice that my hair is touching my shoulders. I believe that qualifies me as someone you would go out with. I think you're adorable, and I've just driven six hours on the possibility that you're available and will live up to our contract. So how about dinner?"

My god, thought Amy, *I can't believe that this hunk is the same Scott from last summer!*

"Well, a deal's a deal. It would be my pleasure to go to dinner with you, Scott. And by the way, I think you look really nice." *I turned this guy down? What was I thinking?* "Give me ten minutes, and I'll be right down."

Scott and Amy spent almost every weekend together. They wrote and phoned each other on weeks they couldn't arrange to see each other, and as soon as Amy graduated, they were married.

Over the last two years, they had become very close with Karen and Michael. When Michael went job hunting, Scott introduced him to his boss, and just like that, they were working together. The girls, needless to say, were delighted.

Scott and Amy lived off Columbus Avenue on Eighty-Third Street, and so naturally when Karen went apartment hunting with Amy, they looked in the same area and found a one-bedroom apartment on Eighty-First Street between Broadway and West End Avenue. Amy knew she wanted a family, so working as an assistant at her father's firm was perfect. She would probably work another month or so and then work on pregnancy.

Karen had no problems with employment. She was a talented artist and could get work anywhere, but she also wanted a family, and so she found a job as an illustrator at a publishing company. They knew she wouldn't be with them long, but after she showed them her portfolio, they decided they would keep her as long as possible.

And so the transition from Rhode Island to New York City was flawless.

CHAPTER 7

August 2007

Karen and Michael were out to dinner at their favorite restaurant, Il Mulino, celebrating with their closest friends Amy and Scott. It had taken them one month to get a table for four on a Saturday night as Il Mulino was one of if not the best Italian restaurants in New York City. Their lobster in garlic sauce was so incredible that it was impossible not to lick your fingers after each bite. With a reservation at 8:00 p.m., they had just been seated at 9:00 p.m. and were happy to have only waited one hour.

Karen had just learned that she was pregnant and called Amy (in her third month) so they could meet for dinner. It was funny; this was just the way they had planned it—meeting the right guys, marriage after school, settling down, having kids. It was as if they were following a script.

"Amy," said Karen, "who is that older man at the bar and why is he waving at you?"

"That's the mayor of New York, Michael Bloomberg. He's waving at me because the last time we ate here he was sitting at the next table, and he must think if we're here all the time, we must be rich."

Amy waved back and then turned her attention back to her friends.

This is such an incredible place, Amy thought. *It takes a month to get a reservation. When you show up, you're lucky if you get seated an hour or more after your reservation time. While you wait, it's practically impossible to get a drink at the bar as it's five deep from the bar to the door. If you try to move forward toward the tables past people who have been waiting longer than you have, you are literally taking your life in your hands. Finally, you are seated. The tables are so close together that the waiters must get on their toes to slide from one table to another. The meal is so expensive you can only laugh unless you've had a few bottles of wine in which case you might cry. The next day, you will see your friends and say the same thing you say every time you eat at Il Mulino: "Tell me that wasn't the best meal you've ever had!"*

Scott had been working for a real estate firm after graduating from law school in Manhattan and had introduced Michael to his boss. Now they were both selling commercial real estates, and even in this down market, they were both doing well.

Amy gave birth in November to a baby girl whom they named Samantha. Karen was at the hospital the next morning and told Amy how selfish she was not to have waited so they could have given birth at the same time. Amy burst out crying, and no matter how many times she said she was joking, Amy couldn't stop crying, and they had to give her a sedative. It was just another memory they would laugh about in the years to come.

Karen not only caught up to Amy, she did her one better. Todd and Adam were born on May 25. Now they walked up and down the west side with their strollers and tried to decide if they wanted to send the kids all the way to the University of Rhode Island or maybe look into Columbia and keep them close to home.

"Then again," said Karen, "Samantha could go wherever she liked, while Todd and Adam would probably be getting basketball scholarships."

"You know," said Amy, "we should have this conversation again when the kids are eight or nine."

"That's why I love you, Amy. You're always thinking ahead." They both laughed. Life was good!

It was on a Sunday afternoon. The four of them were having brunch at O'Neil's balloon on Sixty-Fourth Street down the block from Lincoln Center. Previously known as O'Neil's Pub, it had been a gathering place for ballet dancers for many years. They sat at a table for six: four chairs and two baby carriages, one a double. They had split up the *New York Times*, and Michael suddenly said, "This is the place. This is where I want to live and raise kids." He passed the section to Karen, who smiled and passed it to Amy. By the time Scott started reading, it was a done deal: a combination of single-family homes and townhouses to be built in Mason, Colorado. The houses would have four bedrooms each, 5,000 feet above sea level, all with panoramic views that defied the imagination. Mason was fifteen miles from Aspen where their real estate firm already had offices. There was no crime, no pollution, no traffic; just fresh air and serenity. And the dream continued.

CHAPTER 8

January 2007

Nathaniel and Whitney Whitcup lived in a penthouse on the fortieth floor of the Odeon Towers, Main Line, Philadelphia. To be more precise, they owned the fortieth floor—5,000 square feet overlooking the city.

Nate's great-great-grandfather came over on the *Mayflower*. The Whitcups had been business leaders in Philadelphia ever since. Rumor has it that Nate's great-great-grandfather had been instrumental in hanging the Original Liberty Bell and had the papers in the vault, proving ownership. (Only a rumor, but who knows!)

Nate did his undergrad at George Washington and returned to Temple for his master's in business. He graduated in the fall of 2004 and, in the tradition of all Whitcups, spent the following year abroad. Mostly he crisscrossed Europe by boat and plane, although he did visit several Asian companies the family did business with.

He returned home and immediately began fulfilling his obligation—entering the firm of Whitcup, Whitcup, and Whitcup as the fourth generation to begin his apprenticeship. Inevitably, he would take the helm and guide his company into the next generation.

WW&W, as they were referred to on the New York Stock Exchange, generated gross profits in the hundreds of millions of dollars. Their interests were unlimited—from retail stores, to hospitals, to oil and gas pipelines. They had a hand in almost anything that made money. WW&W was a well-oiled machine.

By the time Nathaniel took over the helm, he could put the business on autopilot, and that's exactly what he did.

He joined Merion, the premier golf and country club in Philadelphia. He took golf lessons three afternoons a week and played in regular games on the weekend. He went to the theatre on a regular basis—a must for a Whitcup—and he supported a multitude of charities and causes that depended on the Whitcup Philanthropies for their survival.

He never neglected the family business, but, of course, there was not a lot to stay on top of it. He had two executive secretaries, either of whom could have been CEO and run the business in his absence (something they did occasionally), and five vice presidents, equally capable of running the company, and all making seven-figure salaries. There was a lot of money to spread around, and that was one of the things that WW&W did well.

CHAPTER 9

In order to understand Nathaniel Whitcup, the man, one must first take a look at Nathaniel Whitcup, the boy.

He was aware, of course, that he was well-off. He attended private school and knew that most children in Philadelphia attended public schools. He had friends who lived well but not nearly on the level that his family enjoyed. Of course, being a mere child, all this was meaningless to him.

In Nathaniel's tenth year, all this changed. The change might have been more subtle. It would have dawned on him eventually that he was not going to live the same life as most other children. In this instance, however, the acknowledgement came hard and fast.

He decided that he would play in the Little League. He had been practicing in his basement all year and loved to fire the ball with all his strength into a square he had outlined on the wall. He was going to play in high school and college, get a contract with the Philadelphia Phillies, and eventually go into the Hall of Fame as one of the greatest pitchers to ever play the game.

Now, aside from the dream—all kids have dream scenarios that are equally beyond the scope of possibility—Nate actually had an incredible arm. The first week he attended practice, the coach lined all the kids up to check out their abilities and decide where to position them in the field. Nate raised his hand and yelled out, "I'm a pitcher."

"Okay, son, we'll find out soon enough what you are. In the meantime, we've been doing this for a few years, so bear with us, and we'll figure it all out." Nate slumped his shoulders and went through two weekends of playing infield, outfield, catching, and so on. On the second Sunday, the coaches asked anyone who thought they could pitch to go to the pitcher's mound. Nate got on line. He'd never pitched before, not to a person with a bat anyway. He had, however, thrown a ball in his basement (almost the size of a baseball field) to the exact specifications of a baseball mound.

It was his turn, and he stood on the mound, looking at Glen Schmidt, the best batter on the club. Glen was almost thirteen, and he had a sneer on his face that said, "I'm going to take your head off when I hit this pitch." He waved the bat at Nate, and there was definitely a little tension in Nate's neck. This wasn't exactly the same thing as throwing at that batter's box in the basement. I mean, if he missed inside now, Glen was going to hit this kid in the chest or the face. Nate reached back, threw as hard as he could, and let go of a rocket that sailed over the batter's head, over the backstop, and across the street onto a neighbor's lawn.

Everyone broke out laughing, including the coaches. One of them yelled out, "Okay, Nolan Ryan, now let's slow that down a mite, and lower your trajectory around ten feet or so, and let's try to get the ball near that white square thing that the batter is standing next to."

Everyone was doubled over and laughing just as hard when Nate threw the next pitch. It was chest-high and landed in the catcher's mitt with a loud pop. The batter thought he was about to lose his head and dove to the ground, the catcher dropped his glove with the ball in it so he could rub his aching left hand, and the coach shouted loud enough for everyone to hear, "Strike one."

There was no more laughing. The coach called over to Nate, "Any chance you could throw another pitch like that." Nate grabbed the ball and got himself set. This time the batter was not simply standing beside the plate; he was crouching over it with every bit of concentration he possessed, focusing on the hand that was holding the ball. It was possible that this pitch could once again sail across the street, come ripping across the plate, or break his nose. However it came, he would be ready!

Nathaniel concentrated on the catcher's glove. He kicked up his left leg as high as he could and released the ball. Glen saw this one coming. He swung hard, but just before his bat came off his shoulder, there was that sound again. *Pop!* "Strike two!" yelled the coach.

"What do you think, Glen? You've got one strike left."

Glen was a long way past being embarrassed, but now that he knew how fast this kid was, he would gauge the speed and be ready for him.

Nate rubbed the ball in his hands the way he had watched pitchers did on TV. He stared at the batter. He knew Glen was a little intimidated by his speed and still a little worried about his chin. This was probably a good time to try that curveball pitch his uncle had taught him. *What the hell! You only live once!*

He gripped the ball by the seams with his second and third fingers the way his uncle John had taught him and whipped that ball right at Glen Schmidt's face. Glen saw that ball on a path to take his head off and dove to the ground. At just about that time, the ball began to curve, and continued to curve, until it landed in the catcher's mitt like a feather. "Strike three!" screamed the coach.

"First game is next Saturday, Whitcup. You are this team's starting pitcher. I know you're not ten years old, and I am fairly certain you've been playing semipro ball somewhere under a different name, but I won't tell anyone if you won't."

As soon as Nate got home, he called his uncle John and told him about his outing. "It was great, Uncle John! You should have seen the look on this kid's face when my curve slid into the glove! My first game is next Saturday. Will you come?"

There was a long pause. Finally, John came out with it, "Nate, have you asked your father if you can play Little League?"

"What are you talking about, Uncle John? Why wouldn't father let me play?"

"It's not for me to say, Nate, but before you start making any plans, talk to him."

Nate went down for dinner that night, still excited but nervous. He had not been at the table for less than ten seconds when his father turned to him and said, "I heard about the Little League tryouts, Nate. You should have mentioned you were planning on going out for the team.

"I know this will be difficult for you to understand, but one day you will. This family has a great responsibility to this city. Hundreds, more like thousands of families, depend on what we do and who we are.

"First off, you are in private school and will always be in private school. This means you will not be free to play in most of these games, and they are by no means more important than your schooling. As you continue your education, you will have less and less time for extracurricular activities, so a sports career is not something a Whitcup can ever hope to achieve. Of course, you can play on weekends. There's nothing wrong with tennis or golf when you have the chance, but on a regular basis, well, you understand, don't you?"

"But, Father, I'm really good at this, and I think if I continued to play, I could really be a great pitcher. You would be proud of me, Father!"

"And one day I will be, Nathaniel, but as for now, there will be no Little League."

The coaches came by the following day to appeal to Mr. Whitcup, but Nate's baseball career was over.

It was, however, a lesson learned. There was only one true course for Nathaniel. He had approximately fifteen years to groom himself to take over a huge conglomerate. His path was already chosen, and there would be few electives along the way. He could have as many good times as were humanly possible, but he could never do anything to embarrass the family name or anything that would get in the way of his becoming CEO of Whitcup, Whitcup, and Whitcup.

Chapter 10

So that was exactly what Nathaniel did. He applied himself at school and excelled, as all Whitcups were expected to excel. He graduated high school with excellent grades and repeated that performance at George Washington University. He then graduated with honors as his father had done before him and collected his masters from Temple University. He followed with his mandatory year of travel and returned to Philadelphia to begin his career.

He totally immersed himself in his new life. He familiarized himself with every department and department head. He worked alongside supervisors and performed basic work in order to learn the ropes from the bottom-up. He sat with the president of their CPA firm and made himself aware of the tax issues that affected WW&W. He had each division head report to his office once a month for his first twelve months and explain ad nauseam what made their division profitable. In essence, he worked himself to a point of total fatigue.

His mother probably saved him from having a breakdown. She called him one afternoon with an unusual request. The fact that she called him at work was in itself highly irregular, but the purpose of the phone call was even further from the norm.

"Nathaniel, my love. I am afraid I have stuck my nose where it doesn't belong and have now obligated you."

"Mother, I am quite busy this afternoon. Perhaps I could speak with you this evening, and you can tell me all about your little indiscretion."

She recognized the tone immediately. It was the same way one spoke down to a parent just before checking them into a convenient nursing home.

"Nathaniel, sweetheart, this might surprise you, as the men in this family are all under the misapprehension that only they are in possession of any brain cells, but I am aware of the fact that you are presently at work. You should also be aware that I do not have Alzheimer's disease quite yet and am cognizant of the fact that you will have to take a five-minute break in order to hear me out. That being said, may I continue?"

"Of course, Mother. Sorry, if I was out of line."

"Apology accepted. Now, as I was saying, I was speaking with a friend of mine at the club this afternoon. She mentioned that her daughter had graduated from the University of Pennsylvania last year. She was living in the city and refused to date just for the sake of dating and so was home most evenings, reading or some such thing. I remember her daughter being quite lovely and so I said, 'I have just the thing!'"

"Mother, don't tell me you gave your friend my number."

"Of course not, my love."

"That's a relief."

"I took her daughter's address and told her that you would pick her up at eight o'clock this evening and take her to dinner at La Minette."

"Why would you do that, Mother? What if I had plans? It so happens. I was planning to work until seven and then go home and have a long hot bath."

"Number one, I knew you had no plans because all you do is work, and number two, you sound like an old man, going home to have a hot bath. I gave my word, Nathaniel, and I never ask anything of you, so I expect you to be pleasant and show this girl a nice evening. Tomorrow you can go back to fifteen-hour workdays and no life, if you so desire!"

The phone disconnected, and Nathaniel sat in his chair, holding the phone in front of him, and thought, *What a perfect way to end an exhausting day! An evening of small talk with a society girl with a weight problem and a butt the size of Virginia!*

Chapter 11

He arrived at 7:50 p.m. to pick up Ms. Whitney Appleton at her apartment house on City Line. It was a nice building, not too big with a comfortable waiting area. There were several couches and chairs situated on both sides of the entranceway. He left his name with the concierge and found a lone chair in a corner where he could best prepare himself for what would undoubtedly be an evening to forget.

The concierge signaled to alert him to the fact that Ms. Appleton would be down in ten minutes, which of course turned into twenty. During the last of those twenty minutes, three girls had walked toward him from the bank of elevators, and each time he said to himself, "I knew this was coming, only to be in error each time."

Whitney exited the elevator and immediately spotted him in the corner and waved. He noticed that she was pleasant-looking but refused to consider the possibility that she was more than that. She walked over and held out her hand.

"Hi, you must be Nathaniel," she said in a friendly manner.

"Exactly," he responded, with just enough coldness to accentuate the fact that he was not a willing participant in the evening's festivities.

She did not say another word but got into his car and sat quietly as they drove in silence to the restaurant. They arrived at La Minette in five or six minutes. He parked in front. The restaurant had valet, but Nathaniel did not like strangers driving his car. He reached for the door and was about to get out when Whitney cut off his exit with a somewhat cold and calculating voice.

"Excuse me, but would you mind closing the door? I'd like to clear a few things up before we go in. If that's all right with you?"

Nathaniel, completely caught off guard, closed the door and sat back.

"I don't need my mother to find me a dinner date," Whitney continued, "as I'm sure you don't need your mother to find you one. I believe your mother meant well, and I didn't think it would be too painful, so I agreed. This was obviously more of an imposition on you, judging from the painful way the first ten minutes have gone. I'm going to save you from another hour or two of anguish, Mr. Whitcup. I'm really not that hungry nor am I that desperate. I would appreciate it if you would drop me back at my apartment or have the doorman call me a taxi, whatever's easiest."

Nathaniel was blown away. He stopped and took a long look at her. She looked like a taller version of Jennifer Anniston. Beneath that scowling look was a very attractive woman. He had behaved like a spoiled teenager, and he was embarrassed to say the least.

"Will you at least allow me a few quick thoughts before you go?" said Nathaniel. "I assure you, I won't take but a minute."

"I think I could handle one more minute," Whitney replied sarcastically.

"Okay, here goes. I don't blame you for wanting to leave, but if you do leave, I will most likely spend the next thirty or forty years working my butt off and being the same arrogant obnoxious ass you spent the past fifteen minutes with."

She bit her tongue to keep the corners of her mouth from beginning to curve upward.

"Could you live with yourself, knowing that you were condemning me to a lifetime in hell? I suggest you give me one chance to redeem myself, and if at the end of the evening, you are not completely satisfied, I believe you would then be justified in calling my mother and voicing your displeasure."

"I'm not sure exactly what you are referring to when you say I will be completely satisfied, but I will admit I have never been given the option of calling my date's mother to discuss his inadequacies, and I am getting rather hungry!"

They talked throughout dinner and into the evening. He told her of his structured life and obligations, and she told him about the burden of coming out as a debutante and having to watch every word she said and every move she made.

She told him that her friends called her Winnie, and he liked that. He told her that his family called him Nathaniel, and she smiled and called him Nate.

He told her about the premature end of his baseball career. She told him that her children would pursue any avenues they chose including baseball and no one would ever say different.

They left the restaurant at 10:30, and Winnie invited Nate up for coffee. They sat on the terrace and continued their conversation.

"So tell me, Winnie. Why have you been staying home when there must be dozens of men dying to take you out?"

"I started traveling with my parents when I was twelve, Nate. My father worked for the State Department, and I was lucky to have spent time in a great many wonderful cities as a teenager. My mother loved Paris. We kept an apartment on the Champs-Elysees, and I went to school there and learned the language. We summered in Cannes until I began my freshman year at the University of Pennsylvania. My parents thought I should have more in common with my peers, and so we began spending summers in Palm Springs. They felt that was more American. In any event I graduated and began working toward my masters in design, and I found it difficult to date twenty-five-year-olds who were just starting out in the world. Don't get me wrong. A lot of them were nice. It's just that after an hour or so, we ran out of conversation. Maybe that's what made tonight so interesting. You're the first man I've ever dated who started off the evening by telling me how much he wished he was somewhere else."

"I was an idiot!"

"True, but tell me, is that the way you start most of your social engagements?"

"Actually, I don't really have the time or the inclination to date much. I meet women through work, and occasionally some of those meetings turn into relationships, but I always have too much on my plate to sustain them. My days are filled with meetings and conferences. I normally skip lunch because by the time it's delivered, I'm somewhere else. People depend on me, and my decisions affect the lives of a great many people. Why are you laughing?"

"Did you memorize that speech, or do you make up that nonsense as you go."

"What do you mean?" Nate replied indignantly.

"Have you ever heard of delegating responsibility? You have a staff in your company that could run a small country. I'll bet there's not one member of your staff that skips lunch, has no social life, and has no time for a life outside of WW&W."

"The people who work for me all have a lot on their plates and are hard workers!" Nate responded emphatically.

"I'm sorry. I didn't mean to offend you. In any event, I've got to kick you out. It's late, and I have work tomorrow." She walked Nate to the elevator. "I want you to know that I had a wonderful time tonight." She got up on her tiptoes and gave him a soft kiss on the lips. He walked into the elevator, and she held the door open.

"I think you're terrific, Nate, but I want you to understand. I have no desire to spend any time with that guy who picked me up this evening. If the man I had dinner with tonight only shows up when a business meeting gets cancelled and he has a two-hour opening to fill, then I've made a mistake and wasted an evening. Call me if you can fit me into your schedule."

The elevator door closed, and Nate rode it to the lobby, more than a bit confused.

The next morning, Nate was at the airport at 7:00 a.m., flying the company plane to New York City where he met with several associates, organizing a new division in Manhattan. He got back to Philadelphia at 10:00 p.m. and was entering his apartment at 11:15 p.m. when he realized he hadn't called Winnie. It was too late. *Damn*, he thought. He wanted her to know that he wanted her to be a part of his life, and once again he let his business dictate his life. Tomorrow he would definitely call. He'd tell his secretary to remind him in the morning.

He arrived at his office at 7:30 a.m. as usual. Nora, his personal assistant, brought him his coffee and muffin and his schedule for the day.

"Sorry, sir, but you already had an impossible day scheduled today. I just added a telephone conference with the New York investors at 11:00 a.m. that should last from forty-five minutes to an hour, and our lawyers are insisting on thirty minutes this afternoon. Mostly they need your signatures on a few dozen tax forms. Tell me when you've finished your muffin and I'll send in your first appointment."

"Thank you, Nora. Let's not waste any time. Who's first?"

"Harry Gelkof leads off, sir. He's our oil and gas manager. He wants to talk to you about expanding into Louisiana. The paperwork is on your desk."

"Thanks, Nora. Send him in."

Nate worked straight through the morning without a break until 12:15 p.m., at which time he finished his conference call with the New York investors.

"I'll work straight through the lunch break, Nora. Send in the accountants, please, and order me a sandwich."

"Before I send them in, sir, there's a woman in reception who says she would like to speak with you. I told her you had no time and she would need to make an appointment. I believe her exact words were 'Ask him if he'll see me, and if he says no, I will disappear immediately.' Her name is Whitney Appleton."

"Tell the accountants to sit tight and send her in, please, Nora."

"You're already behind schedule, sir. As it is, you will be here until 6:00 or 7:00 p.m."

"Thank you, Nora, please send her in."

"Yes, sir," she replied with a bewildered look on her face.

Nate came around the front of his desk and met Winnie as she entered his office.

"What a pleasant surprise, Winnie. I wasn't expecting you to drop by."

"Actually, I was fairly certain I was going to hear from you yesterday, and when I didn't, I thought I would stop by and find out why."

"I'm sorry. I was in New York all day and didn't get home until eleven or so."

"And you haven't called me because . . ."

"I was just so busy. I actually reminded my secretary this morning to make sure I called you today."

"I see. So I shouldn't be upset with you. I should be upset with your secretary."

"I didn't mean it exactly like that."

"No problem. You can make it up to me now. Take me to lunch, and we'll figure out how to improve our communication problems."

"Winnie, I would love to take you to lunch, but I have appointments straight through until six or seven tonight. Maybe when I leave the office, I could stop by your apartment for a nightcap?"

Winnie said nothing for thirty seconds or so and just stood at the window, looking out at the city. Then she sat down in the chair next to Nate's desk and motioned Nate to sit down.

"I hope you don't think I'm unreasonable, but I've given this a lot of thought and I want you to understand exactly how I feel. This is too important to screw up because one of us interpreted something the wrong way, so if I can have five minutes, I would like to make my intentions perfectly clear."

"Hold my calls, Nora. I'll tell you when to send in the accountants. Okay, Winnie, I'm all yours."

"It's like this, Nate. I've got pretty good instincts, and I think you're the man I've been waiting for. You made a pretty good speech Monday night before we went in for dinner, and I understood exactly what you were saying, so I took a chance. Last night I spent the better part of the evening on the Internet reading everything that was available on Nathaniel Whitcup and the Whitcup Corporation. You and your corporation have a hand in so many pies at the same time that you could conceivably work seven days a week for the next five years and still not catch up. I could come back five years from now and you'd tell me you're going to call me as soon as you complete the purchase of some country in South America. Things will never change for the Whitcup Corporation. It's a monster with an insatiable appetite.

"I think I'm your heroine, Nate. I'm riding in on my white horse and riding off with you into the sunset. Normally it's the guy that does the rescuing, but this is my story. I'm offering you a life—happiness, love, children, the whole ball of wax. I think we can make a good team, but I can't make this happen unless you feel the same way."

"I do feel the same way, Winnie. Let me catch up this week, and next week we'll sit down and talk about us."

"I don't think so, Nate."

"What does that mean? You just said you thought we could have a future together."

"The only way it works, Nate, is if you let your vice presidents run their divisions. If you try to run them all, you will never have any time for me or children or a life outside of the office. The only family you will ever have will be sitting in your boardroom. Here's my deal. I'm going downstairs, and I'm going to wait ten minutes in the lobby for you to come and take me to lunch so we can start our life together. If you don't come downstairs, I will assume you have something more important to do. I will not see you again and will begin looking for someone who thinks I come first. I'll be downstairs with my white horse. I hope you make the right decision, Nate." Winnie turned and walked out, closing the door behind her.

Absurd! What am I supposed to do? Turn my world upside down because she wants to have lunch in ten minutes.

"Nora, send in the accountants."

They were all seated and were explaining the tax ramifications of the takeover when Nate raised his hand and stopped them. He picked up the phone and dialed Ed Harris, a senior partner.

"Ed, Nathaniel here. Are you up to date on this New York deal we're involved in? I know you stay up to date on all our deals. I didn't mean it that way. I'm giving you the reins on this takeover. I have other things on my plate at the moment.

It's all yours. I'm sending in the accounting team right now. I'm sure it will go smoothly. Thank you, Ed."

"Gentlemen, please go down to Ed Harris's office. Thank you." Nate walked out behind them and waited by the elevator.

"Excuse me, sir, but what's going on?"

"I'm delegating authority, Nora. Ed's handling the takeover, and I'm going out for lunch. I'll be back in a few hours."

Nora stood in front of the elevator as the door closed, with a stunned look on her face, unable to think of a thing to say.

Nate exited the elevator in time to see Winnie exiting through the revolving doors. He ran through the lobby and through the side door and grabbed her hand as she was reaching for the door of a taxi.

"It's only nine minutes," he yelled.

"What's nine minutes?" she yelled back.

"You gave me ten minutes to show up in the lobby. I made it in nine. Where's your white horse?"

"Right here," she said, opening the door of the taxi. They both jumped in and immediately went after the Guinness World Record for the longest single kiss without a breath.

After patiently waiting for what must have been two or three minutes, the driver turned around and said, "Okay, folks, if this doesn't end soon and I don't begin taking you somewhere, I will be forced to turn off the meter and charge you for a room."

"An interesting choice of words," said Nate. "Take us to the Four Seasons."

They ordered up lunch and a bottle of champagne, and two hour later, after dropping Winnie off at her apartment, Nate was heading back to the office. As he entered the lobby, his phone rang.

"Hi, Winnie. Do you miss me already?"

"As a matter of fact, I do, but that's not why I'm calling. I stopped by your office today so we could have lunch and talk, and we neglected to do either of those things, although I thought the champagne was excellent. So when you get done today, I'll make us a late dinner, and maybe we'll talk afterward."

"Sounds like a plan, but if we're having the same thing for dinner as we had for lunch, there's a good chance I won't be eating until breakfast."

Nate and Winnie were married six months later—a small but extremely elegant affair. Six months later, she was pregnant, and eight months or so after that, Emma was born.

They maintained a full-time baby nurse for the first six months. After that, Winnie insisted on letting her go and taking control of her daughter. That was the first adjustment. The second was the family domain. It was simply too expansive for the three of them or even the four of them. She and Nate discussed this on a weekly basis, but it wasn't until Nate's mother once again stepped in that it all came together.

Her friend Sally's son, who lived in Chicago, had just told his mother of his intention to move into a community that was being built in Mason, Colorado. She would get all the information, which she did, and one more family made their way west.

CHAPTER 12

Kenny and Carol Panzer sat in the waiting room of Howard Rosenberg, attorney at law. Mr. Rosenberg had come in on his day off to meet with them on a Sunday, as it would afford them the time and privacy their case deserved.

They wanted to adopt. It was the missing piece in an otherwise perfect marriage. Kenny had started a carpentry business in Seattle, Washington, and was so talented that within five years, he had opened two more stores in neighboring cities and was extremely successful. The only thing missing was a child.

They weren't concerned until a few years had passed and Carol had not conceived. To be on the safe side, they made an appointment with a specialist and, to their chagrin, found out that Carol was not capable of having children. As difficult as this was to handle, theirs was a strong marriage, and after digesting everything, they discussed their options and realized that they were fine with the adoption process.

Several weeks later, they made an appointment at an adoption agency and walked out an hour later in a state of shock. To begin with, the counselor explained, adopting a white American baby (newborn to several months old) involved a great deal of paperwork, a significant amount of money, an attorney, a wait of up to one year, and a lot of luck. You could probably cut that time in half if you were willing to adopt a non-Caucasian child and in half again if you would adopt a black child, and if you were willing to adopt a child of say eight or nine, you could adopt within a month. If you insisted on an infant, the only way to adopt that quickly would be to look in third world countries.

Carol was on the verge of tears when the counselor cleared her throat to indicate she wasn't quite finished.

"Now for the bad news!"

"That wasn't the bad news?" Kenny asked incredulously.

"No, I'm sorry, the bad news is that the two of you would never be allowed to adopt in this country. I read your file, Mr. Panzer, and you served time in an institution for the sale and distribution of narcotics. That would make any adoption completely impossible!"

Carol was ashen and seconds away from going into shock. "Excuse me," she said, "did she just say you were in prison for selling drugs?"

Kenny got up from his chair and knelt down besides his wife.

"I should have told you, but it happened when I was fifteen years old. I hung with a few tough kids, and one of them asked me to pick up a package and give it to him at school. It was marijuana. They caught both of us at school, which made the transgression that much worse. I was sent to a farm for juvenile delinquents for thirty days and served two years' probation. That's all of it, I swear. I certainly never thought it would come back to haunt me."

Later that night, Kenny turned to Carol and said, "Carol, I swear to you we will adopt a child. This world revolves around money, and luckily we have plenty. Tomorrow, I will make a few calls and find out how to go about it. Trust me. It's all going to work out."

Chapter 13

The next day, Kenny called every friend and connection he knew until he found someone who knew someone who knew Howard Rosenberg. Mr. Rosenberg's firm specialized in difficult adoptions. He had already read through Kenny's entire file, and after he and Carol were served coffee and biscotti and were a little more at ease, Mr. Rosenberg explained how these things worked.

In the first place, Mr. Rosenberg explained, everything that they were going to do would be completely legal. It would not be possible for them to adopt an infant as the waiting lists were never ending, and with Kenny's legal problem, it would just about be impossible. That being said, the best and fastest way for them to adopt a Caucasian child in the US was to adopt a child between the ages of twenty-four and thirty-two months whose family had recently perished. The most common of these occurrences were through plane and or automobile crashes. It was called survivor adoption, and if the Panzers gave him the green light, he would begin searching for their child. Due to the expense of having people around the country able to move on a moment's notice, the cost of this type of adoption, if consummated, was three times the cost of a normal adoption or $125,000. In addition, the contract called for complete secrecy on the part of the Panzers, as Mr. Rosenberg's firm did not want it known that they involved themselves in these types of adoptions.

Mr. Panzer shook Mr. Rosenberg's hand and handed him a nonrefundable check for $25,000—the rest to be paid upon the completion of the adoption.

Three months later, the Panzers received a call from Mr. Rosenberg's office, advising them that their daughter would be arriving the following week and to make the necessary preparations. The call came the following Tuesday morning, and the Panzers went to pick her up.

According to Mr. Rosenberg, the little girl, twenty-eight months old, had been in the back seat of her parents' car when it was totaled. Miraculously, she was unharmed, although she had gone into shock and was still heavily sedated. The doctors had advised them that although they had done everything they could, they still weren't sure exactly how much she would remember. Depending on how vivid her memory of the accident was, she might require therapy at some point. They would need to hire a full-time nurse for her over the next month or so until the sedatives were completely out of her system.

They fell in love with her the moment they laid eyes on her and knew that they would do whatever was necessary to make sure this girl had a second chance.

Kenny made out a check for the balance, an additional hundred thousand dollars, and gingerly carried Emma out to the car with Carol to start the rest of their lives together as a family.

CHAPTER 14

Dominic "the fist" Merano, the youngest of three brothers, grew up in Newark, New Jersey. His father was a laborer and made enough to support his family and pay the mortgage on his three—bedroom house. There was never much left after the bills were paid for new clothes or new sneakers, or new anything. The Meranos went to church every Sunday and made a donation when the hat was passed. Mr. Merano took pride in his house and in his lawn and in his family. That was the way he was brought up. You worked hard. You took care of your family, and you protected your own. Life was simple, and any disturbances could be remedied with the back of your hand.

Dom, as he was referred to by his friends, was fourteen and in eighth grade when he was stopped on his way home from school by three older boys.

"Yo, Merano, I hear some change in your pocket belongs to me. You gonna hand it over or would you like to spend some time at the dentist getting your teeth put back in your mouth?"

"That's a good one, Rocco. How's about this—when we get through taking your face apart, you's gonna need a plastic surgeon to put it back together?"

While the third member of the group was trying to think of something clever to say, Dominic hit the first boy in the face and broke his nose. He punched the second boy on the side of the head and left him whimpering on the sidewalk; the third boy was still running.

Dominic went home and told his father what had happened and how they had tried to take his spending money. His father kissed him on the top of his head, turned to his other two sons, and said, "I disapprove of violence, but when someone tries to take what is yours, you fight with your last breath. Capice?"

The next day at school, Dominic learned another lesson—with violence comes respect! People he didn't know came up to him or passed him in the halls, smiled, and said, "Yo fist! Ain't nobody takin' your money?" By the end of the day, rumor had it that Dominic beat up an entire gang and sent most of them to the hospital. It also marked the inauguration of his nickname, the fist—a helpful moniker when you need to survive on your own.

He never became a bully. He didn't have to. Kids gave him their lunches. The rich kids loaned him money, knowing they would never see it again, but figured it was worth it if that was what it took to keep your nose on straight.

In his sophomore year, the boys came to Newark, looking for local talent and of course who would you want to handle your business, other than someone who instilled fear with just the mention of his name.

That June, Dom graduated high school (he was sixteen at the time). Okay, maybe he just stopped going, but at the time, he was bringing home more money than his father. And he always gave his mother money and always dropped paper money in the hat at church. He was a good son.

Chapter 15

The next year, they cracked down on the local mobs, and they needed someone to throw to the prosecutors—who better than an underage, first-time offender like Dominic Merano?

He did three years of good time (he kept his mouth shut), and when he got out at twenty, he was rewarded with a territory in Passaic. He had five men working under him, and they used six or seven high school kids to peddle their goods. They never let him get too big, delivered the same amount of coke each week, and kept Dominic satisfied but not happy. He never got too far. He got by. Every time it looked like he might be making some decent money, he got busted. This was no way to make a living. He was wasting the best years of his life, and all he had to show for it, everything he owned, he carried in his pocket.

Timing is everything. If he had been approached a few weeks ago, he would never have considered it, but this week, he needed to have a shot at something, and so when he was asked to start his own distribution group on the west side of Manhattan, he jumped on it.

The payoff was huge. On this first score, after paying off the buyer and his people, he would walk away with close to $200,000. Two weeks work, no selling, no distributing. This time he was on top. He would purchase the product, cut it up, and hand it off. His people paid him. He paid the source, a trip to the vault, and the process would start all over again.

He knew all the players except the source, who had to be good. Feds don't walk around with a million dollars in cocaine looking for a game. He took his time and made sure everything was done the right way. The exchange would take place at a busy restaurant on route 4 in Fair Lawn, New Jersey. The exchange was called for 8:00 p.m., so he had men in the adjacent parking lot at 3:00 p.m., watching for anything out of the ordinary. He had a man inside at the bar chatting up the bartender. Everything would go down on his turf. His people would watch all the roads and the perimeter, and no one would be in the area that wasn't part of the buy.

So Dominic was lying on his bunk at Rahway State Penitentiary, in the ninth year of a mandatory ten-year sentence for trafficking, going over that night for the 100th time. Every fucking time the story ended the same way—with him on a cot on his back at Rahway State Penitentiary, staring up at the dirty fucking ceiling!

He drove around the restaurant three times and there were no utility trucks double-parked. There were no signs of unmarked cars in the area. He nodded at his men in the adjacent parking lot and got a nod back. He walked into the River Palm Steak House in Fair Lawn, New Jersey. He nodded to his man at the bar and got thumbs-up. He signaled his men at the table by the men's room, and two of them joined up with him as he walked into the john. Five feds with automatics and shotguns yelled, "Freeze, scumbag," and here he was back at Rahway, looking up at the dirty fuckin' ceiling.

One, if you do the time, the least they could do is tell you how you fucked up, and two, there was no reason for that fed to call him a scumbag. "I tell you, the caliber of law enforcement these days is going straight downhill!"

Chapter 16

The Fist had no problem doing his time at Rahway. In the first place, he was connected. He knew more people inside Rahway than out. Secondly he had a rep. The Fist was known as a man who liked to hit and would kill you as likely as knock you down—a sadistic bastard with no conscience and no allegiances. You did something nice for him last week didn't mean he wouldn't stick a fork in your eye this week. Men of this nature are not usually bothered in the prison system.

So he's done most of his time, and because they had more bandits than bunks, he would be released after the minimum ten years. Maybe he would try politics; most of those guys were crooks, and they made big bucks. There's the garbage business. There was a lot of bread in that business, but to cut into some wise guys territory is not the way to safely break back into society.

You'd think after spending nine years with every type of criminal known to man, he could have found something that interested him, but he hadn't.

With three months to go before his release, he was transferred to a minimum-security facility. The prisons were overcrowded, and the thinking was that an inmate about to be released three months short of finishing a ten-year sentence was not a high risk. It made sense to Dominic. There was no way he would screw up his release by causing trouble.

His roommate at the farm was Steven Carlyle, an internist from Great Neck, Long Island, serving a one-year sentence for Medicaid fraud. Live and learn. Dominic had been busting his ass dealing with the scum of the earth and making a hundred grand a year, if he was lucky, while this guy typed in a few fictitious tests onto the billing records of his older patients and was clearing seven figures a year. He got caught for the first time in his life and was given a one-year sentence. Justice my ass!

They talked every day, and Dominic picked his brain. Steve may have only committed Medicaid fraud, but he knew more about screwing over the system than anyone Dominic had ever talked with. In addition, though some of Dominic's schemes might have been interesting to Steve, he would never use them as they involved physical risk, and there was no way that Steve would ever make a drug buy. So they became friends.

Dom explained what it was like running a drug operation, and it was obvious that Steve was not going to be finishing his year at the farm and running out to score cocaine. Chances were, Steve most likely already had a stash somewhere and wouldn't have to worry about money for quite some time.

Steve, on the other hand, realized immediately that his cellmate was looking for a new field to play on, and he had just the ticket. Adoption!

"Let's go through this from the beginning," Steve explained. "How do you make money from cocaine?"

"People want it. They don't sell it at Walmart! So they come to me."

"Okay, now let's say there's no cocaine around and your customers can't get any?"

"Easy. We still have our supply, except now more people want it and are willing to pay more. So we charge more."

"What if the pipeline dries up and there's no cocaine to be had?"

"That would fall under 'name your price,' but what's that got to do with me? There is no cocaine shortage, and I'm not in a position to influence the quantities of cocaine available anyway."

"I'm giving you an analogy."

"Maybe you should cover your mouth when you cough 'cause I don't need to be sick when I walk outta here."

"An analogy," Steve replied patiently, "is a means of comparing two separate ideas. The first idea is cocaine distribution and the second idea is selling children for adoption."

"I get the economics, but selling children gives me bumps up and down my back. People get all kinds of pissed off when you mess with their kids."

"That's because you know nothing about the subject. Once I give you an education, the bumps will go away."

"What do you get out of this, Steve? I've got no money, and I'm not giving you my cigarettes."

"Simple, Dom, I've got ten months left here and you'll be here for the first three. Make sure I stay in one piece while you're here and hand the job over to someone you trust to take over when you leave. Do we have a deal?"

"That we do, Steve."

"Okay, let's start at the beginning. Explain to me how a person becomes an addict?"

"They probably smoked marijuana. They liked getting high and had heard about cocaine, or their friends were using, and decided to try it. Try it a few times, and it owns you."

"Okay," Steve said, "my turn. A married couple, both husband and wife, grew up in families with brothers and/or sisters and always wanted a family of their own. Now they get married and want kids of their own."

"Okay," Dom continues, "so they try cocaine and they like it. Pretty soon, it's part of their diet. They do a few lines before work and a few lines at lunch. They do some in the evening, and it becomes a part of their sex life. He does a few lines, and he's a stallion for hours."

"Back to me," Steve continued. "They assume that the wife will get pregnant simply because they aren't using protection. After a period, they increase the number of times they have intercourse, and eventually if nothing happens, they go to a fertility expert. The doctor tells them that the wife will never be able to give birth for one reason or another and suggests adoption."

"This is where you can take your analogy you know where. The stories stop following each other 'cause as long as my customer has money, he can buy coke."

"Okay, Dom, let's say your customer loses his job and can no longer afford to buy cocaine, but he's already hooked on it. What does he do?"

"Whatever he has to! Depends on the customer. Some will go to a detox clinic and go cold turkey. Some will try cutting down and hope they can make it until things turn around, and some will buy a gun and get the money any way they can!"

"My turn. The couple tries to adopt, and for a large percentage, that's a possibility. Adoption is expensive, however. So that rules out a large percentage of people. Those people with financial problems don't concern us anyway, so I will skip over them. Those that have the funds contact adoption agencies, hire lawyers, and eventually become parents of adopted children."

"I'm losing you here, Steve. You think I should open an adoption agency?"

"Give me five more minutes, Dom. We're almost home. These people who have adopted children are like your customer who has lost his dealer and then found another one. The customer who cannot adopt for a variety of reasons is the one we want. You, for example, just served time, so you can never adopt. Our friend Tiny down the hall who has been undergoing psychotherapy for the last few years would not be able to adopt. A woman with a history of driving under the influence would never be able to adopt."

"You're losing me again," said Dom. "Where are we?"

"We are back with your customer who can't get his cocaine and will do anything to get it. He's got the money, but he cannot find cocaine. You're not even getting your delivery. He's willing to pay three times the going prices. Will he score at that price?"

"At three times the market, I will find him cocaine if I have to fly down to South America myself. Are you telling me there's a way for these people to adopt children illegally if they have enough money?"

"The light bulb finally went off. Yes, Dom, people will pay whatever they have to in order to adopt. No one is telling them it will be illegal, so even though they have a pretty good idea that they are skirting the law, they want their kid! The legal end is simple. There are snakes or lawyers all over that will make an illegal adoption legal. All that's required is a lot of money and a baby. I know the lawyers. If you can figure out the rest, you're in business." Steve stopped talking because he saw the look on Dominic's face and knew his mind was miles away, working out the possibilities.

Chapter 17

The next morning, Steve hadn't opened his eyes when Dominic asked, "Give me a number, Steve. What's the going rate on a baby for adoption?"

"Here's where it gets a little tricky, Dom. For the most part, the price is determined by age and color. If you can deliver a white child, under three months old, you've hit the jackpot, but that's almost impossible. The people who monitor these things are extremely vigilant, and this is their Fort Knox, guards on duty, at all times. There are still plenty of people willing to adopt children under the age of two, and those lines are a mile long. There's a mile of lawyers out there that make a fortune, locating these babies and setting them up for adoption. Try to muscle in on their business, and you will see why lawyers are called sharks."

The conversation was starting to piss Dom off. Maybe he should forget this adoption shit and donate little Steve to the boys in the shower room.

"So now you're telling me I'm not going to be able to find any kids to sell!"

"That's not what I'm telling you. I'm telling you that there is a category of orphaned child that exists, which includes children of twenty to twenty-six months old who have lost their families in an accident, car crash, plane crash, and the like. This category is called survivor adoption. Normally, when parents are killed in an accident, there are other relatives to take over, so the number of children that fall into this category is small, and the legislation and the safe guards to protect these children are not as tough. Therefore, it is possible to take a child from the clutches of an adoption agency, by way of an orphanage or children's protective services, and move them directly to a family in need. This is accomplished by using a law firm such as the one I am going to write down for you, with a letter of introduction from me."

"Wait, wait, wait, wait," said Dominic, now on his feet. "If there are only a few of these survivor kids out there, assuming I can find them and get them adopted, by the time I transport them to wherever this lawyer does his magic and makes it all legal, what's left in the pot. I must be missing something, but this almost seems like a legitimate line of work. If I do really well at this, I could end up with a kiss on the cheek and a key to the city. Forget the fact that I still won't have enough bread left over for a cheap hooker."

"Don't take this the wrong way, Dom, but for a guy who's been working the corners and cutting the vig, you're not too quick on the update."

"You know, Steve, I could be wrong here, but I think you just insulted me, and our deal doesn't begin until I know what the fuck the deal is. Capice?"

"I didn't mean to insult you, Dom. Let me explain it in dollars and cents. The average survivor adoption that is handled by this lawyer I am putting you in touch with goes for between 100,000 and 150,000 dollars. The lawyer gets fifty thousand. You get the rest. These children are not going to call you and say, 'My parents just crashed. I'm on the side of route 80, by exit 135 in Clark, New Jersey. Come and get me.' You are going to have to find these kids. And that, my good friend Dominic Merano, is all the school you get. What you do with it is up to you." Dominic was no longer listening. He was doing some serious thinking.

CHAPTER 18

March 2007

After years of planning and searching for the right location, William Everett Langston was going to do something no architect had ever done before. He was going to build a work of art. He already had the perfect location. Now, he would use all the skills he possessed, put together all the right people, and make this development one that could never be replicated. After interviewing dozens of architects and twice as many builders, he had found the perfect matches. After turning down funds from dozens of banks and private institutions, all of which wanted their names to be associated with this project, he had raised the money himself. He wanted total control. No one would give him completion dates or insist the project follow the agenda of their bank or board.

This was his dream, and he was about to make it a reality. This was not about selling houses or developing land. This was every architect's fantasy, the quest for perfection. There would be nothing in this development that was not unique. Every home would be a work of art. Every room in that home would set off the next. The light that filtered through each home would seemingly caress the home itself, and of course, standing in front of any window in any of the homes, one would look out for miles with nothing to infringe on the view but nature's natural wonders.

Mr. Langston had been visiting his friend Alicia, in Aspen, the summer before. They had always had a very special relationship. They had lived together for three years in the late nineties. They had a great physical relationship, a great intellectual relationship, and a great work relationship in that they both loved their work. The only problem was that, his work was at that time entirely in the city of Chicago and the only place Alicia did not want to be was in a city. They always remained the best of friends, and it was an unusual year if they didn't see each other at least two or three times. Alicia was an artist, and she knew that although William had never touched a brush to canvas, they both possessed the same love of aesthetics and the same sense of awe when confronted with ultimate beauty and balance.

He spent a week with her, and during that time, she told him to save himself for the last day of the trip as she was saving a big surprise for his last day. He pleaded with her to elaborate, but she simply smiled and told him to wait. It would be worth it.

On that last morning, she filled a picnic basket with a light lunch and an excellent Pinot Noir and drove him fifteen miles north of Aspen, at which point she made a hard right up a fairly steep hill.

"Where are we going?" he asked.

"Up," she replied, and then she proceeded to drive over one half mile on a beautifully manicured road, constantly ascending, until she reached a plateau and drove to the middle and stopped the car.

"Close your mouth, William!"

"Where are we, Alicia?"

"We are sitting in and on the town of Mason, Colorado. We are over five thousand feet above sea level. This entire mountain was donated to the State of Colorado by John Jacob Astor in 1840 and includes everything, with the exception of this square mile or so of land we are standing on now. Before he donated the land, he built outlooks coming up and around the entire property so people could stop and admire the incredible beauty of the land he so loved. He ran sanitation lines up the mountain and included rest stations for hikers so over time people wouldn't destroy the beauty of Mason, Colorado. The land was donated with the proviso that it could not be sold, leveled, plowed, or, in any way, altered from its natural state."

They opened the wine and sat in almost complete silence for some time until William asked, "Who owns this land now, and is it obtainable?"

"I'm sorry, William, I never thought to look into that. As it's Sunday, I guess you'll have to make some calls tomorrow when you get back to Chicago."

They finished their lunch hardly speaking at all but simply gazing at the vistas that stretched out before them. It was so awe-inspiring that William couldn't think of a thing to say.

Alicia drove him to the airport, and when he grabbed his bag out of the trunk, he gave her a hug and thanked her for everything, especially the last few hours. He apologized for being so quiet, but he was blown away. He started to walk away when she called him back.

"I almost forgot, William. Do me a favor, and take a look at this during your flight. You might find it interesting."

"What is it?"

"William, you know me. Just another idea of mine. Give me a call when you've looked at it and tell me what you think."

"Will do, Alicia, and thanks again." He gave her a soft kiss on the lips and a long squeeze. She was getting more and more difficult to leave.

When the plane reached cruising altitude, William opened the manila envelope. On the first page was a picture that Alicia had drawn in pencil of herself laughing. That was all it was supposed to be, but William could not help but notice that the drawing was exquisite. Then again, Alicia was always exquisite. He turned the page and read as follows:

"Dear William,

The first time I drove up to Mason, Colorado, I knew instantaneously that the only reason I was there was to bring you back. In my mind's eye, I pictured homes on that plateau that would be right out of a dream. Not a collection of houses and developments that you might find anywhere in the country, but a community unto itself that would include some magnificent homes for those who were well-off but by no means rich, and some townhouses for those people just getting started who could never, before Mason, have afforded to live in a place so beautiful.

"If you do not share my enthusiasm or think my idea is nothing but the creative mind of an artist run amok, give the envelope to the stewardess to add to the trash as she goes by. If, on the other hand, you cannot stop thinking about it either, I have enclosed the name of the sales agent for the property and their attorney. If you need me to do anything for you until you return, just call. That's what friends are for. Love Alicia."

"Yes," he cried out and nearly sent the elderly woman beside him into cardiac arrest.

Chapter 19

In May 2008, almost two years after the purchase of the land, the first house was completed. The speed in which the house was built was startling in itself, but what was more incredible was the amount of work that was completed in such a short time—the sewage and sanitation work, the lighting for the community, and the electrical foundation. They had, after all, started with woods and rocks, miles from the nearest town. AT&T adjusted one of its towers in the Aspen area to accommodate wireless service. Until that was completed, they communicated with each other by screaming at the work site and leaving messages on each other's windshields.

Everyone was psyched and couldn't wait to see the dream take shape. No one took breaks. Work stopped when you couldn't see what you were doing anymore. They were creating a work of art, and they knew it. This was an inspiration!

When they had finished, they all stood in front and said nothing. It was as if they had just finished a painting and were admiring their work.

William stood in front, deep in thought.

"Do you approve, William?" his foreman asked.

"I definitely love it, but I'm not sure if I'm satisfied. I feel like I'm missing something. Let's take tomorrow morning off. You guys sleep late, and we'll meet at the diner for a late breakfast at around eleven."

"Eleven it is. See you in the morning."

William picked up the phone and called Alicia. "Hi, love, I need a favor."

"Sorry, Will, I gave all my money to my last boyfriend."

"Cute. Can you take a ride here now and sit with me for a while? I need your eyes."

"Are you going to feed me or is this a freebie?"

"Dinner included."

"Give me an hour. I'll meet you at the house."

"Thanks."

Chapter 20

They both leaned against her car. Once in a while, one of them would walk to the left or right to get a better perspective. Neither spoke. Finally Alicia said, "I love it, William, but you're right. There's something missing. Let's go for dinner and not think about it for a while. We'll come back up later."

They were having coffee after dinner. William asked for the check, and as he was pulling out his credit card, he said, "Tell me something, Alicia. You are such a wonderful person—so warm and giving. You would make a great parent. Why is it that you never settled down and had a family?"

"William, you are such an idiot!"

"Alicia, believe me, I didn't mean that to be insulting in any way. I was just . . ."

"Stop. I didn't settle down because I love what I do, and the timing was never right. You're an idiot because that's what's missing! We forgot about the kids. All the people who buy these homes are going to have little kids. These little kids are going to be living over a mile above sea level. We might as well put a sign up that says 'Live here at you own risk' or 'Watch your step. This fall could kill you!'"

"How can I make a community that sits on top of a mountain child-proof?" William asked.

"You can't, but you can make it safe up to a point. It's okay to leave the landscaping up to the people who buy, but if we can get hold of a few tons of fairly large boulders and enclose the neighborhood, it would not only serve as a preventative, keeping kids from getting near a dangerous area, but it would be 100 percent natural. You could throw a few boulders near the corner of each driveway to lend some continuity. Can you visualize it, William, large open homes with beautiful landscaping? Each lot will be about an acre?"

"Just about."

"And the backyard of each home will be set off with twenty yards or so of beautifully free-structured boulders, and beyond that, the sky. Oh, and one other thing. This mountain has always been a haven for hikers, and you can't prevent them from coming all the way up as Mr. Astor intended. You will have young families and little kids living here, so I think you should consider a guardhouse right at the top of the road. There's a last rest stop a few hundred yards before you reach the top with a scenic view. The only way up from there is straight up the road through the guardhouse. If I had a family up here, I would insist on that."

"Alicia, I don't know how to thank you. This whole idea was actually yours. I insist on giving you some of the credit when we finish this project."

"Seriously," Alicia replied, "I was the one who found this place and set you up with the sales agent. I was the one who brought you here and placed it in your lap. I think I should get at least 5 percent of the profit."

"Alicia, how can I promise you a percentage of the profit when I don't even know what the costs are yet? After all, the homes are . . ."

"Time-out! How long have we known each other? Fifteen years? You are such a blockhead, Will. It was my pleasure to help you. I loved every minute of it. If this makes you as fulfilled as I believe it will, I will consider this a very profitable venture. If you're feeling guilty about my working for free, come home with me now and make love to me until I tell you to stop."

William didn't say another word. He just got into the car and drove. He might have been a blockhead, but he wasn't brain-dead!

Chapter 21

Michael Corritore grew up in Opa Locka, Florida. He and his mother, Florence, lived in a garden apartment about two miles north of the airport in Fort Lauderdale. His mother walked three blocks to the bus stop each morning and took the bus to the airport where she managed a coffee shop in the American Airlines terminal. She got home each night around seven, in time to make dinner for Michael.

He never knew his father. His mother said he died in Afghanistan, but Michael wasn't so sure, not that it mattered at this point. He and his mother got by just fine. He was an average student. He stayed out of trouble and always picked up odd jobs to help out. He did a paper route for two years when he was in junior high and got a job at the Pancake House off I-95 when he was a freshman in high school. He liked to work hard. It kept him from thinking about all the things he couldn't afford, and it made him feel good, knowing he was making things easier for his mom who was always working.

When Michael was finishing his senior year in high school, his mother got serious with a man who had a union job at the airport, and Michael knew he had better make plans. There was no way he was going to share a house with his mother and her boyfriend or maybe husband, and if he took all his savings, he could maybe survive for a month. The other alternative was to pack a bag, hop on a bus to the west coast (the frozen north was out of the question), and find a job. He wasn't crazy about the idea—no friends, no money, and minimum wage—but it beat sleeping on some guy's couch, listening to him put your mother away each night.

It was getting close to decision time when fate played her hand. It was Sunday night and Michael had closed the Pancake House at 9:30 p.m. He had been one of two managers for the past six months and worked alongside the owner, Big Ed (he had never known his last name). He was making $400 a week with a little cash on the side, which was pretty good for a seventeen-year-old kid.

The phone rang, and it was Big Ed's wife. Michael had met her dozens of times at work. She must have been in her fifties and had always been nice to Michael, but he knew immediately that something must be seriously wrong if she was calling him at home.

Big Ed came home that afternoon, she said, kissed her hello, and dropped dead before he made it to the couch. She needed to speak to him in person and asked if he could come over. She gave him the address, and thirty minutes later, he was sitting in her living room and listening to her plan.

Big Ed owned this franchise, she said, and in this economy, if she sold it, she'd be on poverty row within three years. She'd watched him over the years and knew that nobody worked harder. Big Ed told her if push came to shove, she could trust him. She offered to pay Michael $600 a week. The last two years Big Ed had made $100,000 a year plus some cash. She offered Michael one third of whatever the Pancake House brought in for the year. The extra cash was mine. She could live fine on $65,000 a year, she said. Oh, and if Michael stayed for a minimum of five years, he would own one third of the franchise free and clear.

She waited to see if he thought it was enough while he was thinking he'd never had more than $2,000 in the bank and he was going to be rich.

He immediately moved into his own apartment within walking distance of the Pancake House. His mother moved in with her boyfriend one month later. Michael had dinner with them every Sunday but was thankful he had his own place.

Chapter 22

That's how Michael got started. Four years later, Big Ed's widow remarried a guy with serious money. Michael had just turned twenty-two. She transferred the entire ownership of the Pancake franchise to him free and clear. He worked there for two more years until on one particularly slow afternoon as he was surfing the Internet, looking for business opportunities, He had practically every penny he had earned over the past five years sitting in a savings account. It was an this advertisement for a restaurant in Aspen, Colorado. The name on top of the ad said Sam and Linda Palazzole. Underneath it said, "My wife and I have owned and run Sammy's for thirty years and have loved making all our friends a little fatter. We thank you all for making us a part of your lives and we will be on the beach in Naples, Florida, if you would like to visit. Anyone interested in purchasing Sammy's can call us at the above number during working hours. If we make a deal, Linda and I would be more than willing to work with you for a few months (on salary, of course) until you feel comfortable."

Michael knew that Sam was speaking to him when he read this ad, and he picked up the phone immediately and called.

"Hello, Sammy's, reservations for this evening?"

"Is this Sam, I say?"

"Hang on a second."

"Hello, this is Sam."

"Sam, my name is Michael. I own a Pancake House in Fort Lauderdale, and as soon as I can sell it, I would like to drive out to Aspen, work out a deal with you, and become the new owner of Sammy's."

"Take a breath, Michael. We haven't met. You don't know how much I want for my restaurant. You don't know what the condition of the restaurant is. In other words, you know nothin'. Maybe you should slow down!"

"Sam, give me sixty seconds, and if you still think I'm wasting your time, I'll leave you alone."

"It's your dime, Michael. I'm listening."

"I am the only son of a single mother who has worked her entire life. I began working at twelve to help with the expenses. I have worked seven days a week for the past six years and have no problem continuing the schedule for another six years or more. I was not looking for a restaurant and have never been outside the state of Florida in my entire life, but I knew, when I read your ad, that you were talking to me. I will put my Pancake House up for sale with an agent (they are an easy sell in Fort Lauderdale), and I will pack up and leave by the end of the week. Give me two weeks from today, and if you are not satisfied that I am your man, I will walk away."

There was a long silence at the other end.

"Sam, are you still there?"

"Michael, you've got two weeks."

"Thank you, Sam. You won't be sorry!"

"From your mouth to god's ear. One last thing, Michael. Do you have a last name?"

"Corritore. Michael Corritore."

As the phone was on its way to the cradle, Michael heard Sammy say, "At least he's Italian!"

Chapter 23

Michael had dinner with his mother that night and told her everything. She was thrilled for him.

"You're incredible," she said. "I gave you next to nothing and you've turned out to be the most responsible, respectful, best man I could ever have hoped for. I couldn't be prouder of you. Now, go and make yourself happy and rich in that order."

He left quickly before he had to wipe his eyes and began packing that night. He took care of all his business and left for Colorado. He was so pumped that it wasn't until he was halfway there that he realized he was heading to the frozen north.

It took him twenty hours to get to Aspen. He arrived at 10:00 p.m. and checked into a motel outside of town. Accommodations in Aspen were too expensive for his budget. He had a light bite, hit the bed, and was asleep before he had a chance to get nervous about how tomorrow would go.

He walked into Sammy's at 3:00 p.m. He knew that would be a quiet time, and he didn't want there to be too many distractions. It was an old-fashioned restaurant—high ceilings, a lot of light in the middle, and some great areas toward the windows. It was very romantic with red and white tablecloths and candles on all the tables. There was also a nice-sized bar, and that was where he sat down. There was no one in the restaurant except Michael, but eventually a middle-aged man, carrying a pretty good stomach and a larger smile, walked behind the bar.

"What can I do for you, my friend?"

I'd like to buy this place if it's still for sale," Michael said, trying not to let his smile take over his face.

"Linda," Sammy called out, "come and meet Michael Corritore."

Linda walked out of the kitchen and stopped in her tracks. "Oh shit," she muttered.

Sammy laughed. "Linda, is that any way to speak to the man who wants to buy our restaurant?"

"I'm sorry," said Michael, "have I offended you? Should I have called first?"

"Not your fault, Michael," said Sammy. "Let's just forget it for now, and I'll explain it to you another time."

They spent two hours, talking. The numbers were fair, and both the Palazzoles and Michael were satisfied.

Over the next few days, the Palazzoles' lawyer drew up a contract. Sam was adamant that Michael have his own lawyer, but Michael was just as adamant that he trusted Sam and was going to need every dime he had to get the restaurant started.

By the following week, Michael was running his own restaurant with the Palazzoles teaching him the difference between a Pancake House and an upscale Italian restaurant.

It was on Tuesday that Sam called Michael in the morning to say he and Linda were going to meet their daughter at the restaurant. She would probably be there before them, and Sam asked Michael if he would keep her company until they arrived.

"You never mentioned you have a daughter or that she lives around here?"

"There are two reasons you've never met her. One is that she's a ski instructor on the big mountain and the only time we see her is when it's raining."

"What's the other reason?"

"I'll tell you later."

"Again, you'll tell me later? I'm starting to get worried. Does she kill people for a living?"

"Bye, Michael."

At eleven o'clock, Michael walked out of the kitchen and nearly knocked over a girl standing by the bar.

"I'm sorry," said Michael, "I didn't realize anyone was here."

"No problem. You must be Michael. I'm Sam and Linda's daughter, Marie."

Now he had some idea of what Sam was not telling him. Marie was 5'3" tall with green eyes and jet-black hair. She had an incredible figure and hot as a firecracker.

"Excuse me, but if you're done checking me out, I think I'll sit down until my parents get here."

"I'm sorry. Of course, have a seat. It's just that I hadn't known, I mean I wasn't expecting you to, uh . . ."

"It's okay, Michael, take a breath before you faint."

"Can I get you something? Coffee, a drink?"

"No, thanks, I'm good. I'll just wait out here."

"Okay, call if you need anything." Michael walked back into the kitchen, talking to himself, "Great impression, Michael. What are you? Fifteen years old?"

He stuck his head out fifteen minutes later, and Marie was gone.

Sam and Linda came back at four to start getting ready for the dinner crowd, and Michael said, "I met Marie, you know."

"Really, I wasn't sure she came in," Linda said. "Probably not your type, though."

"I don't know. Why do you say that?"

"It's just a guess, but in the last two minutes, you put two bottles of red wine in the dishwasher, and if I'm not mistaken, that is Sweet' N Low you're filling the salt shakers with, isn't it? Of course, it's your restaurant. I'm just trying to be helpful!"

When Sam stopped laughing, he walked over and handed Michael a sealed envelope. "From the contract killer," he said.

Michael walked outside and read the note.

"Dear Michael, my mother knows what I look for in a man, so I was prepared when you walked into the bar today. Obviously, you weren't! Here's my phone number. If I don't hear from you within forty-eight hours, I will have you killed. Marie."

Michael walked back into the kitchen, carrying the smile with him. Linda looked over and said, "Oh shit."

"Hey, Michael," Sam said, "you got it now"?

Chapter 24

The next morning, Marie met her best friend Tracy and her husband Paul for breakfast at the hotel. Tracy managed the hotel restaurant and was married to Paul who ran the children's ski school. They had been married for two years, but even with both their salaries, decent rentals in Aspen were out of their price range. They rented a room by the month at the Ramada Inn, which was thirty minutes outside of town. Marie lived in one of the staff rooms the hotel provided for its employees—small but clean.

"We're going to have a quick bite and then catch a late movie tonight," Tracy said. "Why don't you join us?"

"I can't tonight," said Marie. "I'm pretty sure I have plans."

"What does that mean? When will you know if you have plans or not?"

"As soon as he calls me," said Marie.

"Whoa! Let's back up a second. What did I miss since yesterday afternoon?"

"Well, this guy just bought my parents' restaurant. He looks sort of like my old boyfriend, Joe, but taller. You remember Joe, don't you?"

"Let me see," said Tracy. "About 5'9", longish hair, brown eyes. Thought he was God's gift but treated you like garbage and loved to admire himself in the mirror. That's the guy?"

"Pretty close," said Marie. "You know how every guy you meet in Aspen comes from money. They're all smooth as silk. Skiers since they're five years old. If they drove here, it's at least a Mercedes, and all of them have an iPhone attached to their ear."

"Don't tell me you found another one of them, Marie," said Paul. "We're just getting over your getting over, the last one."

"Michael. His name's Michael. He has never had any of those things. He has never owned anything or been anywhere. I doubt he's ever had a serious girlfriend. He has worked all his life to survive and has saved every cent he's ever earned. He's taking a loan from the bank because he doesn't have nearly enough to buy Sammy's on his own, and my parents are letting him pay off notes so he can afford the purchase."

"Why would they take that risk?" Paul asked.

"My father loves him."

"Didn't they just meet?" Paul asked.

"Yes, they did. Oh, and take me off the winter teaching schedule. I'm pretty sure Michael's going to need help after my parents leave."

"Whoa! One more time, you can't go out with us tonight, and you're quitting your job at the hotel this winter, but so far, he hasn't called you?"

"I think you've got it," smiled Marie.

"Okay, listen," said Paul. "Tracy and I are taking a walk into town. If you decide to get married while we're gone, call me on my cell and we'll rush right back. I'd call you to check, but I don't want to tie up your phone in case Michael's trying to get through."

Tracy and Paul walked away, laughing, but it had no effect on Marie. She'd had that same smile on her face since she ran into Michael at the restaurant.

Chapter 25

It was 4:00 p.m., and Michael and the Palazzoles were preparing the kitchen for dinner.

"You know, Michael, Monday nights are the slowest nights of the week. If you want to take off early, this might be your best night," said Sam.

"Maybe I could leave around seven," Michael replied. "Would that be okay?"

"Seven's fine," Sam replied.

Michael walked outside and called Marie. He cleared his throat a few times and tried to think of something to say so he wouldn't start off stammering the way he did yesterday.

"Hello," Marie answered on the first ring.

"Hello, Marie, it's Michael."

"Well, Michael, you finally decided to call. Do you know how long I've been waiting? Were you too busy to call me this morning? Didn't want to seem too anxious?"

"Marie! You probably do this a lot. I don't. So could you cut me a little slack? This is my first break, and I am using it to call you. If you are free, would you like to have dinner with me tonight?"

"Sorry, I thought you would call me earlier, and I was getting upset. Dinner would be great. What time?"

"I'll pick you up at the hotel at 7:15 p.m. Okay? I won't keep you waiting this time."

Michael got to the hotel at 7:00 p.m. and sat there just in case Marie was early. He stood by the car until Marie came out at ten after. She walked over and immediately gave him a kiss on the cheek.

"Did you miss me?" Marie said.

"I haven't stopped thinking about you for a second," he replied.

"We could stay here and talk," said Marie, "but I believe the doorman would like you to move this car, or what's left of it, away from the hotel. I don't think I've ever seen a car like this. What is it?"

"Well, it used to be a Chevy, but it was totaled, and the Chevy parts were no longer available, so they used parts from an old Pontiac to put it back together. A friend of mine promised it would get me to Colorado, and it did. Cost me next to nothing."

"I should hope so," said Marie. "Listen I don't care if we walk, but tomorrow you are going to drive this wreck somewhere and give it a proper burial. You are the new owner of a beautiful Italian restaurant in the snobby rich city of Aspen. If people see you in this corroded mess, they're going to think that your restaurant is run the same way. I'll take you to a friend of my father and he'll give you a good deal on a monthly lease with nothing down. You can lease a new Toyota for under $200 a month. Is that okay?"

"That would be great. Thanks."

"You're welcome. Where are we going for dinner?"

"I was hoping you could suggest some place," Michael replied. "I have no idea what you like, and if I did, I wouldn't know how to get there anyway."

"Well," Marie said, "there's a little place on Anderson that makes a good cheeseburger. How does that sound?"

Michael breathed a sigh of relief. He was hoping she wouldn't pick one of the fancy restaurants in town. "Sounds perfect."

They pulled up to the the Woody Creek Tavern, Aspen's infamous hamburger joint. The hostess seated them at a corner table, and they ordered two cheeseburgers, fries, and two cokes. They then proceeded to fill each other in on what they'd both been doing for the last twenty odd years until the waitress came over to inform them that no one had ever taken this long to consume two cheeseburgers and that if they wouldn't mind, there were people waiting in line for their table.

They spent the rest of the evening walking through Aspen, holding hands and staring into each other's eyes.

It was about 1:00 a.m. when Michael dropped Marie off in front of the hotel.

"You know," Marie said, "I think it would be a good idea if you hired me as a waitress, and then when my parents leave for Naples, I can become your manager. What do you think?"

"I think, Marie, that I might able to handle your working as my waitress, but I'm not sure I can afford to hire a manager just yet."

"Look at it as an investment in our future." She laughed and planted a hot long, lingering kiss on his mouth. She was in the lobby of the hotel and turned to see that he still hadn't moved from the door of his car. Maybe, she thought, he was just waiting for his legs to start working again.

Chapter 26

The next two months were like nothing Michael had ever experienced. He was the owner of a successful restaurant. He not only worked in one of the most beautiful cities in the US, but for the first time in his life, he was respected. Everywhere he went, people stopped to ask how the restaurant was going and how things were with Marie. And of course, he was in love with a beautiful girl.

He would probably wait a year or two until he had a little more money saved before thinking of settling down, but it was simply a question of when. With most girls, this plan would be fine, but Marie was not most girls.

Marie's parents were leaving on November 15 for Naples. That was six weeks away, said Marie, and she would like to be engaged by the time they left so they could all go out and celebrate.

"Hold on a second, Marie. Aren't I the one that proposes to you and buys the ring and asks you to get married?"

"Exactly," Marie cooed as she ran her fingers through his hair. "That's your job, and mine is to tell you when."

They were engaged on November 6, and the engagement party was held at Sammy's the following weekend. Michael sent his mother pictures of the party. She refused to waste so much money on a weekend trip, even if Michael had offered to pay her airfare. She did promise that she would not miss the wedding.

There were two surprise announcements at the party. The first was by Tracy, who informed everyone that in case anyone thought she was putting on a few pounds, she was actually ten weeks pregnant; and the second was by Marie, who announced that she and Michael would be getting married on New Year's Eve.

Her parents were thrilled, and Michael was in shock as he, of course, was hearing about it for the first time. Two days later, Sam and Linda left for Florida, and Michael and Marie moved into the Ramada Inn with Paul and Tracy.

The following week, the four of them went into town together. Michael and Marie were witness to an argument between their friends, an extremely unusual occurrence. Paul was explaining that the baby would be born in May and if they saved their money, maybe they would be able to find a decent apartment before the baby started to walk. Tracy insisted that they find a place to live before she gave birth. She was not going to start her child's life in a Ramada Inn and immediately began to cry. Marie took her for a walk to calm her down.

"What are you going to do, Paul? It costs a fortune to live out here."

65

"You're not kidding, Michael. We've looked everywhere and haven't seen anything close to affordable!"

"You know, Paul, I had the mayor at the restaurant for dinner last week. He was early, and he was telling me about a plan he's considering to provide affordable housing for some of the people who work in Aspen. He was talking about houses, not apartments."

"Well, I certainly can't afford a house."

"The next time he comes in, I'll see what I can find out. Can't hurt!"

"Thanks, Michael. I appreciate that."

"Let's not mention it to Tracy unless something comes of it."

"No problem."

Chapter 27

A few weeks before the wedding, Michael's mother flew in and stayed with them at the Ramada. She got to meet Marie, whom she loved immediately, and Paul and Tracy and the rest of their friends. Sam and Linda flew in the next day and took Florence with them wherever they went.

Michael threw a dinner for his family and friends at the restaurant the night before, and Sam and Linda made the wedding on New Year's Eve. Everyone cried, everyone danced, drank, and celebrated, and then they all went home to Fort Lauderdale, Naples, and Aspen, and life continued on as before.

On Valentine's Day, Marie gave Michael a card that read, "You think I'm difficult? Wait until you meet my daughter." The Ramada would soon need a day care center.

That night, the mayor and his wife came in for Valentine's dinner.

"Nice to see you, Mayor Bradley. Haven't seen you in a while."

"Call me Tom, Michael, and I've been tied up with this housing project we've been working on. As a matter of fact, this could directly impact you and maybe your friends at the hotel. Stop by my office this week, and we'll talk."

"Thank you, Mayor, I mean Tom. I appreciate your trying to help."

Michael took Paul with him on Wednesday afternoon. Michael was pretty good with food and figures, but Paul graduated with a degree in business from Ohio University. Michael was hoping that if the mayor had something to offer them, Paul would know whether it was the right move for them.

One hour later, the two of them walked out of the mayor's office in a daze.

"We have to explain this to the girls together, Paul. For one thing, I'm not sure I understand it completely myself, and for another, you'll have to vouch for me. Marie will think I made it up."

They sat over dinner, and Paul laid it out.

"It's unbelievable! We just saw pictures of the first house completed in Mason."

"I never heard of Mason," Tracy responded.

"It's ten miles south, off route 82."

"I've been down route 82," said Marie. "There's nothing there except a huge Exxon depot. There's no town there."

"Did you ever notice that huge mountain that seems to go straight up alongside the gasoline tanks?"

"Seriously," said Tracy, "are you guys pulling our legs?"

67

"I swear, Tracy, this is no joke. Let me explain. A little over one year ago, an architect named William Everett Langston got the inspiration to clear the area on top of that mountain. The mountain was donated to the state, but the area on top, a few square miles, was sold to Langston. His idea was to create something that had never been built before. It would be his work of art, his masterpiece.

"One house has been completed. Over the next two years, nine more houses in this price range will be built. These homes will sell for approximately 1.5 million each. There will be three larger homes selling for about three million each, and ten townhouses that will range from $800,000 to one million."

"That's fascinating," Tracy jumped in. "At the rate you're going, it will be sometime tomorrow afternoon when you get to something we can consider!"

"Give me five minutes, Tracy, and then you can tell me what you think. Okay?"

"Sorry, continue."

"Okay, this is a very unusual development, in that the main goal is not profit. They'll make money. Don't get me wrong, but less than these homes would normally bring. Here's why. Number one, homes like these would normally carry huge taxes, but because the mountain was donated to the state and because the only business in the entire town of Mason is the Exxon oil depot, the taxes are ridiculously low. Number two, in an effort to help the city of Aspen, not the millionaires but the people who work in Aspen and can't afford to raise their families here. In other words, us. The mayor has worked out a deal with the developer. The community of Mason will allow the city of Aspen to purchase four of these townhouses and rent them out to employees with an option to buy."

"That sounds great," Marie cut in, "but could we have that in English, please? Twenty five words or less!"

"We can pay slightly more per month than we are now paying at the Ramada. If at the end of two years we want to walk away, no problem. If, however, we decide to buy the house for the original price, all the rent we have paid is credited toward the purchase."

Both girls sat in silence for thirty seconds or so until Tracy said, "Oh my god!"

They thought the surprise was over until the following day when they drove up to check the town out.

"This is a dream," said Marie. "This is the most beautiful place I've ever seen, and I don't even know what my house is going to look like yet!"

So they continued with their lives, waiting for their new homes to be completed and their children to be born.

CHAPTER 28

At the minimum-security facility in Langston, Pennsylvania, Dominic was packing up the remnants of ten years in the system and waiting for his number to be called for release. Everything he owned fit into one small duffle bag—two T-shirts, six packs of Marlboros, and the Windbreaker that was on his back when he began his sentence ten years before. Of course, his gold bracelet and ring and his gold chain somehow got misplaced. He had a total of eighty-five dollars in his pocket. The rest of ten years of minimum prison wage had gone for smokes and dope.

"Prisoner #33115, report to the front gate immediately." Seconds after the announcement came over the loudspeaker, his cell was opened and a guard stood outside, waiting for him.

Dominic needed no second announcement. He was at the front gate within minutes.

The guard opened the gate, muttered good luck into the dirt, and clanged the gate shut, missing Dominic's head by inches.

There was no one to meet him. The sign directly in front of him with an arrow pointing to the left said Civilization Three Miles by Foot. He followed the road and the instructions from the prison, which led him to a rooming house with a room reserved in his name—$20 a week. The room was almost as nice as his prison cell.

He had forty-eight hours to report to his parole officer and twenty-four hours after that to report to the cleaners in town for his arranged job. He did as he was told. He needed the week to make phone calls and get the rest of his life started before he pulled his Houdini act and vanished from the face of the earth.

His first and most important call was to Seattle, Washington, and the law firm of Rosenberg and Flakowitz. As per his instructions, he said, "Hello, I'm getting settled in," and left his address and room number. He also included his clothing and shoe sizes. He spent the next few days checking in with his parole office and beginning his new job as steam dryer at the local laundry.

One week later, he received a FedEx package from Seattle. It included hair dye, instant tan (guaranteed to remove the ashen pallor of ten years in prison), and two pairs of blue jeans with matching shirts, one pair of loafers, and three pairs of socks. In the pocket of the jeans, there was a driver's license under the name of John Scully—5'11" tall, brown eyes and hair, 185 pounds, born in Sacramento on June 11, 1975. That would make him thirty-three, close enough.

There were also a library card, a voter's registration card, a plane ticket to Seattle, in the name of John Scully, for Saturday morning, and the address of the Fairmont Motor Inn, where John Scully had a room reserved in his name paid up through the following month. His appointment with Mr. Rosenberg was for Monday night at 8:00 p.m. at his office in Seattle, and there was $1,000 in cash.

Damn, thought Dominic, *these guys are good.*

He went to work at the cleaners on Friday; this way, no one would come looking for him until Monday afternoon. After dinner that night, he applied the hair dye and the twenty-four-hour tanning solution. He packed his duffle bag, woke up at 5:00 a.m., and got out of the rooming house before the sun came up on Saturday morning. He was sitting on the 6:00 a.m. flight to Seattle as the jet began to roll.

The Fist was dead. Long live the Fist!

Chapter 29

John Scully walked down Eastlake Avenue. The weather in August was a little cooler in Seattle than in New York, but aside from that, he felt as if he was back in the city. He loved the action—everyone running in different directions, everyone in a hurry, a million things going on at the same time.

He entered the Conway building at 7:45 p.m. The Rosenberg and Flakowitz offices were on the twenty-fifth floor, and if nothing else, Scully was punctual. He entered the office and called out as no one was sitting at the reception desk.

"Back here," a voice responded from the back.

Scully walked through to the back conference room and was greeted by two men, maybe in their mid-forties, and a worn but not unattractive woman, closer to his age.

The man closest to him stuck out his hand and said, "John Scully, I presume? I am Howard Rosenberg, and this is my partner, Ed Flakowitz. Ed takes care of the personal injury side of our firm, and I take care of the adoption business. This lady is Trudy Miller. In her first life, Trudy was a nurse. She was a good nurse and would still be practicing that profession but for one small problem. More of the medication prescribed for her patients ended up in her mouth than theirs. She's been clean for years, with the exception of a small variety of recreational drugs, if you know what I mean. She can never work professionally again. That is why she works for me and is invaluable in taking care of adoptions before we are able to permanently place them."

John, as he would refer to himself going forward, thought that Trudy looked pretty good, and it looked as though Trudy had the same thoughts about him.

"Before we go any further, I would like to have a few moments with Mr. Scully. Why don't you escort Trudy to the kitchen, Ed, and make her a cup of coffee? Give me fifteen minutes."

"No problem, Howard," and he walked Trudy out and closed the door.

After they had gone, Howard sat for a few minutes, staring out at the city.

"Would you like a drink, John?"

"Whatever your drinking will be fine," he said.

"Now, John, you don't mind if I call you John, do you?"

"You're the one who gave me the name. Be my guest."

"I don't want there to be any misunderstanding here, John. I know everything there is to know about you. I want you to know something about me also. Do you understand what I mean, John?"

"You want us to be friends, Howard?"

"That's funny, John. Let's cut the bullshit, and I'll tell you what kind of friend I need you to be."

"Whenever you're ready, Howard!"

"I got a call from Steven Carlyle when the two of you were on the farm in New Jersey. He told me everything he knew about you, and I found out the rest. I know you did three years of hard time and never gave up a name, and I know about your reputation. Carlyle said you would be a good fit here, and that's why I have invested in you. He told me about the deal he made with you. I thought it was very clever of him. He could never do a year with blue-collar convicts and make it out in one piece. He sets you up, and you promise him protection in return when you're gone. I think that was a good deal for both of you. Did you live up to your end of the deal, John?"

"I took care of my end."

"You promised a thousand a month to Joey Needles to make sure Carlyle stayed healthy."

"How do you know that? I didn't even tell Steve who was lookin' out for him."

"I make it my business to know everything that's going on, John. A man like Steve Carlyle could never be part of an organization like this. The first time he was squeezed, he'd sing like a canary. I have too much at stake to hope he never talks about his cellmate that he helped get set up in Seattle."

"I don't think Steve would ever say anything. He knows what would happen to him if he did."

"You're probably right, John, but I feel better knowing that we don't have to worry about that possibility. You see, Steve had an accident this afternoon in the laundry. He was careless and got his head caught under a steam iron. Joey said it was unbelievable how long it took him to die. By the way, I'll take over Joey's payments as soon as he gets out of solitary. Are you okay with my eliminating Carlyle? Are you going to be mad at me now because I killed your friend?"

"He wasn't my friend. You can kill everyone in New Jersey for all I care. I couldn't give a fuck. Is that why you wanted to talk to me so you could tell me how tough you are? Good for you. I'm impressed."

"Good, John. I want you to be impressed. You're now working for an organization that has people all over the country. Somebody fucks with us, anywhere, and they're history. I'm going to make you very rich, but I wanted you to understand before you set one foot into my organization that if you fuck up in Seattle, it's no different than fucking up in Newark. Dead is dead, John. Capice?"

"It wasn't necessary to read me the beginner's manual. I've been around the block enough times to know how it works. No one will ever hear anything about you from me, and just so we understand each other, if I ever thought that you or anyone else here was a loose end, I'd eliminate them faster than you can say Steve Carlyle."

"Well said, John. I think we can be friends now." They shook hands and called in Ed and Trudy.

For the time being, Mr. Rosenberg continued, "The two of you will work together. I have your first assignment, John. You and Trudy will drive down to Spokane. There is a shelter there, and I have been informed that a two-year-old boy, whose mother died during childbirth, was recently abandoned by the child's father. The boy was picked up by children's protective services and left at the shelter. Now, normally, this child would be lost in the shuffle and might get tossed around for a few years while they figured out what to do with him. Lucky for the boy, I am going to get involved and get him a home. You, Mr. Scully, will speak to my acquaintance at the shelter, give him this envelope, and take the boy. If he gives you a hard time, Mr. Scully, I expect you will show him why it makes sense not to give us a hard time. Trudy will tend to the boy on the ride back, and when the boy has been adopted, Mr. Scully, you will be paid fifteen thousand dollars."

"I don't want to seem ungrateful, Mr. Rosenberg, but I was led to believe the figure would be much higher."

"Yes, I see where you might be confused. What you are doing for me in this instance, John, is running an errand. I have made almost all the arrangements. You are taking my car and, with the help of another of my employees, picking up a child and dropping him off. In the future, if you should get to the point where you find a child, extract him from his living arrangement, and deliver him to me so that I might find him a new family, we will be operating under the numbers to which I believe you are referring. Are we on the same page, John?"

"Most definitely, Howard."

Trudy escorted John to the garage where they climbed into a Ford Station Wagon and set off for Spokane.

They arrived at the halfway house at 3:00 p.m. and immediately asked for Mr. Pryor.

Mr. Pryor walked them back outside and explained that he might have gotten a little ahead of himself. It seemed that the people involved had told him they would get back to him in a few weeks and see about a more permanent placement. He didn't want to get into any trouble, and now he wasn't so sure he had the right to allow an adoptive process to begin.

"Mr. Pryor," Trudy responded, "we have just driven several hours, and our firm has invested time and money as a result of your promises!"

"I'm sorry to mess up your plans," said Pryor, "and you can tell your boss I'll be more careful next time, but I can't go through with this today."

"Excuse me, Trudy, but would you allow me two minutes to talk this over with Mr. Pryor, man to man?"

"Whatever, I'll wait for you in the car."

Ten minutes later, John got into the station wagon with a bag of clothes in his right hand and a two-year-old boy in his left.

"What did you say to him, John? It sounded as though he would never change his mind!"

"Just used my powers of persuasion, Trudy. Now let's get this little one to Seattle before he wakes up."

Trudy was impressed, and John Scully had found a way to make a living that beat the hell out of selling cocaine!

Chapter 30

Tracy was due in May 2008. Although she was ecstatic about the new townhouse they would be moving into in July 2010, she still was upset at spending two years of her life raising a child at the Ramada Inn. By the time they moved to Mason, their child would think it was routine for two hundred strangers to come in and out of your life every few days. On the other hand, she was married to a great guy, and Paul knew exactly how she felt; there was no use in making him feel he was letting her down. She'd get through it. At least she had Marie to complain to.

Paul was just finishing his day at the hotel and was about to get to his car when he spotted one of his best customers sitting alone in the lounge. Jim Karieunitas had five children. Over the past several years, they had all been members of Paul's ski school, and he had formed a close attachment with all of them. The oldest child, who was nine years old, had gone out after class and tried to make an intermediate ski jump, a move he was years away from. He landed with all his weight on his left leg and broke his femur; the surgery went fine, and the family was preparing to return to New York.

"Hello, Jim, what are you doing here all alone? Susan leave you for another skier?"

"Actually, she hired a sitter for the evening, and we're going to spend a quiet evening at the lodge. These past few days with Troy's leg have really been emotionally draining. Speaking of the past few days, you've been terrific, taking them on extra runs and keeping them with you through lunch. I don't know how to thank you."

"Don't mention it," Paul replied. "I love your kids. I had just as much fun with them as they did with me."

"I just want you to know we appreciate it. How's Tracy doing? She must be getting close?"

"A few months. She's due in May."

"Whatever happened with that townhouse you were telling me about, Paul? Did it amount to anything?"

"Actually it was a home run. The city of Aspen is sponsoring the purchase of four of the townhouses, which by the way are gorgeous. It's a two-year rental with an option to buy at the end. We should be able to move in around July 2010."

"That sounds great, Paul. Is Tracy good with spending the next two years at the Ramada? If I remember correctly, she wanted to be in her own place when the baby was born."

"I know, and don't think I'm not upset about it, but there really are no alternatives that we can afford right now. She's terrific, though. I know she's upset about it, and she hasn't said a word. We'll be fine. Listen, if I don't see you guys before you leave, please say good-bye to the kids for me, and tell Troy that when his leg is strong enough, I'll teach him how to jump and not break his arms and legs."

"I will. Take care of yourself, Paul, and say good-bye to Tracy for us."

Chapter 31

The next morning, Paul and Tracy arrived at the lodge and sat down for breakfast. One of the perks of managing at the lodge was that the food was on the house. They were just having their coffee when they looked up at Jim and Sue Karieunitas.

"I thought you guys were leaving this morning," said Paul.

"We are, but we needed to speak with you before we left. Susan and I were discussing your situation over dinner, and we think we may have a solution."

"What situation is that?" responded Tracy, a little upset that Paul was discussing their personal lives with his clients.

"Now, don't get upset," Susan responded gently. "We knew that you were looking at that new home near Aspen and that you were also upset about the possibility of giving birth and not having your own place. While we were having dinner last night, we came up with a very good proposition for the two of you."

"It's like this," Jim continued. "Our little girls are just starting school and Troy is not going to see a ski slope for close to two years, according to his doctor. We own a five-bedroom ski chalet in Aspen and have no intention of letting strangers trash the place. We pay a monthly maintenance charge to the hotel. I know your friends Michael and Marie are in almost the same circumstance, so if the four of you will take care of my monthly maintenance for the next two years, which I believe is less than the Ramada Inn is charging for the month, and if you promise to return it to us in the same condition, it's yours until your house is ready."

"That's ridiculous," Paul said. "You could rent your place for five times the maintenance."

"Actually, more like ten, but as I said, we don't want strangers in our home. We think you guys are terrific and would love to help you get started. The fact of the matter is it would be totally wasted if you and your friends don't use it, and we have no intentions of renting it. So do we have a deal?"

Paul got up and hugged Jim, while Susan wrapped her arms around Tracy, who was crying hysterically and couldn't talk.

"Here are two sets of keys," said Jim. "Make more if you need them. Here are all our telephone numbers if you have any questions or need help with something. That's it. Have a healthy baby, and we'll keep in touch. Oh, and we might fly out occasionally. If you could keep the fifth bedroom for us, we wouldn't bother you too much."

77

"I think we could handle that. This is the most generous thing anyone has ever done for me," said Tracy. "I can't wait to tell Marie. She'll flip out."

They drove over to the restaurant at 11:00 p.m. That was about when they normally closed up. The last four people were just getting up from their table when Paul and Tracy walked in.

"What are you guys doing here?" Marie yelled from the other side of the table. "The kitchen's closed." She laughed.

"We have some exciting news. Open up a good bottle of red and have a seat."

Michael opened a bottle and brought four glasses to the table.

"I can't hold it for another second," said Tracy. "This Monday morning I am going in late and Paul has no ski school. You and Michael can have someone open and still be here in the early afternoon."

"What are we doing?" asked Michael.

"I'm going to tell you," said Tracy with a huge smile on her face, "but I'm trying to drag it out. We are moving out of the Ramada Inn and moving into a five-bedroom ski chalet at the bottom of the mountain."

"You're insane," cried Marie. "Those chalets go for about $20,000 a month in season and $7,500 a month during the summer."

"Except," said Paul, "this chalet is owned by a family I have known for the last five years. They are asking us to pay the maintenance and look after the place, and they might visit once in a while for the next two years or until our townhouses are ready. The maintenance, by the way, is a little less than we are paying for these two rooms we live in now."

"I hope I wasn't speaking out of turn," Paul said, trying not to let his smile run away with his face, "but I accepted the offer for both of us."

And then all four of them began to laugh, and cry, and hug each other until they could no longer stand.

As it turned out, the chalet was barely able to house them. Tracy gave birth to Charlie In June 2008 and Marie gave birth to Gina in November of the same year. All was perfect at the chalet until Tracy added Charlotte to the guest list in November 2009.

The beautiful chalet was starting to look like a day care center, but it was still spectacular. To add to their already magnificent gesture, the Karieunitas family rented a ski house in Switzerland for the last winter, which allowed Tracy to convert the fifth bedroom into a nursery.

Chapter 32

On July 10, 2010, William Everett Langston's dream became a reality. The entire project had been sold out years ago. All the buyers had been given move-in dates spaced out over the next four weeks. This was unusual, but due to the unusual location and the difficulty of access to large vehicles, it was the only way.

William did not involve himself in the realty side of the business. When the last house was completed and all the roads and landscaping backdrops had been laid, William was essentially done. A few final touches remained such as the guardhouse, the landscaping of the common areas, and the last pieces to be delivered—the swings and monkey bars that would go in the kiddie park.

William was currently designing a twenty-five story building in the city of Chicago but took time off to put the final touches on Mason and witness its completion firsthand. He called Alicia, and they planned the week together, spending the last few days welcoming the families to their new homes.

On Tuesday morning, they drove up to meet their first two buyers: Michael and Karen Barnum, and Scott and Amy Fisher. Both families had purchased their homes the first week the advertisements ran in the national papers. The Barnums had twin boys, and the Fishers had a little girl. This was just what William had envisioned—a community of young people just starting out, who would experience the best living experience ever and not have to wait until they were older and financially secure.

William gave them a tour of the entire community before he walked them through their individual homes. He explained how little it would cost them to heat the homes in winter due to the solar paneling and how, due to the cross winds and the constant movement of air at this altitude, they would not need air-conditioning units. He walked them to the back of their property and explained how, no matter what type of landscaping they decided upon, due to Alicia's foresight, the twenty yards that separated them from the edge of the mountain was practically impossible to reach due to the tons of boulders that encircled the properties. He showed them his children's park and the security system, starting with the guardhouse. An added perk, one that Alicia came up with only months before, was the community center—a three-room, one-story children's center located two blocks north of the community entrance. Alicia had considered the ages of the children who would be moving in and realized they were almost all too young for preschool and that if the community had its own center—it's was only cost being a counselor and maybe an assistant—these young couples would enjoy freedom that most new parents seldom experienced. The gates of heaven were open.

On Thursday, William welcomed two couples from the Midwest. They were both in their early to mid-thirties, and their children would be starting kindergarten in September. They loved their homes and the fact that practically all their neighbors would be young parents.

That afternoon, he met Nathaniel and Whitney Whitcup. Nathaniel was pleasant, although a little tight around the collar, and Whitney was an angel.

"You know, Nathaniel, I have done work in Philadelphia for a large corporation known as WW&W."

"You are referring to my firm, sir, and I am fully aware of the work you have done for us. Needless to say, had it not been satisfactory, we would not be standing here having this conversation."

"Excuse me, Nate," Whitney courteously injected, "but Mr. Langston is not looking for a reference. He is simply showing us a development that he created and is proud of. Let's not interview him. Let's just thank him for a beautiful creation."

"Mr. Whitcup," said William, "I have only known you thirty minutes and already I envy you."

The Whitcups home was one of the largest homes in the development—large by most standards but, compared to their former homes, simply average. It sat sitting slightly higher than the other homes and provided Whitney and Nate with an incredible panoramic view.

On July 21, William welcomed Michael and Marie Corritore, along with their friends Paul and Tracy Byrnne to Mason. The Corritores brought their little girl, Gina, and the Byrnnes, their son, Charlie. These were two of the families taking advantage of Aspen's "rent with an option to buy" program. William was skeptical at first, but looking at the two couples in front of him, he completely changed his mind. These were lovely people. There was no doubt in his mind they would end up permanent residents.

They all walked around the community, and William did some background, describing the community center and the new stretch van they had purchased. He really didn't have to say much as both women were so enthralled that he doubted they were listening to much of what he was saying anyway.

On August 8, William called Alicia.

"Well, Alicia, we're done. Tomorrow I am welcoming our last homeowner."

"That's great, Will. Is it everything you thought it would be?"

"It's perfect, Alicia. I've never been so fulfilled with a project. That reminds me. Do you remember when I came out here three years ago and you asked me to wait until the last day for a surprise?"

"Of course, I remember. Why do you ask?"

"Tomorrow is my last day. I have to get back to Chicago on the 10th, and I would like us to spend tomorrow together so that I might return the gesture!"

"I'd love to. Can I meet you up on top at 12:00 p.m. or so?"

"That would be perfect," William replied.

"Alicia, my love, you look beautiful as always."

"As do you, William. I hardly saw you at all this last month. I'm beginning to think you're tiring of me."

"I thought of you every day, but these last four weeks have been quite hectic to say the least. I thought we'd have one final tour before I leave tomorrow, just in case there's some little thing we missed."

"Lead on, Sir William. I shall scrutinize every last detail." So they walked up to, through, and around each and every home and yard until they came to the last house back at the start of their tour.

"Either I'm confused or I've lost count, William. Didn't you tell me everyone had moved in as of yesterday?"

"Yes, that's true."

"This house still looks empty. Who lives here?"

"That, my love, is the surprise. My work is predominantly in the city as you know, and I don't know how much time I can spend in Colorado. I do know, beyond any doubt, that any time I do have, I want to spend with you. It wouldn't be fair of me to marry you and not see you for months at a time, but if you want marriage, just say the word. In the meantime, Alicia, this house is yours. No strings! If you can't stand the sight of me at some time in the future, send me packing. If we are never tired of each other, let's share this dream we created together. What do you think?"

"I do."

And so Mason, Colorado, began to breathe.

Chapter 33

The first meeting of the town of Mason, Colorado, was held on Sunday, August 15, 2010, at the community center. The temporary chairman and only nonparent in attendance, Alicia Fine, called the meeting to order.

"Hi, everyone, my name is Alicia Fine, and I live in number one Mason Lane. My significant other, William Everett Langston, your architect, has asked me to start things off here. I am not in charge. Once we get to know one another, we can vote or make up a committee, whatever we like. The important thing is that we take advantage of all the benefits of this incredible community and that we are all aware of everything and anything that affects our homes and our families.

"Now let me introduce the manager of our children's program, Angela Graham. Angela has a bachelor of arts degree from UCLA and taught first grade for six years before moving to Colorado with her husband. Her daughter has just entered the public school system, which has allowed Mrs. Graham to return to work. Why don't I let her tell you, Mrs. Graham . . ."

"Hi, everyone. You've just heard my life story in thirty seconds. Let me just add that I love to work with children. The average age of the children that we will have here is close to two years old, which is very young even for a pre-school program. However, I will have a trainee, Miriam Young, who is presently going for her teaching degree, and as long as we keep the number under fifteen, I think we'll be fine.

"The community of Mason has purchased its own specially outfitted Lexus SUV. It comes with special tires for the mountain roads, four-wheel drive, and six rows of seats with eighteen individual seat belts. The SUV will not start if any of the eighteen seats belts is not fastened. We have hired a local driver, recently retired from the Aspen Police Department. He will take care of the car and make sure it is in excellent condition at all times.

"One of the parents asked me if it wasn't dangerous driving up and down this mountain. Let me assure you that even though the city cleans and salts these roads at the first sign of inclement weather, we will be monitoring the weather as well. If there are any signs that these roads are unsafe, we will close the community center until we get an all clear.

"I'm sure all of you have done your due diligence and know that we have some of the most modern snow and ice clearing machinery known to man. That being said, if we get hit by one of those god-awful blizzards, you'd best have a large supply of canned goods and water and an equal amount of patience.

"Now, while you adults are discussing your new homes, I would like to take this chance to see all my boys and girls in the other room. So if you will bring them in and let me introduce them to all the toys and games we have waiting for them, I would appreciate that.

"Hi, boys and girls. My name is Angela, and I'm going to be your teacher when you come here every day. On the desks in front of you are all your name tags. So if you find yours, have your mom or dad stick it on your shirt so we can all get to know one another."

After all the tags were on, Angela went around the room, checking off children against her roster: number one, Jonathan Stark; number two, Emma Whitcup; number three, Samantha Fisher; number four, Todd Barnum; number five, Adam Barnum; number six, Arnold Pierce; number seven, Hillary Jonas; number eight, Charlie Byrnne; number nine, Gina Corritore; number ten, Martin Harriman; number eleven, Rachael Block; and number twelve, Steven Wells.

"Okay, now, is everyone from Colorado?"

"I'm from New York City," responded Samantha Fisher.

"Us too," said Adam Barnum, pointing at his twin brother, Todd.

"I'm in Colorado," yelled Charlie Byrnne, "and my friend Gina too."

Gina looked up when Charlie mentioned her name. She was the youngest in the group, one year and nine months, and obviously a little young to be in any sort of day care.

"When you tell somebody where you come from, Charlie, you use the word *from*. You say 'I am from Colorado.' Okay?"

"Okay." Charlie smiled at her.

This was more like a family than a day care center as everyone knew and looked out for everyone else.

"How about you, Steven? Where are you from?"

"Steven's from Michigan," his mother answered. "He really doesn't say much yet."

"Once he gets started, I'm sure you'll have a hard time stopping him," said Angela.

"Well, kids, our school opens the day after Labor Day, which is September 5. We are all going to have a lot of fun together, and I look forward to seeing you all then. I would appreciate it if all the parents would pick up an envelope on their way out, one per family. I've made a list of a few of the things your children will need when we start classes.

"I haven't forgotten you, older children. Although these classes will be for children two years old and younger, we also have an activities room for you across the hall. You are always welcome here, and if you or your parents have any requests or ideas, please come and talk to me about them. My door is always open. Thank you all for coming. If you need to contact me, my number is in the letter, and I am always available."

Chapter 34

In the next few weeks, most of the families got to know and like each other. Amy, being a New Yorker, and perhaps the most outgoing of the group, became the leader. They drew out the other women and brought them into the circle. Winnie Whitcup, for example, was from the upper class and extremely wealthy, but they loved her immediately. Nathaniel, on the other hand, found it hard to come down to their level. Amy had a long talk with Winnie. They wanted to include Winnie in everything, but the guys were having a hard time making conversation with Nathaniel. After two cups of coffee, the girls organized the Mason monthly baseball league. Mason would get a team together and challenge surrounding towns. At the first practice, they discussed positions, and from the back of the group came an unfamiliar voice, "I'm a pitcher." And wonder of wonders, Nate became one of the boys.

It wasn't quite that easy. Ira and Helena Pierce, for example, had no desire to be part of their group. Ira ran one of the largest hedge funds in the country. He worked eighteen hours a day and had no extra time for socializing. Helena made sure everything was perfect during the six hours that Ira rested. During the day, she could be found reading a book, usually with a title none of them had heard of. They assumed this was so because no one would approach her and say, "I heard that was a good book." As you would expect, her son also kept to himself. Arnold was quiet and exceptionally shy and a nice boy, and hopefully he would gain some self-confidence, but it would be a tough road.

The following weekend, after baseball practice, Paul invited all the parents that were interested to come to the mountain for ski lessons. He got the parents a special discount and took all the kids into one of his "first time on skis" classes for free. The day was a huge success. They were, after all, in Aspen. They might as well learn to ski.

Michael and Marie hosted a party at Sammy's once the older kids were in school and the younger ones were getting used to being away from their mothers during the day. They were closed on Mondays, so they held it the last Monday in September. Everyone had a great time, and it brought those families that were on the fringe a little closer to the middle.

Michael Barnum and Scott Fisher were now running the western realty division. Things were settling into a routine. They went in about 10:00 a.m. to be close to East Coast Time, which ran two hours behind. They loved the town and the clean fresh air, and coming home every night was a bonus.

Nate opened an office in Aspen and still worked like an animal, except every few hours, he'd stop, take a breath, allow a smile to transform his face, and look up at the mountains in the distance.

His friends here had been lucky—Scott Fisher and Michael Barnum, and Paul Byrnne and Michael Corritore, not to mention William; they had all found charming pretty wives and were starting families and living in this incredible place, but they weren't in his league. He had been destined to work himself to the bone, to have no life other than his company, and lead a lonely miserable existence, were it not for one dinner that had changed his entire life. He had a beautiful daughter in Emma, an angel that forced him to enjoy his life every day regardless of his obligations at work. His life was nothing short of a miracle. Maybe he'd pick up flowers for his women on the way home—tulips for Winnie and daffodils for Emma.

The first winter in Mason could not have gotten off to a better start. The little kids who were one-and-a-half to two years old loved to slide down the baby slopes, and the four and five-year-olds were already firing down the beginner slopes. Those parents who loved to ski would often take some runs in the mornings while the children were at the community center, and the husbands would steal away when they had the time.

For the Corritores and the Byrnnes, it was a smooth transition. They had spent the past two years living in a magnificent chalet at the bottom of the hill in Aspen. They loved the chalet, and Tracy and Paul were like family, but moving into their own home, their first real home with Gina, was a dream comes true.

Marie never expected anything less. Her parents had been hardworking people who enjoyed the profits of their labor, and Marie always thought she'd settle down one day with her Prince Charming and it would go something like this, so she was happy; but Michael grew up hoping his mother had a job, always seeing the strain in her face, and worrying that something would happen to her and he'd be left alone, never experiencing a normal family life. Now, to be living on top of a mountain in Colorado, owning his own restaurant, having a beautiful partner in life and a baby girl, was so incredible that he couldn't think about it without beaming.

And he was a father. When Marie first mentioned she was pregnant, he would wake up in the middle of the night with nightmares about Gina growing up without a father or his being a failure as a parent. He spent month after month panicking at the thought of being anything like his own father but never mentioned his fears to Marie, keeping everything bottled up inside.

In November, the day that Gina came into the world, he would never forget the moment when Marie lifted Gina off her chest and placed her in his arms. He looked down at her and couldn't think of anything except how much he loved these five pounds of nothing that was resting so comfortably in his arms. That was the last time he ever doubted himself.

The first year at the ski house was nothing less than incredible. The house looked out over the mountain with glorious views from all sides. Every night, they would build a fire and relax in the living room with the babies lying on the rug. Charlie would tickle Gina, and her laugh was so contagious that soon they would all be laughing.

Despite the fact that both Marie and Michael worked long hours at the restaurant, they always managed to pick each other up after a particularly difficult night. For the most part, however, Gina was as easy a child as you could wish for. She was almost always happy. When she was about six-month old she developed a delicious mannerism of holding people by their face. Each time a friend or a perfect stranger came into the restaurant and leaned down to look into her face and say what a beautiful girl she was or how much she resembled her mother, Gina would place both her hands on each side of that person's face, look them straight in the eye, and deliver a heart-breaking smile. To say she had her parents wrapped around her little finger was putting it mildly.

Speaking of children who command attention, little Emma Whitney, a small version of Winnie with her short blond hair and bright blue eyes, had a series of facial expressions that were so delectable that it was impossible to keep a straight face. There was her mad face. If she asked to hear a story or go to the kiddie park and was told to wait a few minutes, she placed her hands on her hips and scrunched up her face. Winnie swore she never made that face, and Emma did not get it from her. Her second face materialized when she was being reprimanded. Instead of the tearful expression most children would demonstrate, she would tilt her head to one side and adapt an expression that seem to say "You can't be serious." In any event, it was practically impossible for Nate and Winnie to discipline their daughter when everything she did made them laugh.

As far as Nate was concerned, spending time with Emma was akin to going for therapy. He spent most of his work day involved in one large deal after another and came home and sat in the grass at the kiddie park and built sand castles with Emma. Her favorite parts of the park were climbing the monkey bars and riding Nate the bull, who crawled all over the park until he collapsed from exhaustion. That meant the ride was over and Emma would pull Nate up and brush the grass off his pants.

During the day when Nate was working, Emma would sit with her mother and her friends and watch them paint. She would try to paint sometimes, but she preferred the monkey bars.

On one occasion, Nate held his annual board meeting at the Aspen Hotel. In the middle of the meeting, Emma walked into the conference room, casually strolled past the twenty board members in attendance, and climbed onto Nate's lap.

"Excuse me, sir, but with all due respect, do you really think this is the right time and place to entertain your children?"

"Actually, Howard, Emma, in addition to being my daughter, also happens to be one of the largest stockholders in this company even if her shares are all in trust."

Emma turned and stared at Howard for a few moments. She put her hands on her hips and made one of her funny faces at him.

Just then Winnie appeared at the door.

"Sorry, one minute she was playing at the desk and the next she was attending your board meeting. Come with Mommy, Emma. Let Daddy finish his meeting." Emma slid off Nate's lap and was halfway to the door when Nate yelled.

"Hold it right there, young lady. I think you forgot something."

Emma ran back, laughing, and planted a wet one on Nate's face. Then she ran back to Winnie who picked her up and left the meeting but not before rewarding Nate with a big smile.

William Edward Langston's Garden of Eden did indeed exist in Mason, Colorado, but then, like all things that make an attempt at perfection . . .

Chapter 35

It was on Friday, 9 October, when Karen Barnum got the call.

"Hello, Karen?"

"Angela? What's wrong?"

"The kids should have been here twenty minutes ago, Karen! Can you look outside and see if Ben's SUV is still on top?"

Karen dropped the phone and ran outside. Ben wasn't there. She ran back and grabbed the phone. "Maybe he stopped at the pharmacy or he was low on gas?"

"He doesn't do that, Karen. He's too responsible, and he's never more than five minutes late. I'm going to call Winnie. Emma is his last pickup. Maybe there was a delay. In the meantime, it would make me feel a lot better if you would drive down. Maybe the car broke down. Maybe he's sick. I don't know. Please just drive down here, okay?"

"I'm leaving immediately, Angela!"

Karen backed out of her garage much too fast and just missed her mailbox. "Slow down, you idiot. Driving like a moron won't help." She slowed down to a normal speed and started down the hill. She was no more than fifty yards past the guardhouse when she saw the smoke. *Oh my god*, she thought, *how can one car cause that much smoke?* She opened her window, and the smell was both toxic and overbearing. "Please, God, don't let my boys be hurt." She slowed down as the tears were blurring her vision.

She was more than half way down when she saw the opening in the guardrail on her right. She pulled over and walked to the opening. Below her, the smoke was funneling from the Exxon storage tank straight up into the sky. There was no sign of anything, and then she saw Ben's hat, hanging onto a limb a short way down. She walked back to her car in shock, got in, and drove down the mountain to the community center.

Angela was waiting for her in the parking lot. She saw Karen's face and knew immediately that something terrible had happened. She helped Karen out of her car and sat her down in the office. She called 911 and then Alicia.

"Alicia, this is Angela at the community center." She told her what she thought had happened and asked her to please contact everyone. She was going to wait with Karen.

Within an hour, the community center was filled with police, parents, reporters, and firemen. The police chief took control in the front of the room.

"Excuse me, everyone, please. If you will all stop shouting, I will explain what we know so far and then you can ask your questions." In five or ten seconds, there was absolute silence.

"Approximately an hour and fifteen minutes ago, at approximately 9:15 a.m., a Lexus SUV carrying twelve children and one adult either skidded on its own or, in an attempt to avoid an animal, went off the road approximately an eighth of a mile from the bottom of Mason mountain. The SUV dropped straight down into the Exxon oil depot. We have fire engines there now, as close as possible, as the inferno is reaching incredibly high degrees of heat. As far as we are able to discern at this time, the SUV was consumed in this gas and oil explosion and completely incinerated. Aside from extending our condolences to all the families involved, the only consoling information I have is that the heat and resulting explosion would have been so tremendous that death would have been instantaneous. No one would have suffered. My men have searched the upper hillside and will search the lower areas when the temperature permits, but at this point, I have no hope whatsoever that there is anyone still alive."

Everyone was together at this point, and a bus was brought in to take them all to the local hospital where they were sedated. Professionals were brought in to talk to the parents who were so far into shock that no one was permitted to drive home.

The next day, the police chief came to the hospital to talk with the parents and try to at least make some sense of what had transpired.

'Hello, everyone. My name is Lieutenant William Gowan. Let me first express my condolences and extend my wife's prayers and my own to you and your families. I've never seen anything worse in all my years on the force.

"To the best of our knowledge, here's what we think happened. Yesterday, October 9, 2010, at 9:15 a.m., Ben Webster, a capable man, in reasonably good health, was driving down the Mason Hill. We observed skid marks, where he had veered to the right, which leads us to believe that either an elk or a deer jumped out right in front of him or some physical condition, heart attack, kidney stone, and the like, caused him to lose control of the SUV.

There is no way, once that vehicle went off the road and began to free fall an eighth of a mile, that anyone could have survived, but what defies the imagination is that it fell directly into an Exxon storage tank. That tank is forty yards by forty yards, but still, from so far up, it boggles the mind, and yet, that is exactly what had happened. We located Ben's hat some thirty yards down from the road, which is consistent with a vehicle falling straight down and an article getting caught in the draft. The temperature of that storage tank once it exploded, I am told, is in thousands of degrees, which is more than enough to melt gold, which is why we do not have the slightest trace of anything in the way of evidence. Our tech team did take a sample of the residue in the tank and determined that there was a high metallic reading, which once again is consistent with the absorption of a motor vehicle.

"Once again, on behalf of my family and my entire department, our prayers go with you. God bless you all."

Alicia stood up in the front of the room. "Thank you, Lieutenant, for all your help. This Sunday services will be held here at the community center. All denominations will be represented. There will be a graveside service also. I will contact everyone and tell you what we are doing. Afterward, unless anyone feels differently, I thought it would be a good idea to meet at my house and be together." Several people nodded. Some sat frozen, not hearing or seeing anything, while others fought off, losing it completely.

On Sunday, the parents of the twelve children gathered at the kiddie park. Also attending the funeral was Michael Corritore's mother, who flew in from Florida along with Sam and Linda Palazzole; Nathaniel's mother along with Whitney's; Tracy and Paul's parents, along with Michael Barnum's mother and father; and Amy and Scott's parents.

Half of the park had been converted into a monument with twelve small tombstones stretching straight across. It was impossible to actually listen to the funeral service as the anguished cries constantly escaped the lips of all those parents, who were beyond pain.

Karen turned to her husband and said, "How can I possibly go on with my life? Our boys are gone! Michael, they're gone."

"We'll get through this together, Karen. We will lean on each other until we can breathe again, and when the pain becomes unbearable, we will go over to Scott and Amy and help them get through the day, and then we'll do the same for Nate and Winnie until we are all able to breathe again."

"We'll do this together because we have no choice!"

William and Alicia stood behind the mourners. They had not lost their own children, but they had lost all their children.

"We tried to show them heaven, Alicia, and instead we gave them hell!"

Book II

CHAPTER 36

One year after the accident, they welcomed a new neighbor to Mason. Laura Orzo was a money manager from Los Angeles who made enough money to buy one of the houses, and her husband Steve was a treasury agent with the Federal Bureau of Investigation and made enough money to live in the house with Laura; but they were super-nice and quickly became a part of the circle of friends. They also had a one-year-old son, named Daniel, who fit right in.

Steve Orzo was thirty-four years old and had worked for all seven of his years with the FBI in the Treasury Department. Having gone through all the training the FBI offered, he still possessed that natural distrust of anything that wasn't supported with facts. He had heard all the stories of the crash and had even thrown his credentials around a little to get all the official reports.

He sat down with William one night.

"Listen, William, I would never bring this up with the others because there's absolutely no evidence to suggest another scenario, but let me throw a few thoughts at you. Maybe I'm missing something."

"Fire away, Steve."

"Okay. I've looked at that guardrail that runs down the mountain, and I've read the work orders. There was no section of that guardrail that was more than four years old. The guardrails are inspected every year. I looked at the adjacent guardrails, and it looks to me as if a garbage truck couldn't have gotten through those rails in one pass. Don't even mention the odds on an SUV smashing through and falling an eighth of a mile and landing in a gas storage drum. Obviously it's a possibility, but I would have loved to see that guardrail. The helicopters picked it up off the hill. As there was no investigation other than an accident, unfortunately, it was dumped and never examined."

"You know, Steve, I tried to think of another reason for this, but I couldn't come up with a thing. How about you, anything?"

"I tried to look at the kidnapping angle. I even considered the possibility that the driver, being an ex-cop, had been targeted by someone in his past. I kept hitting the same stonewalls. One, they're too old for adoption. They'd scream for their mothers. What could they do? Drug a dozen two-year-olds? I don't think so. And second, what do you do if you set this up? Shoot an SUV through a guardrail and it falls and misses the storage tank? Police are there within thirty minutes. They see the SUV is empty and put out on all points for anything large enough to

93

carry a dozen kids. No chance. And yet, William, I am not buying what went down here."

"Please don't mention this to any of the families, Steve. They are just about surviving with the loss as it is. If they thought their kids were tortured, in pain, sold to other people, whatever, and couldn't prove anything or do anything about it, I think they'd fall apart."

"Don't worry, William. Anything I do, I'll do on my own, and I'll be very careful to keep it to myself. Thanks for listening."

As Steve walked away, William thought to himself, *Damn, I've been thinking the same fucking thing for two years and I still can't make sense of it.* He considered Ben again. *He was an ex-cop and in good shape. He loved those kids and never would have let anything happen to them. Was he the reason this had happened? If he was, where's his body? None of this made any sense!*

Chapter 37

March 2014

Kenny and Carol Panzer lived in an east side suburb of Seattle, Clyde Hill, approximately two miles east of Seattle. The average housing lot in Clyde Hills was 5,000 square feet. All the suburbs near Seattle were magnificent, scenic, and upper class. One of their neighbors was Bill Gates of Microsoft. Kenny's businesses were still flourishing, and now that they had Patricia, life was especially good.

It had been about three-and-a-half years since they adopted Patricia, and every moment was ingrained in their memories. The first week when they brought her home, they were expecting a frightened little girl who would get used to them and settle in, not quite!

The first night they spent in her room. She kept waking up and screaming "No, no, go away!" They tried to calm her down but didn't know what drugs she had been given and were afraid. Her eyes were too yellow, and Carol said she felt clammy, and she definitely had a fever.

First thing in the morning, they brought her to their family doctor. He couldn't believe her condition and had her hospitalized immediately. They spent three days, cleansing her body of the drugs she had been taking, and an additional week, slowly nursing her back to health. Physically, that is. Patricia was over two years old by this time, and they had very little trust in their attorney and weren't sure if anything he had told them was true.

She wanted her mother, and so the Panzers took the advice of the child psychiatrist at the hospital who told them she was in a tough enough place as it was, without explaining, death to a two-year-old. So they told Patricia that her mother was very sick and her father was taking care of her and that when she was all better, they would talk about getting them back together, but that they had trusted Kenny and Carol with taking care of her, and so they would. In time, Patricia became accustomed to her new surrounding and the constant love she received from the Panzers and their extended family: aunts and uncles, nieces, and two sets of grandparents. There might have been a memory buried down deep, but temporarily that was where it was staying.

The next few years went very smoothly. Patricia made friends and fit in very easily. At almost six years old, they enrolled Patricia in the Clyde Hill Elementary

School. It was a beautiful school in a beautiful suburb, and Patricia, with her hazel eyes and jet-black hair, fit in like a glove.

In August 2014, Patricia stopped sleeping! Every night, at twelve or twelve-thirty, she'd start screaming "Mommy, Mommy. Go away. You're hurting me. Mommy, Mommy," over and over, night after night. They brought her to Seattle Children's Hospital, one of the top pediatric hospitals in the country. They hired Doctor Edwin Heinz, a pediatric psychiatrist with an excellent reputation to tend to her personally.

Over the next few days, Dr. Heinz sat and talked with Patricia for hours. She remembered nothing of the car crash that killed her parents. She couldn't remember being in a car with her parents. She remembered her mother had long black hair like hers and green eyes and was pretty, and she remembered that someone gave her medication and told her to sleep, consistent with therapy for a child in shock, but that was it.

Kenny paid the attorney Howard Rosenberg a visit. There was no private room or coffee and biscotti this trip. If it wasn't business, Rosenberg didn't want to talk about it.

"Listen, Mr. Rosenberg," Kenny pleaded, "my daughter is very sick, and I need to know where she comes from and who her parents were. If it's a graveyard, maybe I can find some pictures of her family. It could help her now."

"I would help you if it was possible, but it's not. In cases like these, the original records are either sealed or destroyed. I don't have the original records nor would I have wanted them. If you recall, Mr. Panzer, I told you that these adoptions were difficult and that they cost three times the amount of a legal adoption. You were fine with that when you wanted your child. Now, you want me to find the sealed adoption records from years ago?"

"You told me that this adoption was legal. You said all your adoptions were legal!"

"And you believed me because you wanted to believe me. Seriously, Mr. Panzer, you're a businessman. Why would you pay me three times the going rate for a two-year-old girl if it were on the up and up? If I recall correctly, you had a record, which we both know makes adoption in the United States both illegal and impossible. Did you conveniently forget all that, Mr. Panzer? I hope your daughter gets better. You know your way out."

Kenny walked down the street, cursing to himself. Of course, he knew it was illegal. *What do I do now?* he thought to himself.

He got back to the hospital and pulled Carol aside and told her everything.

"Listen, honey," Carol said softly. "Don't blame yourself. We both knew what was happening. What we didn't understand was how it was happening? I thought, instead of a child being placed in an orphanage, or even worse, instead of a child going to the next person on the list, we would cheat and get her first. I didn't think about whether it was right or wrong. I just wanted my little girl. I never thought that something worse than that could be happening and now I'm afraid to even consider what had happened to this little girl or her parents so that Rosenberg could make her available for us."

"What can we do now, Carol?"

"I'll tell you what we can do. We can do everything possible to make sure this little girl doesn't grow up scared with nightmares for the rest of her life, and that's exactly what we're going to make sure of!"

"Carol, what we did to get Patricia was not on the up and up. We could get in trouble. We could lose her."

"I hope that never happens, but I'll tell you what we're not going to do. We're not going to sit back and hope she doesn't turn into a psychotic, messed-up adult because we did nothing. Let's straighten her out, and then we'll figure out what to do about the rest of her life. Okay?"

"You're something else, kid. Let's do it."

Kenny and Carol took Patricia to see Dr. Heinz every Monday and Thursday. The three of them sat through every session together. It was important for Patricia to understand that her parents, Kenny and Carol, were going to put out just as much effort as she did to understand what had happened to her and her parents. Together, they would discover who her parents were and where they came from and finally who Patricia was and what these nightmares had to do with her life.

Dr. Heinz explained to Patricia that none of what she was experiencing was in any way her fault, that there were people who had manipulated her for some reason, and that not only were the Panzers and Dr. Heinz working on discovering what had happened to her, but the authorities were investigating as well. She was not alone in this, but she was a part of a large group of people who were all working together to help her find out the truth.

"We will find out the truth, Patricia," said Dr. Heinz, "and when we do, all your nightmares will magically disappear. This I promise you."

Patricia looked back at him, her eyes wide open and her lips curved downward as if she might cry at any moment. "They scare me," she said.

"The dreams scare you, Patricia?"

Patricia nodded.

"Trust me, Patricia. We are going to make those bad dreams go away forever. Okay?"

She looked up at him with her sad face and nodded.

Chapter 38

John Scully lived in Fairview, Washington, in one of five homes bordering Lake Larsen. The house was surrounded on three sides by forest and on the other by the lake. If you boated across the lake, you could say the only part of John Scully's house that was visible was the boathouse. Unless you walked around to the front of the house, you would never know the house was occupied. He knew none of his neighbors, and they had never laid eyes on him. He was invisible, and that was just the way he liked it.

John had been living there for the last two years with Trudy Miller, his lover and accomplice. The arrangement was perfect. On assignments that were provided by the law firm, they drove or flew to wherever they needed to be and returned either to the lake or directly to the law office. There was no one else involved, no driver, no middleman, and no loose ends—just the way John liked it.

Trudy was a perfect partner. She gave him everything he needed physically and emotionally. She was instrumental in handling the kids, and he fulfilled her needs in addition to making sure all her habits were satiated. She depended on him completely—just the way he wanted it.

John had introduced himself to his banker in Seattle as a collector of Americana recently relocated from the East. He was obviously successful in this endeavor as his accounts were in seven figures. He was an excellent customer. His money was deposited on a regular basis; CDs and asset management, nothing that was high risk. On John's end, he was a phantom. He entered the private office of the manager, Simon Truscott, through the private entrance behind the bank. No other bank employee had ever laid eyes on him.

If they needed to see Rosenberg, it took them about an hour to get to Seattle. If they needed to hold children for a few days before delivery, John's house, with the entrance through the garage and no neighbors in either direction for over a mile, was ideal.

It was a perfect symbiotic relationship. Rosenberg and Flakowitz were making money every time Scully scored or ran their errands. They had no conscience. They never asked questions, and they paid on delivery. John, on the other hand, had no conscience and no fear—a combination that bordered very closely on the psychotic. His goal was to acquire ten million dollars. With that kind of money, he would pull one more disappearing act and retire to some country with no extradition agreements. He didn't care how he made the money or who suffered while he was working as long as the numbers kept getting bigger. He figured two more years, and he would be looking for property in Brazil, maybe with company, probably not!

This last job was one of his easiest. They had driven to Montana and returned with two infants whose mother, and only parent, had been killed in a gas explosion that had reduced her small home to little more than ashes. The authorities questioned whether the mother had intentionally killed herself and her children as the gas built up had to have been tremendous to cause such an explosion. Tracy had chloroformed the children originally and then kept them on a steady dose of Valium, which was her usual method. The call came two days later for delivery—one hundred thousand clear for each kid. His doctor friend had the right idea with this adoption business. Dealing drugs was too dangerous. This was a piece of cake.

He sent Trudy to get the kids ready and was about to enter the garage when he heard her cry out. He ran to the bedroom in time to see Trudy pick up one of the children and rock her in her arms.

"What's going on? We've got to get moving!"

"She's dead, John. I must have given her too big a dose."

"What the fuck is wrong with you? You just cost me $100,000. I thought you knew what you were doing?"

"I'm sorry, John. It was an accident. I can't judge the exact dosage to give. We're not in a hospital, you know."

"It's all those pills you take and the Coke and the vodka. It's amazing this hasn't happened more often. Shit! Leave the dead girl here. When we get back, I'll take the boat out. Bring the other one to the garage and try not to drop him." Trudy went back to bring the other child. Her hands were shaking so badly she had to shake them before she trusted herself to pick the child up. She had seen that look in John's eyes before, but they were never centered on her. She would have to pay very close attention in the future. She had seen the sadistic side of John Scully, and she wanted no part of it.

Chapter 39

In Seattle, Kenny and Carol hired Harry Immerman of the Ace detective agency. They explained that they not only wanted to find out every possible connection there could be to Patricia, but they wanted her involved in the discovery process. They bought Patricia a wireless computer so she could work and play on her bed as well as her desk. They brought in a computer expert who insisted that a six-year-old girl was not mature enough to learn the intricacies of the Internet, regardless of how precocious she was. They doubled his salary. He made sure Patricia could handle it. Together they checked the files for every lost girl in the last five years. The FBI supplied them with all their lists of missing children, happy to have help. They checked morgues throughout the country for women and men who could possibly fit into the same age bracket as Patricia's parents. They updated every file on fatal accidents—accidents with multiple bodies and accidents with children involved. They left nothing out. After an entire week of working, they came up with nothing. The Panzers were feeling the frustration until Harry hit them with his enthusiasm.

"You didn't actually think that by going through the same channels as every one else, a name would pop up, did you? That's only on 'missing' or 'law and order.' We did the legwork. Now we don't have to second-guess ourselves and worry that we missed something obvious."

"This is not a fast process, but it's a reliable one. We can't find what we're looking for because either it doesn't exist, which we don't believe, or it was done in such a way that ordinary methods won't work. So what we are going to do is stop looking for the answers and start putting out the questions."

"In English, please," Carol begged.

"We are going to tell our story in several different versions, utilizing several different modes of communications. Here are some examples. We are going to go on Google and hit 'questions asked by adopted kids'. Maybe one of those questions will strike a familiar chord. We are going to enter our own questions. 'I am a six-year-old girl. My parents I've been told were killed in a car crash. I have dark black hair and hazel eyes, and I am just less than four feet tall. I don't know where I was born or my birth name or if I have family anywhere.' We are going to go on Facebook with all the people you know and a world of people you don't know. We're going to say 'I have the same nightmare every night. A dark-haired woman is dragging me out of a car or bus and into another car or bus and she has something over my mouth. When I wake up, she is giving me a needle and I am screaming for my mommy.'

"Now, Patricia, the reason I thought you were too young to undertake this was because you are going to get hundreds if not thousands of responses from children, and maybe adults, from all over the world. Some people will mean well, but they will be of no help, and some will be game players who will try to say exactly what you want to hear even if they make it up, and some will be absolutely crazy. That's why it's essential that you do all this research along with your parents. As a team, the three of you will sort out the crazies from the possibles. And of course, if you need me, I will be here to track down any leads and see if they pan out. There is a great deal of this that you are not going to understand right now. Just know that your parents and I are going to help you, and before you know it, all these nightmares will stop."

"What do you think, Patricia?"

"Mom, can I go watch cartoons?"

"Sure, honey, go upstairs. I'll be right up."

Patricia and her parents did become extremely proficient on the computer, and working together to find out Patricia's roots had a therapeutic effect on her. Her nightmares stopped occurring as often, and within a few months, they stopped all together. This was a great improvement, but it had absolutely no bearing on their search. They were determined, and with heads down, they steamed ahead.

Meanwhile, Steve Orzo had a new hobby. He couldn't get it through his head that this accident was legitimate and woke up nights with new ideas that he looked into the next morning.

His latest fixation was the adoption angle. If these kids were alive somehow, they must be somewhere. So he hit all the computers at headquarters and checked out every adoption between the times of the accident through the next six months. He followed up on any child that could be any one of the twelve but came up with nothing.

He knew it was there—somewhere just beyond his reach. He was going to find it. He just had to keep and open mind and not give up.

Chapter 40

Jill Diamond was seven years old and lived in Central Valley, New York. Her brother, Jason, was twelve years old and played basketball all day long. She wasn't big on basketball, but she loved her brother, so she went to his games and cheered. Aside from basketball, Jason was a computer freak. He created games, played with his friends online, and had all his school work computerized, and if he didn't need a few hours of sleep, he would be on the computer all night. He Facebooked regularly with his close friends and people he never met. When he was bored, he would go into chat rooms and talk sports with people all around the world.

Jill wasn't into computers like Jason, but Jason did teach her the basics. When she was bored, she could go into the adoption chat rooms by herself. She felt like she belonged to that club, but she rarely contributed. She just watched from the outside.

She was watching the day that Patricia Panzer told her story. It was so sad that this girl, her own age, was having nightmares. She thought about Patricia from time to time, but basically Jill was a happy kid and didn't dwell too much on how she ended up in Central Valley, New York, with the Diamond family.

Maybe a week or so later, the Diamonds were sitting around the dinner table and Jill said, "Mom, can I ask you a question?"

"Of course, honey. You can ask me anything."

"What happened to my parents? I mean I know you're my parents. You know what I mean."

Sandi looked over at her husband for help.

"Let me answer that one, Jill," said Robert, her father. "When you were very little, your parents were flying back from an island in the Caribbean on a small plane. They were returning from a vacation, and the plane crashed. Mom and I adopted you shortly after that, and you've been here ever since."

She nodded, obviously trying to understand what he was talking about. That night, as she was falling asleep, she kept thinking about Patricia being pulled from a car, and for some reason, it felt familiar. When she closed her eyes, she could visualize kids being carried out of a car and her waiting for her turn. Then she fell asleep!

That Saturday in Central Valley marked the beginning of the Tom Dowd Memorial Basketball Tournament. Tom Dowd was a local coach who involved himself in all children's sports. On September 11, 2001, Tom Dowd went to work in the Twin Towers and never came back. The tournament was named in his honor. It included all grades and all ages. If you loved basketball, there was a league for you. The tournament ran in several cities on the Eastern Seaboard.

Jason loved the competition and played in the tournament every year. Of course, Jill watched every game and screamed her support. Jason's team had made it through the week and was now in the semifinals against a team from Boca Raton, Florida. It was a great game, but Jason's team lost in the final seconds. A boy much taller than Jason had stuffed the ball, going right over her brother with time running out to win the game. Jill was so mad at him. She ran up to the boy after the game, looked him in the face, and yelled, "You're a big bully!" She turned to storm away and ran smack into another boy who was standing near the grandstand. She actually knocked him to the ground and started to apologize, but when the boy looked at her, she froze.

Jason came over to her and asked what that was all about.

"I don't know. I was mad, and then I ran over this other boy and I saw his face . . . and now I don't remember. Can we go home?"

"Sounds good. You know my neck hurts from guarding that guy all game. Damn, was he tall?" They both laughed and went home.

CHAPTER 41

That night, Jill was half asleep. They had all gotten up at 6:00 a.m. to leave for the tournament and hadn't gotten home until 9:00 p.m. She was exhausted. She was almost asleep, and then she was in the back of a car or a van, and they were coming to take her. There were three of them left, and they were holding on to each other, Jill and two boys. That boy's face at the gym . . . it was that face . . . wait . . . that's why she froze when she saw him. It was the same face. They were twins—Tom and someone. No, not Tom, Todd. Todd and Adam. *Yes,* definitely Todd and Adam.

She ran to her brother's room. "Jason, come into my room."

"As soon as I finish this game, Jill."

"Jason," she screamed, "come into my room this second."

"Holy cow, what is it? Is it a cockroach?"

"I want to talk to Patricia."

"Patricia, the girl from the chat room, who lost her parents?"

"Uh-huh."

"Have you lost your marbles?"

"Just do it."

"Okay, do you want me to type for you on the keyboard if I get through to her?"

"Yes!"

Two minutes later, Patricia had responded with "Who is this?"

"My name is Jill Diamond, and my brother and I read your story yesterday."

Jason typed out Jill's response word for word.

"Thanks, Jill, but it's almost 10:00 p.m., and I have to get to sleep."

"I was in that van!" Jill shouted, as Jason typed the words on the keyboard.

"What do you mean, Jill?"

"At first, it meant nothing to me," Jason typed, "but this last week, I kept seeing myself in a van and thought I must be making that part up. Today, I went to my brother's basketball game, and there was a boy about our age. I went up to him and looked at his face, and it made me shake. I didn't know why. Tonight, when I was falling asleep, I saw myself in the back of a van. The others had been taken, and there were three of us left, and I didn't want to go. I was holding on to the two boys. They were twins, and their names were Adam and Todd. One of them was at the gym today. We were on the same bus, Patricia, weren't we? Patricia? Hello?"

"Adam and Todd, my friends, the twins. Oh my god! Jill, wait a second. I have to get my parents."

"Maaaaaaaaaaa!"

Patricia's parents came, running in. "Is it the nightmare? It's going to be okay, honey."

"No, I'm fine." She took them to her computer. "Read."

They read the conversation.

"I remember those names," Patricia said. "Those were my friends, Adam and Todd. I'm positive!"

"Oh my god! Kenny, what should we do?"

"Let's call Harry. No, first, we have to explain what's going on to Jill's parents."

"They're not even aware that there's a problem."

Kenny went back to the computer. "Hello, Jill, this is Patricia's father. I want to thank you for helping us try to clear this up, but I think I need to speak to your parents. Would you please give them this telephone number and ask them to call me in about fifteen minutes collect. My name is Kenny Panzer."

"Okay, I'll tell them, Mr. Panzer," Jason typed.

"I just called Harry, hon. He'll be right over."

"Okay," Harry said, "everyone calm down. This is just the beginning. If you thought it was chaos before, wait until you see what happens now.

"Before we continue, let me congratulate you. This was incredible. The four of us put our heads together and are getting results. The FBI couldn't have done better. What am I saying, the FBI didn't do better.

"Now, we are out of our league. This girl you are communicating with lives in New York. If you were both in the same bus, van, whatever, then whoever made this happen is able to transport children from one side of the country to the other with no trail. That's scary! It's also dangerous. If this operation is as big as it looks and if they think their operation could be in jeopardy, you get where I'm going?"

"Okay," Kenny responded. "What do you recommend?"

"I think we have to call in the FBI."

"Before we make that call, I have to speak with Jill's parents. They have no idea what's about to happen to them."

Ten minutes later, the call came. Kenny spoke with Jill's father for what seemed like hours. When he came back into the room, he looked ready to pass out.

Carol brought him a glass of Chivas that he knocked off in three sips.

"Tell us, Kenny," Carol gently urged him.

"They don't know our lawyers. They must have a representative or representatives around the country. Their story is almost the same as ours. They wanted a second child before they got older and didn't want to wait. Jill came in the same condition, maybe not as drugged as Patricia, but drugged, and then I had to wait about five minutes as both of Jill's parents were crying. We discussed the possibility that our children might have parents that are alive and that if we pursue this, we could lose our kids. We also both realize that this could be so much bigger than we could ever imagine and to close our eyes would be criminal. We've agreed that we will speak with the FBI tomorrow and give them the Diamonds' name and number when we finish."

"I hope you understand, Carol. What we are doing now is definitely the right thing, but there is a possibility that Patricia's biological parents have been searching for her for several years and will insist that she go back to live with them."

The following morning at 10:00 a.m., Agent Sam Pierce, no relation to the Pierces from Mason, and Agent John Mahoney, two agents from the Federal Bureau of Investigation, sat down in the Panzers' living room. They listened to their entire story. At the same time, another set of agents were interviewing the Diamonds in New York. After two hours, Agent Pierce closed his pad.

Chapter 42

"That's all we need for now. Let me explain what's going to happen next. We are going to coordinate all the information we have received today and combine that with all the information we already have. The most important thing at this point is not to set the gears in motion until we put the fence up. If we grab this lawyer in Seattle, Rosenberg, by the time we lock him up, his entire pipeline, from associate lawyers to the child abductors and their accomplices, will all disappear, not to mention the records that will show us where the rest of the children they've sold are living.

"Have patience. Within a week, this will all come together. So, please, for the time being, not a word to anyone. Do you understand, Patricia? You can't say a word to any of your friends at school. Look at me, Patricia. This is very important. Promise me that you won't say a word."

"I promise."

"That's my girl, Patricia," he said with a smile.

The first thing Monday morning, the project was labeled *Adoption Game* and was forwarded to all FBI offices in the United States. It arrived at the Aspen branch at 10:00 a.m. due to the one-hour time difference and hit Steve Orzo's desk just as he took his first sip of coffee.

"What do we have here, Margaret?"

"Don't know, Steve. Only that it's top priority."

Steve began reading immediately and was only on the second page when he realized what he had, but it was the third page that made him jump up and spill his coffee all over the floor.

"What happened, Steve? Did you burn yourself?"

"Holy shit! Holy shit!"

"I got that part," said Margaret. "Could you be a little more explicit?"

"This little girl in New York remembers being pulled off a bus or van along with a pair of twins named Adam and Todd."

"So," Margaret said, waiting for more.

"Do you remember that van in Mason, Colorado, that went off the side of a mountain and exploded in an oil tank, incinerating the driver and twelve, two-year-old children?"

"Of course, that was the worst accident Aspen had ever seen. It was devastating. All those little kids!"

"My friend's children were on that bus. They were twin boys, and their names were Adam and Todd. I knew it was too far-fetched. It wasn't an accident. It was an abduction. The reason we never saw their names on adoption sheets is because the lawyers who sold these kids to unsuspecting parents as adopted children never filed any adoption papers. The parents would never insist, as they knew the way they got their children was a little shady at best and they had what they wanted. I knew there was something off about the accident, but I'll admit I never believed all those kids could be alive."

"Get me the main office in Washington DC."

"Yes, sir. Pick up line two."

"Hello, this is Agent Steven Orzo in Aspen, Colorado. I need to speak with Agent Sam Pierce."

"This is Agent Pierce."

"This is Agent Steve Orzo in Aspen Colorado. I've got a big piece of your adoption game puzzle. Grab a cup of coffee, sit back, and tell me when you're ready to hear a story."

When he had finished, Agent Pierce said, "Give me fifteen minutes to discuss this with my partner and the CO and I'll get back to you."

"I'll be waiting."

The return call came quickly.

"Okay, Agent Orzo, this is how we are going to proceed. We all have the same objectives: number one, get these kids back safely; number two, take these lawyers down on major counts; and three, shut down their networks and lock up the bad guys that are running it."

"Agent Pierce, I have several close friends who lost their children almost four years ago in that supposed accident. I'm going to see them this evening. How can I spend time with them, knowing their children are probably alive and not tell them?"

"It won't be easy, Steve, but it will be harder if what we are onto leaks, and people, maybe even their children, disappear. Make no mistakes, Steve. We are dealing with millions and millions of dollars, lots of jail time, and possibly death sentences. These people will kill for less."

"Are there any vacant homes where you live, Steve?"

"Actually, there is one home for sale."

"Can you speak with the owner? We'll send a couple down supposedly to buy it, and her sister and husband will move in with them. That will give our original families added protection, although, to be honest, I can't see it ever getting that far."

"I'll take care of that immediately. You can move your couples in this evening."

"Perfect. We have already set up a twenty-four hour watch on both Rosenberg's office in Seattle and on the lawyer's office the Diamonds used in New York."

"The Panzers have invited the Diamonds to spend the week with them in Seattle, and that will make it easy for our artist to drop over and see if we can get either of the girls to come up with a sketch."

"I think I know who Patricia Panzer's birth parents are also. Can you imagine having the knowledge that your friends' supposedly dead children are alive and not being able to tell them?"

"I don't think I could possibly keep it to myself, Steve, but you will. I'll touch base with you later, Agent Orzo, or sooner if something comes up. Call me when we're good to go on that house in Mason."

"We'll do. Bye."

Chapter 43

"William, it's Steve Orzo."

"Hi, Steve, What's up?"

"I need a favor, and I can't tell you why. Only that you can't discuss it."

"Consider it done. What do you need?"

"I need you to close on that empty home, number 6, I believe. The new owner and his wife and her brother and his wife will be moving in this evening. I'll fax you their information in the next hour."

"How long will they be staying, Steve?"

"I'd like to say a week, but it could be a month."

"Should I be nervous?"

"If I told you the reason, you would definitely do this, but I can't tell you the reason. I can only thank you now and explain everything later."

"Fax me the information. The keys will be in the mailbox. I assume you don't want me, welcoming them to the neighborhood."

"You assume correctly, William, and thank you. One day I promise to tell you the entire story. Bye."

No sooner did he hang up on William, than Agent Pierce was back on the line.

"Steve, It's Sam. Let's stick to first names. We're going to be doing a lot of talking this week, and it's a lot easier."

"Sounds good, Sam. I was about to call you. The keys are in the mailbox. Send the information to fax # 646-628-0796."

"You work fast. That's great. Here's some good news for you. We had our artist stop at the Diamond girl's house and got her to make a sketch of the boy she thought was one of the twins. We brought it to the tournament supervisor and have already spoken to Robert and Andrea Kent of Rye, New York. If they had got a girl, they were going to name her Melissa, so this poor kid got to be Melvin.

"Once again, they had used Larry Levin, the same lawyer that the Diamonds had used. The Kents are cooperating. What else are they going to do? They illegally adopted a child. I don't expect any of these parents to give us a hard time. So that's the good news. Our third child from the van is alive. The bad news is we're out of leads. We could put this twins' picture on the news and somewhere the people he was with would see it. Who knows what they would do next. They illegally adopted. They could get in trouble. They could lose their child. Would they come forward? And even if they did, that would make four and we would be back at a dead end."

"There's only one way to do this. Either we get the guys who pulled this off or we get the lawyers, and then we have to hope they talk."

My god! thought Steve. *Both Michael and Karen's sons are alive. From that picture of Patricia in the files, that would have to be Amy's daughter, Samantha, and Jill could definitely be Winnie and Nate's daughter, Emma, although that was more of a guess.*

On Sunday, Steve and Laura and their son Daniel were walking over to the kiddie park when Paul and Tracy stopped their car on the way to the mountain with Charlotte.

"Hey, stranger. You must be involved in something big. I haven't seen you all week," said Tracy.

"I could tell you, but . . ."

"I know, I know, you'd have to kill me. You guys better come up with a new line. That one's about had it. How's everything?"

"We're okay. No sense in complaining. How about you?"

"We're okay. Catch you later."

As they drove off, Steve thought to himself. *I hope their son's alive. How would they stay here if their friends got their children back and they didn't? Forget about staying here. How would they get up in the morning? Please, God, let this one turn out well!*

Chapter 44

John Scully and Trudy parked in the underground garage and took the private elevator up to Rosenberg's office. He was waiting for them when they walked in.

"Where's the other kid? You said two kids, Scully. I've got two sets of parents in the waiting room. Where's the other kid?"

"Trudy fucked up the sedatives! The girl overdosed!"

"Overdosed as in dead?"

"Yeah, as in dead."

"What do you expect me to do now?"

"Well, you could pay me anyway, but I don't think that's gonna happen. You could find me someone to take care of the kids who's not high all the time," and he shot Trudy a look that had murder written all over it.

"Trudy, bring the kid. I'll be back in a few minutes, Scully."

Rosenberg returned alone about ten minutes later.

"Listen, John. I need another kid and soon. These people were expecting a child today. I gave them a long story about the kid's mother changing her mind, but they're ready to freak out! What can you do?"

"I'll find a kid. What can you do about replacing Trudy? She's a liability. I can't have her taking care of these kids. She can't even take care of herself!"

"Give me some time to come up with someone. In the meantime, we have no choice. Keep an eye on her. Here's your money. I'll send Trudy out in a few minutes."

Trudy eventually came out and knew not to walk too close to Scully. When he lost money, she knew anytime in the next few days he could beat the shit out of her with no provocation whatsoever. She had also talked with Rosenberg, who told her she better straighten up, which could only mean John had complained about her when she was inside. Her arrangement with Scully had become very dangerous!

Chapter 45

The two agents parked in the underground garage took a series of pictures of John and Trudy getting in and out of their car and their license plate. They had no idea if they were involved, but their orders were to photograph anyone going into or out of the lawyers' private elevator. Two other agents had the front of the building and the regular entrance covered.

The first hit came with the license plate. The car was registered to a John Scully of Seattle. All his statistics checked out except for one. John Scully was a member of the armed forces and died in Afghanistan in 2007.

Agent Pierce showed up at the Panzers' house the next morning.

"Good Morning, Mr. and Mrs. Panzer, and you must be the Diamonds."

Everyone shook hands and sat down in the living room.

"I need to see the kids. I have some pictures I want them to go through, and there's one woman in particular I want them to look at."

"Who is she?" asked Carol.

"Could be no one. Could be the woman in the van," replied Agent Pierce.

"Kids," Carol called upstairs. "Could you come down a minute?"

Patricia walked over and sat by her mother. Jill walked over and said hello to Agent Pierce.

"How did you get here so fast?"

"The FBI has very fast planes," Agent Pierce replied with a serious face.

"I think you're fooling," said Jill.

"I think you're right, and I think you should call me Sam. That way I can call you Jill, okay?"

"Okay. Can Patricia call you Sam also?"

"Absolutely. Now I would like you both to look at some pictures and tell me if anyone looks familiar. I may be showing you lots of pictures and no one may look familiar, so don't get discouraged. This is how the game is played."

"Okay, can we see the pictures now?" echoed Patricia.

These girls certainly turned out well. They were both adorable, thought Sam as he placed the pictures on the coffee table.

The girls took one picture at a time and looked closely before going to the next picture. They went through the close-ups of John Scully driving the car and then the first close-up of Trudy in the passenger seat. They stared at it for close

113

to thirty seconds before looking at each other. Then they turned to Sam and in unison said, "That's her."

Agent Pierce grabbed his phone and called it in. "We have a match. The woman in the car is the woman in the van. Run the picture. Put everyone on it. Get someone to check out the address on Scully's license. It could be legit. Tell all agents, this is a remote. I don't want any of these people to have any idea we're on to them and panic. Remember, we lose them, we lose the trail that leads to the rest of these kids. Also, everything in these reports goes directly to headquarters for distribution, but I want everything we have now and in the future to be forwarded to Agent Steve Orzo in Aspen. He has direct involvement, and we need him. One last thing. I want wiretaps on the phones in the law offices and the phones at Scully's place wherever that is, and I want them yesterday. Got it? You girls were great. I'm going back to work now and see if we can make sure these people don't hurt any more children."

Patricia walked him to the door.

"Bye, Sam," she said.

"Bye, Patricia."

Chapter 46

Steve got the FBI report fifteen minutes later and was on the phone with Agent Pierce two minutes after that.

"This woman, Sam, we know she's been involved in multiple abductions. We also know that all the abductions we know of involved chloroform and some form of sedation. Jill, for example, ended up in New York. They couldn't have carried sedated children on a plane. Let's assume they don't have their own plane for now, so they're driving across the country and keeping at least a bunch of these kids drugged up for a long period of time. You with me so far?"

"You're on a roll. Keep going."

"Okay, could you do that? Would you know how much of a drug to give a two-year-old and how much to keep giving a two-year-old? Would you know what to do if something went wrong? I think we're looking for someone with a medical background. At least some medical training. Could be a medical school dropout, dental technician, or more like a nurse or nursing assistant. My first thought would be ex. Anyone working today with a license would never do something like this."

"I think you're on the right path, Steve. We're looking for a woman who is no longer working in medicine but did at one point. How do we circulate a picture and description throughout the medical community without someone who knows her seeing it and warning her?"

"Good question, Sam. Let's try this. We start off by contacting every nursing school in the US. We make it 'high priority, extremely sensitive,' and we only contact the heads of these institutions and explain the importance of keeping the information secure. At the same time, we contact the personnel department of every hospital with the same guidelines. I think we have an excellent chance of identifying this woman."

"Let's get the ball rolling."

"Wait! Why are we assuming this woman came with Scully?"

"What are you getting at Steve? We saw them drive to Rosenberg's office and leave together. That would be the natural assumption."

"Yes, it would, but before we check the rest of the country, let's allow for the possibility that Scully, whose identity does not come up in the computer, needed someone to help him with these kids and that someone had to have medical knowledge. Isn't it possible that Rosenberg supplied the woman that Scully now works with?"

"Sure. It's possible. Where does that get us?"

"It might get us to Seattle where Rosenberg has been practicing law or whatever he does for some thirty odd years. I'm suggesting that while you start searching the country, it might be a good idea to look hard at the Seattle area first."

"I like it, Steve. You take Seattle and Washington. I'll take the rest of the states. Call me if you get anything."

"Will do, Sam."

Chapter 47

As soon as John and Trudy got back to the lake, John went into the den and started searching the computer. He wasn't giving up on this hundred thousand so fast. He needed to find one kid quickly and that meant in the northwest, preferably close to Seattle.

Their last grab was easy for two reasons. The girl lived in a remote area, and she was a single mother. The gas explosion simply covered their tracks and eliminated all the loose ends, and he hated loose ends. Maybe, he could explore the same vein. The more he thought about it, the more he liked it.

He hit Craigslist and entered "single mothers." "Let's see. Mother of two boys, five and seven, no. Black girl with infant, no. Mother of fifteen-year-old, no. Widow with three teenagers, shit. This could take all day." And then as if someone was listening, perfection: twenty-five-year-old secretary; 5'2", blond hair, nice figure.

"They say I look like Paris Hilton, with one-year-old son, no father, but if you don't love my son, you can't love me. Looking for mature man with steady job who likes children. Call after 6:00 p.m. Cindy in Portland. Might as well have put my name on the ad. Portland is about 180 miles, Interstate 5 south almost all the way. Sounds like three hours. Today's Tuesday. I can make the date for tomorrow night and make the delivery Thursday. Now, I just have to work out the details."

It was just getting dark. If he was going canoeing, he better hurry before it got too dark to see anything.

"Trudy," he called out. He knew she was hiding in her room. "I'm going to take the canoe out. Why don't you put up a couple of steaks and open a bottle of wine. We can have dinner when I get back."

She breathed a sigh of relief. She wasn't sure if he wanted her on the canoe as well, but now he must have found work and needed her again. Alive for at least another day!

She watched him walk toward the canoe with a burlap sack and some rope. Obviously, he was weighing down the dead girl and dropping her in the lake. "I can't believe I killed that little girl. I hardly gave her anything. Maybe she was sick to begin with. There better be some vodka in the cabinet. I don't think I can do this much longer. Not a problem. John will definitely kill me before I quit. He hates loose ends!"

After dinner, John called Cindy in Portland.

"Hi, Cindy. My name is John. I read your ad on Craigslist, and I think we should get together. I have my own construction business in Tacoma, and I'm going to be in Portland on business Wednesday and Thursday this week. I was married once for four years, but my first wife didn't want any children, and I love kids and always wanted a family."

"Tomorrow is a little short notice for me to get a babysitter, John."

"You don't need a babysitter. I would love to meet your son. I'll pick you both up at 7:00 p.m. I know a nice lobster restaurant in Portland. We'll get a high chair and the three of us will see if we like each other."

"That sounds wonderful, John. You're sure you don't mind?"

"On the contrary. I'm looking forward to it. See you tomorrow at seven, Cindy. Good night."

"Good night, John."

It was like taking candy from a baby.

Chapter 48

Steve did a five-year search of all medical personnel in the state of Washington and came up empty. He went back ten years and started with hospitals only. On his third hospital, Sacred Heart, out popped Trudy Miller, 2003-2006, nursing school graduate. He immediately called the hospital personnel department.

"Afternoon! This is Agent Steve Orzo with the Aspen Federal Bureau of Investigation. Whom am I speaking with?"

"This is Shelly Kingsley."

"Ms. Kingsley, the subject I am inquiring about is involved in the abduction of children. The case she is involved in is high priority and the next few weeks are crucial. The lives of a great many people will be in jeopardy if anything we discuss today is leaked. We are cautioning everyone we speak with that all conversations must remain confidential. If you speak about our investigation to anyone, you would initially be endangering the life of these children, not to mention the possible obstruction of justice, which is a felony. Do you understand what I am saying, Ms. Kingsley?"

"You don't have to hit me over the head with a shovel, Agent Orzo. I've got it. Keep my mouth shut."

"Good, I need everything you can give me on a Trudy Miller. She was a nurse in your hospital from 2003-2006. I'll hold."

A few minutes later, Shelly came back on the line.

"Okay, here it is. She received two warnings for erratic behavior before being stopped, exiting the hospital in possession of narcotics. She was charged with using the hospital's narcotics for her private use or sale. She was terminated and, with that record, could never work in the medical profession again. Is that what you need, Agent?"

"Thank you, Shelly. My office will call you back and give you a number so that you can fax everything you have to us. Thanks again, and remember, your silence could save lives."

"I understand. Good-bye."

Steve's first call was to Sam.

"Sam, I've got her. Three years as a nurse at Sacred Heart Hospital in Washington. Dismissed for stealing narcotics. Out of the nursing profession ever since."

"That's our girl, Steve. Let me bring you up to date. Last night, our wiretap paid off. Scully responded to an ad on Craigslist. He called a girl in Portland, Washington, who's looking for someone to take care of her and her one-year-old son. Scully is picking her up tomorrow, Wednesday at 7:00 p.m. It's a perfect setup for him and, coincidentally, for us. Single parent! He makes her disappear and returns to Seattle with the kid."

"Why not just go in and arrest him now, Sam?"

"Two reasons: number one, we don't know what kind of arsenal he has at that lake house or if he's got some sort of escape route, and two, this way we get Trudy clean. From what we've seen of this guy, she could be the first person he eliminates if he thinks we're on to him. We're putting it together now. I'll keep you up to date."

Chapter 49

John and Trudy left for Portland Wednesday afternoon at 2:00 p.m. They'd get there early and have a bite somewhere before they went to Cindy's. As soon as they got on 5 South, he called Rosenberg.

"This is John Scully. Tell Mr. Rosenberg I'll be dropping off a package Thursday morning at 11:00 a.m."

"Would you like to speak with him, Mr. Scully?"

"I'll speak to him tomorrow," and he hung up.

"Okay, doll. This is how it's going to go down. You haven't done any coke this morning, have you?"

"I haven't done anything. You told me not to get high today, and I didn't."

"That's good, doll, 'cause if you fuck this up, I'm going to fuck you up! Capice? I'm going to park behind her building. You are going to sit in the car and not move an inch. I will return with Cindy and her son. I will tell her we're dropping off my sister, that's you, on the way to dinner. When we get into the car, you will get out and sit behind her, and when I give you the nod, you will reach around and hold the chloroformed towel to her face. I'll throw her in the trunk, and we'll drive back to the lake and take her for a dip. Her kid is one-year-old. Don't sedate him. Give him some food. If anything happens to this kid, I'll take you out to the lake with Cindy, and you can do the dead man's crawl together. You got all this, Trudy. You've got no chances left!"

Trudy nodded her head. She could hardly breathe. Scully wouldn't simply kill her. He would make her suffer. She was stuck between a rock and a hard place. If she stayed with him, he would keep her high when they weren't working, but as soon as he found a replacement, she'd be going for a swim in the lake. If she ran, he'd make it like a game and torture her twice as long. She would be dead. She just wouldn't know when. Her train of thought was broken by the ring of her cell phone.

"Trudy, this is Rosenberg. Thursday is no good. The couple is out of town until the weekend. Make the meeting on Sunday at 11:00 a.m."

"Sunday at 11:00 a.m. Got it."

Chapter 50

"Steve, it's Sam."

"What have we got, Sam?"

"It's all going down tonight. Scully's last call was from the highway leaving Seattle. He's bringing the kid back to his house tonight and delivering him on Sunday at 11:00 a.m. That gives us until Sunday to get this whole package wrapped up."

"I like your optimism, Sam, but there's no fucking way that can be done!"

"Steve Orzo! What would your mother say if she heard you using that kind of language?"

"I'm Italian, Sam. If my mother were listening right now, she'd say 'That's my son the FBI agent. He's got such a big vocabulary.' Seriously, how do you expect to do a month's work in less than five days? We don't even know if we can find the rest of these kids yet? If Scully doesn't show up Sunday, Rosenberg and whoever else is involved will know something's wrong and that will make finding these kids that much more difficult."

"We'll get these two tonight and give them the full-court press. Let's see what we get. Fly up to the Seattle office. We'll meet at 10:00 p.m. tonight and put our heads together."

"I'm on my way."

Chapter 51

Scully stopped at a diner ten miles outside Portland. He had a roast beef sandwich, a large order of fries, and a coke. Trudy had a cup of coffee and tried to keep her hands from shaking. He talked about nothing for thirty minutes, and she nodded whenever she thought it appropriate. At 6:30 p.m., he asked her, "Can you do this? Tell me now if you're gonna fall apart."

"I'm okay. Let's get it over with."

He pulled behind Cindy's building and parked in the shadows.

"Sit still! Don't smoke. Don't get out of the car! Just wait!"

He left her and entered the building. It was a buzz-in. "Good, no doorman."

She buzzed him in, and he rode up to the eighth floor. He found 8e and rang the bell.

Cindy opened the door, and the first thing he thought to himself was *That's why these dating services are so fucked up. Paris Hilton my ass! This girl looked more like Conrad Hilton.*

"Hi, Cindy. It's a pleasure to meet you. I'm John."

"Nice to meet you, John. Would you like to come with me and meet Timmy? He's taking a nap, but he'll be fine."

"I'm sure he will."

Cindy walked Scully into the bedroom and backed away. Three agents with weapons drawn stood inside the room.

"On the ground! Hands behind your head. Now!"

"Mother fucker," Scully muttered to himself as he hit the floor.

After they cuffed him, the female agent called downstairs. "Scully secure," she said.

The other two agents walked to the passenger side of Scully's car. "Trudy Miller! Put your hands on the dash and don't move. You're under arrest for the kidnapping and murder of Arnold Pierce. That will do for now." She sat calmly as they read her rights and placed her in their car.

"Where's Scully?" she asked.

"You're worried about that animal? He's cuffed and on his way to the gas chamber."

The agent watched Trudy's shoulders relax and a small smile creep onto her face.

Chapter 52

They sat in the Seattle office—Agent Sam Pierce, Agent Steve Orzo, Margo Post, a district attorney out of the FBI Washington office, and Trudy Miller.

"Here's where we stand, Ms. Miller. You're an accomplice to numerous counts of kidnapping. We're not sure how many counts of murder among other charges, which at this point don't really matter as you can only be put to death once. Before we even discuss why you shouldn't be in that gas chamber with your friend Scully, let's start with Mason, Colorado, and how you got involved in all this."

"I know how this works," Miller shot back. "I've got nothing to say unless you've got something to give. I'm probably the smallest link in this chain, and I know you want Scully and the people making the money. I know for a fact that Scully won't even tell you his real name, so you're getting nothing from him. As for Rosenberg and Flakowitz, they're not running this operation either. You know what. I'll stop there. Give me a reason to tell you anything!"

Agent Pierce turned to the district attorney. "Mrs. Post?"

Margo got up and walked around the table before she spoke.

"You're a little confused, Ms. Miller. We have you for the murder of Arnold Pierce and a little girl in Montana. In addition, you were an accomplice in every murder John Scully committed. You have been an accomplice to kidnapping and murder several times over. Throw in the kidnapping of dozens of little children, not to mention the selling of those children. I can easily foresee your spending every remaining minute of your life in a federal penitentiary, assuming we can't get the death penalty. Realistically, I can see you getting life with no parole. Personally, I don't think that's long enough, but as you say, you're the little fish, so I will make you one offer that I will leave on the table for thirty seconds after which you can go pick out window treatments for your cell. Here it is. Twenty years, that's twelve years with good behavior, and that only works if we get convictions as a result of your testimony and we get the rest of these children back in one piece. If there is one more fatality among these children, all deals are off. Clocks ticking, Ms. Miller!"

"Accepted," Trudy shot back. "Let's get this over with. Rosenberg hired me to help take care of adopted children before they were delivered to their adoptive parents. I couldn't get work anywhere else as I had lost my nursing license, and he paid in cash. I didn't get a lot of work until he hired this guy right out of prison, sent him money and fake ID under the name of John Scully, and flew him out to Seattle. He had just finished a ten-year sentence on the East Coast. That's all I know about who he is or where he comes from. In the four years we have been working and living together, he has never told me one word about who he is or what he did before he came to Seattle. The only thing I learned on my own is, this is one guy you don't want to get on the wrong side of.

"We did some errands for Rosenberg in the beginning, and then John started putting his own plans together. He read about this dream community that was being built in Colorado. He found out when everyone was moving in and about a community center that was being provided for all the little kids. I had no idea what he had in mind, only that he kept saying 'This is fucking perfect,' over and over again. 'This is fucking perfect.' What did he call it? Oh yeah, Fort Knox in an SUV! We drove down there in a stretch van that John had bought used. He painted it himself at the lake and threw on some phony plates. We camped out there and ate fast food and never spoke with a soul. During the days, we checked out the mountain a couple of times a day, never enough to arouse suspicion. I never saw anything like it. It was like something out of Disneyland. We're driving down this road, and then in the middle of nowhere, there's this huge Exxon refinery. Aside from a few smaller buildings, there was this incredibly huge gasoline drum. I'm talking thirty yards by thirty yards. It must have had twenty thousand gallons in it or more. I'm trying to figure out why we are looking at gasoline drums, and John turns up this road just to the right of it and drives up this mountain. Every day we drove back to the Exxon place and up the mountain. Several of those mornings, we parked at a lookout, maybe a third of the way from the top of the mountain, and watched the SUV go up and down the mountain with the kids. The people who lived and worked off the mountain were always gone by this time. The guard's shift changed at 8:00 a.m., so that wasn't a problem. We knew exactly what time that SUV would be coming down and that we had plenty of time to do whatever needed doing with no interruption. I never understood what the Exxon place had to do with the kids, and John never talked to me when he was working unless he was giving me orders.

"On the morning of the supposed accident, we blocked off the road with our van. John smeared ketchup over the side of my face, and I lay down in the middle of the road. That cop pulled his SUV over and ran to where John was holding my head in his lap. He said, 'What the hell' and before he got out 'happened,' John shot him several times in the face. Then he wrapped him up in a burlap bag and stuck his body in the trunk of our van. I took the kids and transferred them from their van to ours, holding a small amount of chloroform to their faces as I put their seat belts on. When John had cleaned up the road and all the kids were in the van, he got in the SUV and moved it in position in front of the guardrail he had loosened the night before. Then he stuck a large rock on the gas pedal of the SUV, threw it into drive, and jumped out. He told me after we were a few hours away that he knew there was a good chance the SUV would miss the Exxon tank.

We would have had to make a run for it, but it fell straight into the center and made such a big explosion I thought the entire world would be coming for us in seconds. As it turned out, once we turned onto the highway, we were home free.

"I gave all the kids an injection of Valium and knocked them out. We drove to John's house on the lake. It was a long ride, about twelve hours, and I had to inject those kids a few times to keep them under. I set up twelve cots for the kids. One of them had overdosed, and John took him out to the lake with the driver of the SUV. He kept extra burlap bags and weights at the lake for what he called burials at sea.

"Over the next three weeks, we delivered four of the kids to Rosenberg's office in Seattle. I don't think it was his office because we only met at night or on Sundays. He even told the adoptive parents that meeting on Sunday was a good way to protect their privacy and that he didn't want his firm to be known for handling difficult adoptions.

"Aside from seeing some of the people picking up their kids in Rosenberg's office, I have no idea who they are or where they live, and I never saw them again.

"We kept those seven kids hooked up to an IV. I fed them intravenously and sedated them with Valium. Three weeks later, we drove the other seven kids to New York. I was surprised they were all still breathing. We left them at the law office of Larry Levin, someplace in Westchester. I told John that if no one helped those kids, they would never last the night. He told me Levin had seven appointments set up in thirty-minute increments to move them out. He made me stay with the kids until all of them had been picked up, and then we turned around and drove back to Seattle, and that was the last time I ever saw any of those kids again.

"Over the last two years, we only did single or double pickups, never more. John always got rid of the bodies. I was pretty messed up those two years. I'm not making excuses for my actions. I'm just saying I was so fucked up on a day-to-day basis that I'm not really sure whom he did what to. In my condition, I'm amazed that I kept those seven kids alive all the way to New York. I came along after he was done with the jobs that followed and tended to the kids until we delivered them. This last time I was with him was when he took the two kids from a mother in Montana. He walked out of the house with the two kids. They were like six months and eighteen months old. Then he went back inside for ten minutes. As we drove away, the house blew sky high.

"I gave the eighteen month old a dose of Valium to keep her asleep, and she overdosed. John went ballistic. I knew from that point on that it was just a matter of time before he took me out to the lake for one of his burials at sea."

"So you know nothing about the whereabouts of those children you dropped off in New York?"

"Not a thing! I already told you that!"

"That's it for now, Ms. Miller. We'll talk to you again tomorrow. See if you can think of anything additional that might help us."

"You're going to try to find all these kids that were taken, aren't you? They're all over the country, and you won't get anything out of these lawyers. How are you going to do that?"

"Can you help us, Trudy," Steve asked. "Wouldn't you want your kids back? It's over for you now."

"I'll think on it, Agent Orzo, and I'll get back to you tomorrow. Maybe if I think of something helpful, you'll sweeten my deal."

"You're probably where they got the term *angel of Mercy* from, Trudy," Steve said with an obvious look of disgust on this face.

They took Trudy away. Agents Pierce and Orzo remained with the district attorney.

"What can we offer her if she can help us get those kids back, Marge?"

"Let's get everyone down here and see if we can get the information ourselves," Marge replied, "and if we hit a wall, then we'll have this conversation. If we can find them on our own, I would just as soon see this women spend twelve years in jail."

"No argument there, Marge. Let's get the show on the road."

Chapter 53

In Seattle, they entered the twenty-fifth floor offices of Gold and Company at 10:00 a.m. on Thursday. They checked the lobby desk first to make sure the owner, Peter Gold, and his associate partners, Rosenberg and Floakowitz, were in their offices. They arrested the partners at the same time and escorted them out of their offices individually to prevent any conversation between them. After they were safely away, they presented a search warrant and began going through every file on the premise.

Agents Pierce and Orzo sat down with Gladys in the reception area.

"Good morning, Gladys. My partner and I are with the FBI and are investigating the kidnapping and murder of several children. We believe that this firm you work for has been involved in these incidents. Do you have any knowledge of any activity of this nature, Gladys?"

"I swear to you. I know nothing about any of this."

"We believe you, Gladys, but this past Wednesday, you received a call from a John Scully who asked to speak with Howard Rosenberg. Do you know John Scully?"

"I have put through several calls from John Scully to Mr. Rosenberg, but I do not know him personally, and I have never met him."

"How about Ms. Trudy Miller? Do you know her?"

"Again. I have put through several calls from Ms. Trudy Miller to Mr. Rosenberg, but I have never met her either."

"Thank you, Gladys. If we need, you we'll get back to you."

Chapter 54

They returned to the FBI office and started with the owner of the firm, Peter Gold.

"Hello, Mr. Gold. I am Agent Sam Pierce, and this is Agent Steve Orzo. We would like to ask you a few questions. Do you deny that your firm has been dealing in the adoption of children, two years old and younger for the past several years?"

"We do occasionally help out with the legal aspects of an adoption. I don't believe that's against the law."

"We are talking about the kidnapping and murder of children and parents for the sole purpose of adoption sales and the garnering of huge amounts of money made through this endeavor."

"I have no idea what you are talking about, Agent."

"Mr. Gold, we have sworn testimony from several witnesses who swear they picked up their children in your office. Some on Sundays and other in the evenings during the week."

"I couldn't help you there, Agent. I never work on Sundays, and I leave my office at 6:00 p.m. every night. I refuse to stay later—a bonus one gets when one is the boss. As far as adoptions are concerned, you would have to speak with the associates in this firm that handle that area. I do not. I also have nothing further to say to you, so unless you have specific charges against me, I can't see how you could. I believe we are done here. You cannot hold me here more than twenty-four hours without charging me and allowing me a phone call. Although I'm sure you are aware of that, Agent Pierce. My lawyer will be here to remind you just in case you missed that course at FBI school."

They next interviewed Rosenberg and Flakowitz. They both admitted to handling adoptions. They insisted, however, that none of them were illegal. They remembered the Panzer case and would take a look through their records when they were released. They categorically denied any knowledge of a John Scully and a nurse working for them and added that any allegations that they were involved in illegal adoption activities were preposterous.

Pierce knew he could show a connection between Rosenberg and Scully and Miller, but how far could he take that? All the proof was in the missing files. All they had now were four adoptions with no paperwork to support it. They could make a connection between the children they had and the van and Rosenberg, but that would bring them back to square one—Rosenberg alleging he simply made the adoption possible and knew nothing of the circumstances. Of course, the FBI had two witnesses: a career criminal and psychopath, and a drug addict and alcoholic with a record for stealing narcotics. Great case!

Worse still, they were running out of time. If there was a loose end and they didn't find it by the time these lawyers were released, not only would the evidence disappear, but their last chance of finding these kids would be gone also.

Two hours later, the search of the law offices of Peter Gold and his associates was completed; they found absolutely nothing.

"Fucked, Steve. We're completely fucked. By tomorrow, every law firm in the country will know what went down here today and any strand of evidence that might implicate these lawyers will have vanished. I'm desperate. Throw me a long shot!"

"Let's interview Trudy Miller again. Maybe we can squeeze a little something extra out of her. What do we have to lose?"

"Nothing but time, Steve."

Chapter 55

Thirty minutes later, an agent brought Trudy Miller back and put her in the interrogation room.

"She looks ready to fall over, Sam."

"She's an addict, Steve. She hasn't touched anything since Tuesday, that's, three days. She's hitting a wall."

"Send someone downstairs for a half dozen candy bars and two triple espressos. Let's wake her up."

Twenty minutes later, Trudy had knocked off both espressos and half the candy and sat staring at the wall with her eyes wide open and glazed. Agents Pierce and Orzo entered the interrogation room.

"Morning, Trudy. Nice to see you again."

"Yeah, thanks for the breakfast."

"Trudy, we got a little confused with all your testimony yesterday. What we'd like you to do is start at the very beginning and tell us the whole story again. Is that okay?"

"I'm not going anywhere, am I?"

"Good point, Trudy. As long as we're sitting here, we might as well go over everything. Maybe we missed something. Start from the first time you had any connections with this law firm, and go on from there."

"Okay, I was contacted by someone from the law firm and told to come in for an interview. They told me they needed someone with a medical background and they were aware of my record and would overlook it. It was the summer of 2007 and for the first year, or so I didn't do much. I think they did about four adoptions a year, and they would send me to pick up the child at a hospital or an agency, sometimes at a home. After I dropped the kid off with the new parents, I was done."

"Did this always happen at the office in Seattle?"

"Yes, same office, usually on Sunday afternoons, sometimes on a weekday after 8:00 p.m. Then Scully showed up, and the adoption business became a major business. I worked exclusively with Scully from then on and only took orders from John and Rosenberg, but usually from John."

"Before that you only took orders from Rosenberg?"

"Well, yeah, after Edna left."

"I'm sorry, Trudy, but who is Edna again?"

"I didn't mention her because she's been gone a long time, but when I started working in 2007, she ran the office."

"When did she leave, Trudy?"

"Well, she was there when we brought the van in. I remember that because she was interested in one of the kids. Oh yeah, now I remember. She told Rosenberg once, when I was just leaving, that one of these was going to be hers and if they gave her a hard time, she'd bury them. She was one tough bitch!

"I think they gave her one of the twin boys because we never delivered him to new parents. He just stayed there one night. And then about two or three weeks after we had made all the arrangements to drop off the rest of the children from the van, she left. I never saw her again."

"Thanks, Trudy, you've been very helpful. We'll talk to you later."

"Can I take the rest of the candy bars?"

"Be my guest."

As soon as they left the room, Pierce got on the phone and requested the personnel records be brought to his office ASAP.

"I like it, Steve. Let's find this Edna and have a chat with her."

Chapter 56

Edna Collins lived on the third floor of a four-story walk-up on Sycamore St. in downtown Seattle. As they drove downtown, Orzo and Pierce went over her history.

"Listen to this, Sam. Edna Collins worked for Peter Gold for ten years. During that time, she reported only to Gold and did not make one friend in the office. Since the day she left, no one has heard one word from her. Her boss, whom we both know, is the scum of the earth and has been paying her full disability for slipping on the wet floor by the water cooler. Sounds like she's got him by the balls."

"The key word here is *had*. She had him by the balls. At this stage he has no choice. As soon as he gets a phone in his hands, she's history, and I would bet on a large fire that burns the building to the ground."

They walked up to the third floor and knocked on Collins's door.

A male voice said, "Who's there?"

"FBI."

The door opened, and a short heavyset man in a T-shirt said, "Let me see some ID."

They produced their IDs, and he opened the door and let them in.

"My name is Agent Sam Pierce, and this is Agent Steve Orzo. I presume you are the husband of Edna Collins."

"That's right. Frank Collins. What is this about? Wait, Let me guess. The kid?"

"What kid is that, Mr. Collins?"

"You know which kid. Okay, play it your way. My wife comes home with a kid maybe four years ago. She says we just adopted a kid. I'm a construction worker, not a brain surgeon, but even I know you don't come home one night with an adopted kid."

"Did you ask her where the child came from?"

"Of course, I did, and I also asked how we were going to afford this kid with her out of work. She says, 'No problem. I'm not working any more, but they're going to pay me full disability.' I ask her, 'Why would they do that?' She says, 'Because I've been working there for ten years and have enough shit on them to put them in prison for life.'"

"Where is the boy now, Mr. Collins?"

"No idea. Edna takes him out with her every day. He's like her toy. She kept him back from starting school this year so he could keep her company. I don't know who's more fucked up—her or him?"

"Would you have any pictures of the boy, Mr. Collins?"

"Are you kidding? Go into the bedroom. They're all over the fucking wall!"

Steve walked into the bedroom and came out with a picture in his hand and showed it to Sam. They both nodded.

"What is it? What's going on?"

"It's a long story, Mr. Collins. We're going to have someone take you down to our offices and have you make a statement. We'll talk to you later."

Chapter 57

"Let's get a car down here to watch the front door, Steve. I want Edna and her son in custody as soon as they surface. Oh, and let's make sure we have a search warrant."

"I think we should interview her in her apartment, Sam. We arrest her in front, and someone she knows may see what's going on and call someone else. You know how this works. If she's got any information or if she's holding any files that we could use, they could disappear awfully quickly if someone thinks she's about to give them up. Let her enter the building. We'll send the kid uptown, and we'll talk to her alone immediately."

"You realize, Steve, that there's not a lot we can hold over her head. She might have been privy to all the shit that went down, but they weren't her orders. She shows no financial gain from the adoptions. The only thing we have on her is illegal possession of someone else's child, and she will throw herself on the mercy of the court and declare that she thought she was helping a child whose parents had been killed in a crash."

"Let me have her, Sam. I think I can bring her around."

"She's all yours, Steve. Good luck."

Edna Collins and her son arrived at their apartment house at 1:45 p.m. The agent in the car waited for two minutes and then followed them up to their apartment.

The apartment door opened, and Edna Collins and the boy entered. Edna immediately froze as the two agents confronted her. Sam and Steve showed their IDs and asked Mrs. Collins to sit down. The third agent entered behind them and closed the door.

"Simms, we're going to be speaking with Mrs. Collins for quite some time. Would you please frisk her and check her purse for a weapon and then take the boy back to the office with you and call children's protective services? We will follow you in about an hour. Thanks."

"What do you think you're doing? You have no right to break into my apartment, search me, and take my son away. I have a right to call my attorney, and I am demanding that right this instant."

Steve walked over and stood in front of Mrs. Collins. "Let me make the call for you, Edna. Who would you like to call? Let me see. You can't call Peter Gold today because Peter Gold has been arrested and is in a holding cell. You can't call Rosenberg or Flakowitz as they were also arrested this morning. John Scully is already halfway to the gas chamber, and Trudy Miller is following close behind. That leaves you, Edna Collins."

Edna had turned a deep shade of crimson and was visibly shaking at this point.

"You know, Edna, before I get to how ugly the rest of your life is going to be, I would just like to tell you how complex my feelings are right now. My friends supposedly lost their sons Adam and Todd in a terrible crash in 2010, and I've just seen one of them alive and well some four years later. Tell me, Edna, do you know if that boy you've been keeping these last four years is Adam or Todd? Do you care that my friends thought both their children were killed when you arranged their kidnapping, and lastly, do you feel any guilt, taking one of their sons as your own the same way you pick up a stray dog and take it home? The real question is, what kind of monster are you, Edna Collins?

"I'm sure you already know all this, but let me review a few facts quickly. You, Edna Collins, are part of a conspiracy to kidnap and sell children for money. During some of these abductions, we know of two children—one eighteen-month-old boy and one twelve-month-old girl—who overdosed while being transported. There may be other deaths that we are not aware of. There is also the death of the retired detective who was driving the SUV, which coincidentally delivered the boy you kept. I don't even know how to refer to your boy. He's not your son. You never adopted him. Was he your bonus? Whatever, let's return to the moment.

"We have a very interesting situation here, Edna. We have enough evidence to put you away for two lifetimes, assuming they don't give you the gas chamber. As fate would have it, you are the lowest head on the totem pole. In other words, if you can help us put away the big fish, we might not care what happens to the little fish, regardless of how much we would like to see that little fish fry. Nod if you're following me, Edna."

Edna gave a definite nod of her head.

"Okay, Edna, we presently have arrested all the principles involved in this case. We can hold them for twenty-four hours after which they will be free to consult lawyers; and those lawyers will be free to instruct other persons to eliminate any possible trails that would lead back to them. If I were Peter Gold, Edna, I would have someone burn this building down to the ground and make sure no one was left to talk. Are you still following me, Edna?"

Edna followed with another definite nod.

So we have a very small window in which we are going to bring you together with the district attorney of the state of Washington. If you are able to provide us with what we need to put the big fish away and you and the district attorney can make a deal, it's possible that you could actually spend a majority of the rest of your life outside a federal prison. Whether or not you deserve to spend the rest of your life behind bars is a question we will not get into at this time.

"Before we set up this meeting, Edna, I need to know three things: one, are you willing to sit down with the district attorney and make this deal, two, do you have the files, papers, contracts, whatever, to put these lawyers away, and three, will we be able to locate all the children who were sold? If the answer isn't yes to all three questions, Edna, we have nothing further to discuss. We have until 12:00 p.m. tomorrow to bring all this to fruition, so think quickly and give me an answer."

There was no hesitation on Edna's part. She knew enough about the legal system and where she stood to make an immediate decision.

"*Yes*. But I want something in writing before I give you everything I have."

"You will have it, Edna. Let's get Edna up to the Seattle office, Sam. We can call the district attorney and have her meet us there."

Chapter 58

They sat down with Edna Collins and Margo Post, the DA, at 3:00 p.m. in the Seattle office of the FBI.

Agent Pierce began the proceedings.

"Okay, Edna, you're on. This is the district attorney for the state of Washington, and if you convince her that you can provide what we need, she'll make you an offer. Simple as that."

"Okay. I worked for Peter Gold, Howard Rosenberg, and Ed Flakowitz for ten years. They would pressure small orphanages and social workers on the take to turn over young children to them for which they were compensated, and these children in turn were put through the adoption process. We didn't see more than four cases a year, but they were extremely profitable, and the firm hired Trudy Miller to tend to the children until they were delivered. In 2009, the firm hired a man just out of prison, sent him a new identification, and flew him out to Seattle. They teamed him up with Trudy Miller. This John Scully made the firm millions of dollars. He was cunning and ruthless and had absolutely no conscience. I kept a record of every dollar, every abduction, and every child—where they came from and who they ended up with. I have it all."

The agents went out into the hall with the DA.

"It's up to the FBI," said Margo. "She's got everything we need, and we don't have much time. I'm willing to let her walk if we get convictions. Are you?"

"I don't think we have much choice. Let's make the deal."

"Okay, Edna, as the district attorney for the state of Washington, I am offering you full immunity if your information results in the prosecution of Peter Gold, Howard Rosenberg, and Ed Flakowitz and leads us to the missing children. Agents Pierce and Orzo will escort you to your bank vault to retrieve your files."

"I get that in writing?"

"Yes, you do," replied Margo.

They drove to the Washington Federal Savings Bank on Pike Street, and Edna retrieved all her files. She recorded all her statements and affidavits with the district attorney's office. They reunited her with her husband and dropped them both off at their apartment.

"Stay in touch with our office and notify us if you leave the city. You should be fine. All your testimony is now on file and the evidence you gave us is more than enough to put away the lawyers. Once they learn we have the files, you become meaningless. We'll still want you when the trial begins, but until then you're on your own."

Chapter 59

Agents Pierce and Orzo met in the office.

"Okay, where are we, Sam?"

"We've got all the files, Steve. Let's lay everything out and see what we're missing. I can't see us being able to track these kids down by 12:00 p.m. tomorrow. I think we need to keep these guys cut off for a little longer. Can we do that?"

"I'll call Margo. Let's see if she can help us. In the meantime, here is the list of kids that were in the van: (1) Jonathan Stark, (2) Emma Whitcup, (3) Samantha Fisher, (4) Todd Barnum, (5) Adam Barnum, (6) Arnold Pierce, (7) Hillary Jonas, (8) Charlie Byrnne, (9) Gina Corritore, (10) Martin Herrera, (11) Rachael Block, and (12) Steven Wells."

"Okay, Sam, to begin with, I checked the pictures we had on file of Emma Whitcup. No question. Jill Diamond is Emma Whitcup. Patricia Panzer is a dead ringer for her mother Amy, so that's two. We have Melvin Kent in New York and the Collins boy, who are the Barnum twins even if we don't know which is which, and we know that Arnold Pierce overdosed sometime during the transfer to the van or on the way back to Seattle. That leaves five kids in New York with Levin and two kids out of the Seattle office."

"We have an entire office standing by in Westchester, waiting for instructions, and we have plenty of manpower here. Let's go upstairs, Steve, and start going through these files."

"How do you want to handle the parents, Sam? Aside from Edna, all these people think they have an adopted child that has been a part of their family for four years or so. Look at the Panzers and the Diamonds. They love those girls and look like great parents to me."

"Steve, are you forgetting that these kids already have parents? Some of them are actually friends of yours."

"I haven't forgotten. Still, there must be a way to go about this without destroying these people. Imagine, after trying unsuccessfully to have children and then trying to adopt and hitting a wall, a couple finally manages to become parents. They pay a great deal of money to beat the system not to abduct a child. They raise that child and give him all the love they have, never suspecting he or she already has parents. Now, two agents walk up their door, shove a piece of paper in their hands, and take their child away. Sorry, Sam, but there's got to be a better way."

"I'm not arguing with you, Steve. I just don't have an answer. I'm listening. Come up with something feasible, and I'm in."

"Hang on a second. I've got a call. Hello, yes, this is Agent Pierce. Margo, hi, we were just thinking of you. He did? I didn't know that. Hang on one second."

"When did you have the time to call Margo?"

"On the way up when I ran into the men's room."

"Were you dialing with your right hand while you were wiping your ass with your left? That was rhetorical. What can she do for us?"

"Hi, Margo, I'm back. I'm listening. Really? Can we do that? Isn't that denying them their rights? I agree he's lower than slime, but that doesn't mean we can take his phone call away." Sam held the phone for a while and listened. "Oh, okay. Now I've got it. And you think we can get away with that? You're getting me very worked up. Do you date FBI agents? I agree. Bye."

"That was one of the most interesting non-conversations I ever heard," said Steve. "Care to translate?"

"We've got an additional twenty-four hours. We are doing everything by the book. Peter Gold and his two stooges have requested their telephone calls. We are obligated to pass this request on to the warden. The warden is required to inform the guard on duty, who is then required to take them from their cells and deliver them to the telephone facility. The warden's assistant inadvertently puts the orders for their calls in with the outgoing mail and drops it into the mail chute. The mail chute is not opened on Sundays, so the mistake will be discovered forty-eight hours from now, and the warden's assistant will be severely chastised."

"I'm appalled," Steve responded.

"As am I," Sam concurred.

Chapter 60

"We've already broken these files down by location. There are five children on the East Coast. Those families will be interviewed and flown to Seattle by Saturday afternoon. You and I will take the two families in Arizona and Texas and make sure they are in Seattle by Saturday afternoon as well. We already have the Panzers and the Diamonds in Seattle. The FBI has interviewed the Kents and arranged for them to fly out and the Collins boy is already in Seattle with children's protective services. That makes eleven, and the Pierce child makes twelve.

"I know we reminded everyone to be sensitive and to stress the fact that we would connect the families with the hope that a relationship develops, but remind them again. These families are victims also."

Before they opened the first file, Sam called the East Coast and explained how they wanted this handled and what the timetable was.

"Okay, Steve, here's the first file. Michael and Elayne Roizin. They live In Scottsdale, Arizona, in a golf resort called Desert Springs on Acomo Drive. The house address is 118 North Fifty-Sixth Street. They adopted a baby girl. All the ages in the files are listed as two years old, so until we figure out who this girl is, the age is irrelevant.

"Michael Roizin is thirty-eight years old and his wife Elayne is thirty-six. Michael is the president of a computer company. They have no other children. The girl, whose name is Dina, is now six years old, according to this file, and is a member of the dance team at Desert Mountain. We better not ask Dina what she wants to do. She might not want to leave Desert Mountain. I wouldn't.

"Our second set of parents is Robert and Laura Foster of Leander, Texas. Their address is 110 Cedar Park, section # 04. Their child is a six-year-old boy named David.

"Robert Foster is forty-two years old and was the owner of an Internet company. He sold it last year for, let me check this again, $110 million dollars. His wife Laura is thirty years old and married him for his money."

"It doesn't say that, Sam."

"Okay, I made that up. It says he's their only child, but I still want a raise!"

"I suggest we leave first thing tomorrow morning. Let's get a car to the Roizins' home at 6:00 a.m. and tell them it's an FBI matter and keep them in their home until we get there. We can be there by 10:00 a.m. We can leave transportation up to the Scottsdale division, and we can be in Austin by 3:00 p.m., same routine. Keep the Fosters there until we arrive except in this case we can arrange transportation back to Seattle."

"Coffee at 5:00 a.m. at the airport sounds right."

"My favorite time for coffee. See you in a few, Sam."

Chapter 61

The 6:45 flight out of Seattle got into Scottsdale at 9:15 a.m. A company car was waiting for them, and they were at the Roizins at 9:45 a.m. The FBI car was parked in front, and an agent was posted at the door.

Looks like we're right on time, Sam thought to himself. *Now all we have to do is break the hearts of two innocent people and take their child away. No wonder everyone wants this job!*

The two agents entered the Roizin home, acknowledging the agent at the door before walking into the living room. The Roizins were sitting together on the couch. Sam glanced at the second agent, who flicked his eyes upward so that Sam would know the child was upstairs.

"Mr. and Mrs. Roizin, I am agent Sam Pierce, and this is Agent Steve Orzo. I apologize for the cars and agents so early in the morning, but due to time restraints, we really had no choice. It was necessary that all of you were home when we arrived."

"Agent Pierce, I am not one to throw my weight around, but you have made a huge mistake. I am an extremely patriotic man and have done nothing to deserve this treatment."

"There's no easy way to do this, Mr. Roizin. So please bear with me while I tell you why we're here."

"We've been sitting here since 6:00 a.m. That's over four hours, so please make it a very quick story."

"That I will, sir. I have two very good friends. They live in Colorado. Approximately four years ago, their twenty-month-old daughter was killed in an SUV that went off the road and exploded. You might remember the accident. There were twelve children in that SUV. All of them incinerated."

"I remember that accident," said Elayne Roizin. "It was devastating. All those little children and their parents. Even now, I can't even think about it, but what can that have to do with us?"

"Four years ago, Mr. Roizin, you and your wife adopted a twenty-month-old daughter."

"One second, Agent. We went through a reputable law firm, and the adoption of our daughter was totally legitimate."

"Can I ask you why you adopted, Mr. Roizin?"

"Not that it's any of your business, but my wife and I weren't able to have children on our own. It happens to lots of people. Adoption is not a crime, Agent Pierce."

"Why may I ask did you pay so much more than normal to adopt a child?"

"The money meant nothing. I am extremely wealthy. It was the only thing missing from our lives."

"A young couple in Seattle also adopted a girl about four years ago. She was having a difficult time when they first brought her home. Did you have any difficulties when you first brought Dina home?"

"As a matter of fact, she did have some respiratory problems, but she was treated and was fine after a few weeks."

"The Panzers brought their daughter to a psychiatrist who recommended that they try to uncover her past. They hired a private investigator, and they discovered that her real name was Samantha Fisher. She was in the SUV that was incinerated in Mason, Colorado."

"I don't understand," said Mrs. Roizin, "how could she have been one of the children in that SUV in Colorado?"

"She wasn't in the SUV, Mrs. Roizin. There were no children in the SUV."

Mr. Roizin turned to his wife. "Oh my god," he sobbed.

"What is it, Michael? I don't understand!"

"All those children," Agent Pierce continued, "that were supposedly in that SUV were abducted and sold to people around the country that were either desperate to adopt or would never be allowed to adopt. All the lawyers involved have already been arrested. The only thing left is to return the children back to their biological parents."

"You don't mean you're going to take my daughter away? We love her. She loves us. You can't do this. Michael, do something!"

"Agent Pierce, I believe you realize that aside from being naive, we never thought for a second we could be taking someone else's child. Do we have any options? We're not criminals. This is our little girl. We're the only family she knows. She loves us. Ask her. She doesn't want to leave us and go back to people she has no recollection of. We legally adopted her. I have the papers. We're not letting her go!"

"Mr. Roizin, I don't want to be here. We understood how impossible a situation this was before we came, but the fact remains that you illegally adopted someone else's child. If this was your daughter and she was kidnapped and adopted illegally and you found her, wouldn't you want her back?"

Mr. Roizin was sobbing into his hands, and his wife was hysterical.

Sam gave them a few minutes before continuing.

"Here's what Agent Orzo and I have come up with. We knew coming here that this would be heart-wrenching. We knew that people who have adopted a daughter and love her as their own were not going to be okay, giving her up. I would like to suggest that over the next twelve hours, you explain to your daughter what has happened. During that period, the three of you will be coming back to FBI headquarters in Seattle along with all the children and most of the parents that thought they had legally adopted a child. We have to insist that until all the children have been reunited with their parents, you keep everything absolutely quiet. This is for your own protection. Until all statements have been introduced as evidence, you pose a danger to these law firms and their associates. In addition, if word gets out prematurely, it will make it that much more difficult to locate those children we have yet to locate.

"When we are finished with all the legalities, we would like to bring you and your child with us to Mason, Colorado, where we can introduce your daughter's natural parents to their daughter's adoptive parents. What happens from that point on is not the business of the FBI."

"I follow your thinking, Agent. Perhaps, instead of losing our daughter completely, you're thinking we might at least maintain some contact. I'm sure in your mind, that's a compromise, but let me assure you that you are still ripping out our hearts despite your attempt at compassion."

"I'm sorry, Mr. and Mrs. Roizin. It's the best we could come up with."

"Come dear," Mr. Roizin said, helping his wife up. "Let's get ourselves together. This is going to be devastating for Dina. Let's try to support her as much as we can." They walked up the stairs and into their daughter's room without uttering another word.

"We'll see you tomorrow in Seattle," said Agent Pierce.

"Let's get moving, Steve. We've got a plane to catch." As they headed out the door, Sam turned to Steve and said, "That wasn't so difficult. I hope they have plenty of vodka on this plane!"

Chapter 62

They arrived in Austin at 2:00 p.m., jumped into a waiting car, and arrived at the entrance to the Crystal Springs Golf Course in the suburb of Leander, Texas, at 2:30 p.m. They pulled up to the gate and showed their credentials.

"This is the third FBI vehicle I've seen today. You guys having a golf outing?"

"Actually," Sam replied, "we're investigating people who work at the gates of communities like these who don't pay all their taxes. We'll be back in about an hour. Don't go too far."

"A sadistic streak," said Steve. "First time I've seen that side of you."

"That's the house on the right, with the tennis courts," said Sam.

"Why do you build tennis courts when you belong to a golf and tennis club?" Steve responded.

"So you don't have to share them with anyone else, Steve. Don't you know any rich, arrogant people?"

An agent stood outside the Foster home. They exchanged hellos and entered the house. Another agent stood alone in the living room.

"Where is everyone?" Sam asked the agent.

"The Fosters have a standing massage from 2:30-4:00 p.m. on Saturdays, and they told me to tell you they'd be in back by the pool when you got here. The boy is upstairs in his room, playing video games, and has already told me to stay the fuck out of his room. Oh, and in my humble opinion, he's the nicest member of the family. Take a few deep breaths. You're going to need all your patience to handle this trio!"

Sam and Steve walked through the house to the enclosed pool in the back. The Fosters were getting massages alongside one another under a separate canopy.

"Mr. and Mrs. Foster, I'm Agent Pierce, and this is Agent Orzo."

"Is it really necessary to disturb our massages, Agent? We'll be finished in an hour or so."

"Actually, Mr. Foster, your massages are over right now. Agent Thomas will you please escort our two therapists to the door? Thank you."

"You have no right to invade our privacy and walk around our house as if you're in charge. You have no idea who you're dealing with. You could both be unemployed by Monday. I make one call, and you're both collecting unemployment."

147

"Mr. and Mrs. Foster, I would like to speak to both of you in the living room. I'm going to give you ten minutes to throw on something and make an appearance. If you both are not sitting on your couch when those ten minutes have expired, I will handcuff you both, read you your rights, and lock you up until tomorrow when we will try to find the time to interview you when we are in the mood." Sam gave a nod to Steve, and they both reentered the house.

"I told you it would get easier," Steve said with a smirk on his face.

"I'd rather deal with this egomaniac than torture another couple like the Roizins."

"Might as well go see the kid and get it over with all at once." Sam knocked on the boy's door.

"Go away."

"Sorry, son," Sam replied, opening the door. "We wanted to introduce ourselves. I'm Agent Pierce, and this is Agent Orzo. We are going to be flying up to Seattle in an hour or so with you and your parents. I'm sure they will help you pack, but you need to finish whatever you're doing."

"I'm not going anywhere with you. I have a playing lesson tomorrow morning on the blue course at 10:00 a.m. It's too late to cancel, and my father has already paid for it."

"See you in a little while, son," Agent Pierce replied, exiting the room.

As they walked downstairs, Steve said, "It's the age-old debate. Which is more important in framing a child's character, genetics or environment? Here we have the son of Paul and Tracy Byrnne, two of the most sincere, down to earth, loveliest people in the world. You take their two-year-old and have him spend four years with Mr. and Mrs. Entitled, you get a spoiled, ill-mannered brat."

"Your friends will have their hands full with this kid," said Pierce.

"You know what, Sam? If I were a betting man, I'd wager that faster than you could ever imagine, Tracy and Paul will get this boy back on track. He's still a little boy, and something tells me the Fosters won't be making a lot of visits once he's no longer their property."

The Fosters walked into the living room with three minutes to spare, surprising Sam, who was sure he was going to have to drag them out of their rooms.

"Please have a seat," Sam gestured toward the couch.

"I can't wait to hear this. This can't be about my business. I work for a very large corporation, and I can't believe there are irregularities that would concern the government. This can't be a Patriot Act visit. I live in a golf community in Leander, Texas, for God's sake. I give up! What do you want?"

"In the summer of 2010, you and your wife arranged for the adoption of your son with a law firm in Seattle. Whom did you deal with?"

"I spoke with Howard Rosenberg."

"How many times did you see him?"

"We met initially at his office in Seattle. I spoke with him several times on the phone, and about two months after our first meeting, he had us fly up to Seattle and pick up our son. Why is this your business?"

"For the past seven or eight years, the law firm of Peter Gold has been performing adoptions. Many of the adoptions up until 2009 were slightly tainted but not necessarily illegal. In 2009, people under his employ began abducting children, falsifying or simply losing all paperwork connected to them, and selling them in the guise of adoption. In September 2010, there was an SUV that went off the side of a mountain in Colorado in which twelve children and one retired policeman were supposedly incinerated at an Exxon oil facility.

We now believe that all those children are alive and have been sold to families around the country for large sums of money. All the children are being brought to Seattle and will then be returned to their birth parents."

"My wife and I hired a law firm to find a child for adoption. We paid $175,000 to that firm for the service. We did nothing knowingly that was illegal, and I don't think you have any case against us. In any event, I'm going to call my lawyers."

"I'll tell you when you may call your lawyer, Mr. Foster. In the meantime, I will need you to pack a bag for your son, as we will be leaving for Seattle within an hour. We are allowing all the parents to come with their children and meet their biological parents, although you are certainly within your rights to decline."

"So you're taking the kid back. My wife and I are not being charged with anything?"

"That's correct, Mr. Foster."

"Do we have to go with you? Can't you just take the kid?"

"You and your wife will have to sign affidavits and make some statements on the record. At some point after that, your son will be going to Colorado to be reunited with his real parents."

"We certainly don't have to go with him to Colorado?"

"No, you don't. That's entirely your decision. I would guess that you would be free to leave Sunday afternoon after all the children have been reunited with their parents."

"I'm sorry about this, Laura. Are you upset?"

"Well, we're going to Ms. Bonnie Wener's party tonight, and we were supposed to play golf with the Kleins tomorrow morning, but I enjoy Seattle. Why don't we make a mini vacation out of this and stay there a few extra days?"

"Listen, folks, we need you to pack a suitcase for your son, basically essentials, and to be ready to leave in thirty minutes."

Steve couldn't contain himself and had to get the last word in, "We are truly sorry to be taking your son away from you. You are both obviously very broken up about losing him."

"It was a mistake," replied Robert Foster. "As soon as we brought him home, we knew we fucked up, but it was too late. So we gave him a large bedroom, and he pretty much does whatever he wants. He hasn't had it so bad."

"You're a real saint, Mr. Foster. Can we wait outside, Sam? I can't shake this feeling of nausea I get being in this house."

Chapter 63

June 2014, Mason, Colorado

It was almost four years since the crash. The community of Mason still existed, though it was hardly the same. Several families sold their homes and left immediately. Some of them had lost a child and couldn't stand to be reminded every time they drove down the hill, and others simply wanted to get as far away as possible, even those who hadn't suffered a loss.

The Pierces had practically nothing in common with the other families to begin with. After Arnold was taken from them, they never left their house until one afternoon a moving truck pulled up and they were gone.

The basic inner core remained firm. Michael and Marie now had a two-year-old daughter, Lynn. They had both worked straight through the tragedy. It was the mentality of both the Palazzoles and the Corritores—you can be heartbroken, you can feel like the world is coming down on top of you, but first you do your work. Michael especially had lived such a tough life that a tragedy, even the loss of his daughter, was something you lived with. That was not to say that he didn't stop every so often when he was alone and put his head in his hands or that late at night, he didn't hold Marie as she was trembling. Only that they loved more and worked harder.

Sammy's had become Aspen's favorite restaurant. Everyone loved Michael and Marie. Lynn could usually be found coloring or playing games at the bar. Marie converted one of the storage rooms into her private day care center. If she was waiting on a table, one of the other waitresses would cover. Occasionally the patrons complained about the crying but not too loudly. They were both still young and were looking forward to another child.

Scott and Amy's son Sam was three, as was Michael and Karen's daughter, Tammy. Scott and Michael were very successful realtors and were very busy, but they always put plenty of time aside for their wives and their children.

Karen and Amy were fortunate that they had each other. Nothing eases the pain of losing a child, but having a best friend go through it with you can make it survivable. They also had Alicia who was a great friend and as good as any psychiatrist. The three of them and sometimes Winnie and her son Mark would often set up their easels at the playground and paint landscapes as their children played.

They all agreed that Nate was the surprise of the group. By far the wealthiest and originally the most affected of any of them, Nate became the rock. They were amazed at how overt his show of affection was to Winnie and Mark. He was also the best, most considerate friend possible, available to sit and talk with any of them at any time.

During the first winter after the crash, Alicia and William had their first child. They named her Hope. Two months before the birth, Alicia and William gave Mason its first wedding. There was so much emotional baggage that went with the ceremony that during Alicia's vows the service was temporarily halted three times so that all the girls and several of the men could stop sobbing and get themselves together.

It was a new beginning—one that found all its participants barely able to breathe, but still it was a beginning.

Alicia, being there every moment and holding on to everyone for dear life, had created an unbreakable bond. She had not lost a child, but each and every woman who remained in Mason knew that Alicia loved them as if they were family, and the feeling was mutual.

Starting with the week of the crash and continuing forward, the women who remained met every Thursday at the center and let it all go. The first year, they were led by a psychiatrist, Carly Stephens, who literally brought them back from the depths of hell. She left after one year but still returned occasionally to visit. They now ran the sessions themselves, holding on to each other when needed and crying uncontrollably whenever necessary. At times, they held the sessions in the evenings so the husbands could sit in. Alicia was the team leader, and William was an honorary member.

They all loved their children twice as much if that was possible but always stopped at the kiddie park to speak with the children they had lost and had no intention of ever forgetting.

Chapter 64

In Harrison, New York, at the same time as agents were arresting Peter Gold and his associates in Seattle, FBI agents entered the offices of Larry Levin. He owned a small two-family house in a residential area. His office was downstairs.

"Good morning. Please tell Mr. Levin that we'd like to speak with him."

"I'm sorry, but Mr. Levin does not see people off the street. If you'd like to make an appointment?"

Agent Giles placed his credentials on the desk. "We'll only be a minute. Oh, and if I were you, I would lock up the office after we leave and start looking for another job. Mr. Levin may not be returning for quite some time."

They led Mr. Levin out of his office and help him into the back of the car. They drove him to an office they maintained in Scarsdale and sat him in an interrogation room.

Agent Giles entered the room and smiled at Mr. Levin.

"Good morning, sir. I'm Agent Giles. Can I get you some water, cup of coffee?"

"You're confusing me with a common criminal, Agent. I have been a lawyer in New York for twenty-five years and have an excellent reputation. Why am I being harassed in this manner? Are you charging me with a crime? If so, I want to hear the charges, and I am entitled to a telephone call."

"Excuse me for a few minutes, Mr. Levin, but if I don't get a cup of coffee, I'm going to nod off."

Agent Giles came back ten minutes later, carrying a container of coffee.

"Where were we?"

"We were getting me a phone."

"No, I'm pretty sure we weren't doing that. Let me ask you a question, Mr. Levin. What do you plan on doing after you're disbarred? Have you accumulated a great deal of money over the years? What am I talking about? They'll probably take your money and your house. Are your parents still alive? You never know when you're going to need your parents again."

"I've had enough of this shit, Agent Giles. You're starting to piss me off, and I have no intention of letting someone of your intellect harass me!"

"I do apologize, Mr. Levin. I've had a very traumatic morning. They woke me at 5:00 a.m., and I was in this office at 5:30 a.m., going over a file sent from our Seattle office. By 6:30 a.m., I was sick to my stomach—an entire file of little kids all drugged up, some with their mouths hanging open and drooling, other covered in their own vomit, one two-year-old overdosed, and they hadn't gotten rid of his body yet.

"Thank God, my morning improved. I got my orders. Arrest the son of a bitch responsible for torturing these kids and then selling them! Now comes the tough part. I'm supposed to have an intelligent conversation with you and pretend you're a human being and not the lowest piece of shit on earth."

"I want a lawyer, immediately!"

"Lucky for you, Mr. Levin. We all don't get what we want. If we did, your face would be in little pieces all over the wall. I'll be back in five minutes. I can only stand to be in this room with you for five minutes at a time."

Agent Giles went back to his office and called Agent Pierce.

"Hello, Pierce here."

"Agent Pierce, this is Agent Giles in New York."

"What have you got there, Giles?"

"I'm interviewing Larry Levin and need to know what my goals are. Are we looking to bury him or get him to snitch on his boss. Are we offering him a deal? I need a little direction before I go back in there with this garbage."

"Have you told him what we know?"

"I told him we know about the kids being dropped here and then sold. That's where I stopped."

"Good. Get over to Westchester Airport. We have a government plane standing by, which will fly the kids and their parents here this afternoon. Don't say another word to him. Let him sweat until we get him tomorrow morning. See you in Seattle."

"Is that Levin you were talking about, Sam?" asked Steve?

"Yes, we picked him up this morning, and we'll make a decision later with Margo before we interrogate him in the morning."

"Are you sure you want Agent Giles to put Levin on a private plane with six sets of parents who are about to lose their children as a result of his criminal actions?"

"I can't believe I almost did that. Good thing, one of us isn't brain-dead!"

Pierce redialed Agent Giles in New York.

"Agent Giles, Pierce here. I almost did an insanely stupid thing. Do not, I repeat, do not go to Westchester. Use commercial transportation and make sure you're here by tonight. Thanks. I'll see you in the morning."

The other six couples—Beverly and Peter Marx, George and Hali Liss, Al and Penny Katz, Jerry and Lynn Cohen, David and Sandra Kessler, and Robert and Andrea Kent—all met in Westchester with their adopted children and flew to Seattle, each with their own FBI chaperone.

CHAPTER 65

Saturday began with a legal sit-down in the FBI conference room. Attending were District Attorney Margo Post, Agents Pierce and Orzo, Tom Johnson, the prosecutor for the state of Washington, and Althea Jackson, the legal counsel for the bureau. It was a Saturday, but no one minded giving up his or her time.

Margo Post started things off. "We're all thinking the same thing. How can we seriously consider giving light sentences or, God forbid, letting any of these people walk? We get the same answer. We cannot go after everyone at the same time. It's too expensive and time-consuming, and we would run the risk of relying solely on the testimony of one or two witnesses. Those witnesses would be a drug addict and an immoral secretary who actually blackmailed her employer and took home a child to keep her company. We need more. I would like to put this gang of degenerates away until they die of old age, but we can't take the chance of losing the top two.

"John Scully or, as he was known before they gave him a new identity, Dominic Merano, will never see the light of day again. Peter Gold is the man who set this up and ran it. He's our number one. He doesn't get away. If he walks, I become a vigilante and take him out myself. Number two is Howard Rosenberg. Gold pushed the buttons, Rosenberg ran the entire operation. I want to be there when he starts to cry, no deals. Now we come to the reason we had to get up early—Ed Flakowitz and Larry Levin. Let me hear some opinions. What do you think, Sam?"

"I think Flakowitz is a no brainer if he can give us enough. He definitely has knowledge of everything that's gone down. Edna's files and notes have him present for practically all the fake adoptions. That being said, I believe he's a puppet. Had they been selling cosmetics instead of children, he would have done the same thing. I say get him to give up the other two and throw him back."

"Before I start talking about Levin, let me hear what you think so far, Steve. This is your case as much as mine, and you actually have a personal connection. Can you live with letting Flakowitz walk?"

"If it's absolutely necessary, I can live with it. I don't think we have to go that far, though. This guy's been living high, and he knows about the kids that have died in addition to those that were sold to the highest bidder. I want his license, and I want his assets. I have to believe if we offer him five years, two with good behavior to avoid the possibility of a twenty-five-year sentence or worse, he'll jump at it."

155

"I think he's right," Margo replied. "Are we all good so far?"

There was a group nod, and they moved on to Levin.

"Good, now, here's the tough one," Sam continued. "If Levin clams up, we have Gold and Rosenberg throwing the blame back and forth. I would almost be satisfied hanging them, but I can't see letting this guy off. Forget the fact that these kids have made him rich. This prick deserves to burn! I see that look on your face, Margo, and the answer is, if we lose Gold or Rosenberg, I'll never forgive myself, but Levin, in my book, has to do serious time. Steve?"

"I'm with you, Sam. He's got to go down with the other two. Whatever we have to do, he's got to go down."

Margo turned to the prosecutor. "Tom, can we get them all?"

"Margo, I don't think we have any choice. These are the scum of the earth, and that's why we're here to make sure they don't get away with it."

Margo walked toward the door and turned back toward the group. "Better get off your asses, guys, we've got a lot of work to do!"

Chapter 66

Saturday Afternoon

They started with Ed Flakowitz. Ed had become a partner some eight years ago. Rosenberg was handling the behind-the-doors stuff, and they needed a lawyer to handle the mundane matters: deeds, closings, injury claims, and so on. For the most part, that was what he did until Scully joined them. After that, he didn't have much time for the routine cases. The adoption business brought in so much money that they made Flakowitz a partner. He was hesitant at first, but once the money started rolling in, he got into the swing of it."

"Good morning, Mr. Flakowitz," offered Margo Post. "I am the district attorney for the state of Washington. You have been charged with the abduction of minors, in this case, two-year-olds. You have been charged with the falsifying of papers for the purpose of adoption. You have been charged with complicity in the sale of children for profit, and you have been charged with the murders of Ben Webster of Aspen, Colorado, Arnold Pierce, twenty months old of Mason, Colorado, and Brittany Holt and her daughter, Tammy Holt, eighteen months old of Butte, Montana. How do you plead to these offenses, Mr. Flakowitz?"

"I want my lawyer," Flakowitz replied, his face the color of chalk and his voice barely above a whisper.

"Let me see now. I believe that most of the lawyers you know are in a cell downstairs, but even if you have another lawyer stashed away somewhere, you'll have to wait until we have time to release all the people we have locked up, who all of a sudden have this urgent need to use the phone.

"I hope you are aware that in the state of Colorado, murder in the second degree, when it involves infants, that's three-year-olds and under, can be punishable by legal injection if in the judgment of the jury the crime warrants it. I'll be damned if that's not exactly what I'm going to recommend to this jury. A man responsible for the killing of babies for money is right on the top of my death wish list."

Margo knew the look on Flakowitz's face. She'd done this many times, and she could smell the fear when it hit. He had thought about it since Friday and must have concluded that they would throw him something. Now, she seemed to be wrapping up, and he hadn't heard any type of plea deal. He had now entered the depression cycle—that's when you stop telling people who you are and start thinking about who you were.

Margo never looked back at Flakowitz. She gathered her pads and banged on the glass, and as she walked out the door, she casually said, "See you in court, Mr. Flakowitz."

Sam gave Margo a hug as she walked into the mirror side of the interview room. "You are the best."

"Thanks," said Margo, looking content and obviously satisfied with her interview.

Steve was standing up and shaking his head. He hadn't done much of this courtroom stuff. In Treasury, once you got your man, your job was done. "I'm sorry, I realize I'm new at this, but what just happened? You threatened Flakowitz. You scared the shit out of him, and then you left. Why is that good for us?"

The phone rang on the desk, and Margo grabbed it. "Got it, Sergeant. I'll be there in two minutes." She hung up and looked over at Steve. "Guess Mr. Flakowitz has something he would like to discuss with me."

Sam smiled at her as she walked out and looked over at Steve. "Is she smooth or what?" Ten minutes later, Margo walked back into the waiting room.

"One million dollar fine, his house is forfeited, he's never allowed to practice law anywhere in the United States, and he has to serve at least eight years of a fifteen-year sentence in a federal penitentiary. He's been working with Rosenberg primarily, but he's guaranteeing Gold as well."

"Great job, Margo. How do you want to handle Rosenberg and Gold?"

"I'd like to make sure they get everything that's coming to them. It would be easy for us to simply indict them and not tell them what we have, except I'm afraid they would try to eliminate anyone that could implicate them, and with this group, I don't think there's an age limit. So I'm going to bring them up to date and then find some revolting accommodations for them until the trial starts. They will make their phone calls on Monday. That gives you Sunday to set up your meetings and reunions, and by the time the defense lawyers hit the prisons on Monday afternoon, things will be back to normal or as close to normal as this situation allows.

"Agents Pierce and Orzo, I thank you for your dedication and hope we can work together again. Our office will contact you when the trial begins. You should be here for quite a while. Maybe we'll have time for a dinner or two. There's no reason for you to sit through these next two interviews. I know you have a lot on your plate now. Best of luck."

"I know I can speak for Steve when I say that it has been a pleasure to work with you. Put together a good case. We'll see you at the trial."

As they hit the hall, Steve said, "She was definitely looking at you when she mentioned those dinners when the trial starts."

Sam smiled. "I hope so."

Chapter 67

The phone rang two minutes later. "Ms. Post, we have Howard Rosenberg in room one."

"Thank you, Sergeant."

She entered room one and found Rosenberg, legs crossed, with a contemptuous sneer or his face.

"District Attorney Post, are you aware that I requested a telephone call close to twenty-four hours ago? This is a direct violation of my constitutional rights. I will be very forthcoming with the press when I tell them how personal rights are ignored in the state of Washington."

"Nice speech. You'll get your phone call. I wanted to do you the courtesy of bringing you up to date. Once your trial begins, your lawyer will be entitled to know what we have anyway, so what's the harm?

"To begin with, Mr. Rosenberg, you're being charged with conspiracy to kidnap, the illegal adoption of minors, the abduction and sale of children, the murder of Ben Webster of Aspen Colorado, the murder of Arnold Pierce of Mason, Colorado, the murder of Brittany Holt and her daughter, Tammy, eighteen months old. I'm sure we'll come up with a few more charges by the time of the trial, but you get the idea?

"Was there something else? Oh yes, your associate Mr. Flakowitz has turned state's evidence and will testify for the prosecution. We have Trudy Miller's statements, which have been notarized and submitted as evidence. She will also be a prosecution witness."

"That's a great case you've got there, Ms. Post. You've got one addict who would kill her mother for a gram of cocaine and the testimony of my partner who would say anything to stay out of jail. I'll be out of here in time to watch Monday Night Football."

"Did I forget to mention Larry Levin?" Margo replied casually. "He has already confessed to his involvement and, as a result of omitting any charge of murder in his indictment, submitted testimony about you and Peter Gold. Well, that seems to be it. I guess we'll see you in court, Mr. Rosenberg. You should be quite a bit thinner by the time you get out, if you get out. Nothing like prison food to make you healthier.

"I almost forgot. I didn't mention Edna Collins, did I? Anyway she received immunity from prosecution. She delivered all her files, affidavits, and recordings.

159

I don't know how she got recordings. We also have her complete testimony, which we have already had notarized and approved as evidence, just in case she has an accident or some such thing.

"We also took away the child that you gave her as a bonus and have since located all the kidnapped children and their parents, who have also testified and are now in the stage of separating from their supposedly adopted children of four years or more. Some of those parents might be in the immediate area, Mr. Rosenberg. I would be particularly careful not to bump into them on your way out."

Margo rapped on the door, and the sergeant entered. "Please take Mr. Rosenberg back to his cell, Sergeant." She didn't bother to look up.

Rosenberg wouldn't have noticed anyway. His chin was buried in his chest, and his walk was that of a beaten man.

Chapter 68

"Last one, Sergeant. Let's go for the gold!"
He brought Peter Gold in and closed the door behind him.
"Nice to see you again, Mr. Gold."
"Why haven't I been granted a phone call?"
"I assure you the request was made the minute you asked, Mr. Gold. I think it's the system. It's just so unreliable. I was talking with David Roizin earlier. Do you know who David Roizin is, Mr. Gold?"
"I have no idea."
"David Roizin is a man from Texas who tried to find someone to expedite his adoption of a child. He's the president of a computer company, so money was secondary. He paid your firm $175,000 so that he could adopt a little girl and make his wife happy. We just informed him yesterday that they never legally adopted her and so she was going to be taken away from them after four years and returned to her parents. Isn't that a great analogy, Mr. Gold, you know. You demanded a phone call and can't figure out why you haven't been given a phone, and David Roizin paid $175,000 to adopt a child and after four years finds out he never adopted one. I think it's called poetic justice except for the pain which Mr. Roizin has now and forever and your pain which we haven't delivered to you yet.

"In an effort to provide you with a fair trial, Mr. Gold, I would like you to know what has transpired so far. Trudy Miller has made a plea bargain. She has given us her complete statement, going back to her initial hiring at your firm. She has given us any and all information she possessed regarding adoptions before the hiring of John Scully and after. She has told us everything she remembers about her dealings with Flakowitz and Rosenberg, the people who ran the office after Edna left in the winter of 2010. She gave us all the details as to how she and John Scully kidnapped twelve children in Mason, Colorado, after killing the driver. She has told us about the children who overdosed and the people John Scully killed to get children for your firm for what your clients thought were adoptions, but we now realize were the abduction and sale of children.

"Ed Flakowitz has confessed to working for you these last years and with your consent and support has created these bogus adoptions and supported Scully and Miller in their abductions to keep the money flowing.

"Larry Levin has also made a full declaration as to his involvement with you and your partners. Between Levin and Collins, we have located all the remaining

161

SUV children and their adoptive parents. They have all made statements and testified as to your involvement.

"Along with Edna's records of every child you have abducted, every couple you have illegally given children to, and every adult and child that has died as a result of your apathy and greed, I'm going to put you in the smallest box our penal system has to offer for as long as you have a breath left in your body. The only regret I have, Mr. Gold, is that I don't have the means to make you suffer more. The state of Washington is charging you with kidnapping and murder in the first degree, and we are hoping, Mr. Gold, that the judge will grant us special circumstances and allow the jury to give you the death penalty. Either way, Mr. Gold, you will never see the light of day again."

She got up from the table and rapped on the door.

"Sergeant, put Mr. Gold back in his cell and close the door behind you, please." Margo put her head in her hands and let the tears flow. She thought about all the suffering the parents of these children had been put through—four years trying not to shrivel up and die, and now the kids they thought dead, kids that are now six going on seven years old, are going to come back into their lives. *How do you deal with that?* she thought. *Except for the Pierce boy, all the other eleven children would be reunited with their parents, at least they would get them back. These poor kids were abducted, drugged, and traumatized beyond belief and then finally were able to settle down with parents, who for the most part loved them, and now they are going to lose the only parents they have known and go to live with strangers who they will be told are their biological parents. How does a six-year-old cope with that? God, let them find some peace.*

Chapter 69

"Ms. Post, there was a message for you while you were doing your interview. Agent Pierce called and asked if you could meet him at the Grand Hyatt on Pine Street when you finished."

"Thank you, Sergeant," she replied as she dialed Sam's cell.

"Sam, this is Margo. I thought maybe we could grab a bite one night and get to know one another. A hotel is a bit of a rush. Don't you think?"

"Don't get me wrong, Margo. I would love to have dinner with you, but this Grand Hyatt is filled with the parents and their adopted children. We have two agents and two representatives from children's protective services watching over them and they're calling for backup. I'm heading there now with Steve, but we could use your help."

"I'll be there in ten minutes."

She got out of her taxi at the same time as Sam and Steve pulled up in their car. They all ran into the lobby together with Sam leading the way to the elevators. They were met on the third floor by one of their agents who was stationed at the elevator.

"What's going on here?" Sam asked, as soon as the elevator was half open.

"We have eleven children and twenty adults on this floor. We confiscated all cell phones and shut off hotel phone service in the third floor. We explained to all the parents that we would be flying to Aspen first thing in the morning and that it was essential that they not discuss this among themselves until we brief them on the plane in the morning. They all have separate rooms. They all can order room service."

"It sounds like a reasonable plan," Sam offered.

"It was, until Rob Foster started banging on everyone's door and telling them that what we were doing was illegal and that the FBI has no right to hold them against their will! I swear he went on for ten straight minutes without taking a breath!"

They went into the lounge where Foster was still ranting, and others had joined in the discontent.

"Okay, can I have some quiet please? *Hello?* If you want to know what's happening now, please sit down and listen." The muttering died down, and Sam continued, "Can I get my two representatives from children's services to take all the children down the hall? In a short while, I am going to sit down with all of you children, but first I am going to talk with the adults. I know this is very difficult for you to understand, and I hope that when we finish talking, everything will be a little clearer."

The children were now at the other end of the hall, and Sam addressed the parents, "Most of you are going through one of the most traumatic episodes in your lives. Through no fault of your own, you are being forced to go through this as a result of the criminal behavior of others. This is true, but look at the larger picture. A handful of extremely dangerous people, operating in several cities around the country, will go to trial soon and be found guilty. They will most likely never see daylight again or walk the earth as free men. It is likely, therefore, that if there is anything they can do to avoid this end, they will. The easiest way to change the circumstance would be to eliminate the witnesses. In case you're wondering, that would be you. There are four couples I believe who personally did business with Howard Rosenberg, handed him a check, and received a child from him. If the eight of you disappear, who's to say he did any of those things. Once we have your affidavits and they've been notarized and admitted as evidence, you are all out of danger. That's why we have held all the lawyers and their accomplices in solitary from the minute we picked them up and have not allowed them to contact anyone on the outside. Shortly, we will no longer be able to prevent them from making their calls. At that time, hopefully, it will be too late for them to do anything. One phone call before we have finished here and are prepared, there could be serious repercussions.

"The second part of the equation relates to the biological parents of these children. Since that day in September 2010, they have been mourning the deaths of their children. Within the next forty-eight hours, they will learn the truth. We will sit them down and explain everything to all of them at the same time. It has to be done that way. Can you imagine being one of these families driving home tomorrow and hearing on the radio that an SUV that went off the road in September 2010 was a hoax and that your child was alive? That's why no one can say a word until all statements have been recorded and notarized, until all evidence has been submitted, and until all witnesses have testified."

"You can't stop me from talking to anyone, Pierce," responded Robert Foster. "Building a case against these lawyers is your problem, not mine. Let's go, Laura, we're out of here!"

"You know, Foster, I hate to admit this, but it gives me great pleasure to place you under arrest for obstruction of justice, and Mrs. Foster, if you get in that elevator, I will have to include you in that obstruction charge."

"You can't shut me up. I will have you fired, Pierce. You'll be working at McDonalds the next time I see you!"

"Take them to a nice quiet cell, Agent, and if they say one more word, tape their mouths shut."

"Margo, if you would talk to the children for me, I would appreciate it."

"No problem, Sam."

They walked over to the children at the end of the hall. "Hi, kids, my name is Margo Post, and I am the district attorney for the state of Washington. I'm not sure exactly what your parents have told you, but I'm going to go over it one more time. If you have any questions when I'm finished, we'll talk about it. Okay?

"Four years ago, all eleven of you lived in Colorado. Your parents were all neighbors, and most of them were friends. They moved into new homes in the same community, and all of you were picked up every morning by a van and taken to a community center at the bottom of the mountain you lived on. One morning, the van that took you to the community center went off the road and fell a long way. It crashed into a storage tank at an Exxon facility. The driver and everyone inside the van was burned in such an intense heat that there was nothing left of the bus or the children except gases and ashes. A funeral was held for the twelve children in that van. Each of the parents who attended that funeral would never get over the unbearable pain of losing their child in such a terrible accident, and they have not been the same since."

Heather Katz raised her hand and said, "That doesn't make any sense. If we were all in that van that fell from way up on that mountain and exploded into flames, how can we be sitting here now?"

"Good question," replied Margo. "The answer is that the people who did this wanted everyone to think you were in that van when it went off the road, and everyone did. Just before the accident, however, all of you were taken off that van and driven away."

Harry Marx called out, "That was a mean thing to do. Why would anyone want to make parents think their kids were dead?"

"There were two reasons: the first is because no one would start searching for twelve children if the police report says they were all killed in an automobile accident, and number two is, so the lawyers who sold you as adopted children would never have to worry about people looking for their children. If your real parents thought there was even the tiniest possibility that you were still alive, they would have searched heaven and earth to find you."

Patricia Panzer raised her hand. "What's going to happen? We don't even know these people. You're going to make us go to live with strangers and leave our parents?"

"You kids are so smart," replied Margo. "We tried to think of some way to make this impossible situation bearable. We realize that today most of you have a very strong bond with the only parents you've ever known. You have to understand that your real parents have a legal right to take you back, and believe me they loved you before you disappeared and they will love you even more when they get you back. Tomorrow we are going to go back to your original homes and tell your parents exactly what had happened for the first time. They know absolutely nothing about your being alive. After they get over the initial shock, we will introduce them to the people who have been taking care of their children for the last four years or so, and after that, we hope that some kind of understanding and maybe friendship develops. In other words, we hope that instead of losing your family, it simply gets bigger."

Patricia raised her hand again. "What does that mean? I don't want to live in Colorado. I want to go home!"

Margo looked at her for a short time before replying. "Patricia, I can't answer that question for you. If I were you, I would meet your real parents and talk to them and talk to your family now and tell them how you feel and see what happens. Tomorrow, you are going to have two more people who love you with all their hearts and that, Patricia, is a good thing."

CHAPTER 70

They got all the families back to their rooms, had them all fill out room service menus for 7:30 a.m., and arranged for all tickets for the 9:30 a.m. flight to Aspen to be delivered and held by the FBI agent in charge.

Sam, Steve, and Margo walked out of the Grand Hyatt together at 8:30 p.m.

"I suggest," said Sam, "that the three of us grab a quick bite somewhere and go over what we have and what's going down tomorrow. There's a diner down the block."

"Good idea," Margo responded.

Steve nodded in agreement, and they walked to the diner together.

Once they were seated, Margo started the conversation, "Here's the legal end of it. We will get those phone call requests at 3:00 p.m. tomorrow afternoon. We will get them to the parties that will be no earlier than 4:00 p.m. Your Aspen meeting is set for 3:00 p.m. so we should be good there.

"Robert Foster and his wife Laura were both arrested this evening and charged with obstruction. They will also get their phone call after 4:00 p.m. tomorrow. On Monday morning, we will indict everyone involved. We will start with the plea bargains that will get Edna Collins, Trudy Miller, and Ed Flakowitz out of the way.

"We will then indict Larry Levin, Howard Rosenberg, Peter Gold, and, John Scully with no deals. Anyone have anything to add?"

"I think we're good with that," said Sam.

Steve nodded. "Well, Margo, I want to thank you for everything. You've done a great job. I'll be going with Sam to Aspen, but I'll be back for the trials. In the meantime, if you two don't mind, I'm not hungry, and I'm going to get some rest. I'll see you in the morning, Sam. Good luck with the trials, Margo."

Sam and Margo finished eating and walked out to the street.

"You know, Margo, I want you to know that this case is going to be complicated enough without you and I making it more complicated. That being said, I would love to see you again. What do you say we have dinner as soon as this case is finished and we'll see where that leads?"

"You are intelligent as well as cute, Sam Pierce. Consider it a date."

Book III

Chapter 71

FBI headquarters, Washington DC
Wednesday, October 5, 2:30 p.m.

"Good afternoon, gentlemen. My name is Dan Schulman, and I am the coordinating agent in charge of adoption game. There are twenty agents including me that will be involved in this operation. There is no need at this time to get into specifics, but I will bring you up to date and we can get into details as we go.

"You have all read the file, which makes you current as of this morning. I will fill you in on what has happened this afternoon and what our objectives will be going forward.

"John Scully has contacted Howard Rosenberg and arranged for a drop-off at 11:00 a.m. this Sunday, the 9th of October. He and Trudy Miller are scheduled to meet with our agent at her apartment at 7:00 p.m. for their date tonight, at which point Mr. Scully and Ms. Miller will be arrested.

"That's when the clock starts running. We have three-and-a-half days. By Sunday, all those involved will have been indicted and incarcerated. We are running everything legal out of our Seattle office. The district attorney there will deal with all arrests, indictments, plea bargains, and so on.

"All the children who were supposedly killed in the Mason, Colorado, accident will be brought to Seattle by Saturday afternoon, where they will be briefed, as will the parents who thought they had adopted them legally four years ago. On Sunday, these parents and the children they supposedly adopted will be flown to Mason, Colorado. The children will be reunited with their biological parents. They will have an opportunity to say good-bye to the people who supposedly adopted them four years ago, and both sets of parents will have a chance to speak with each other.

"This entire operation is being coordinated so that not one word gets out until all files are entered into evidence, all witnesses have given their sworn testimony, all the children have been reunited with their parents, and all those responsible have been put away. We want to be certain that no parent finds out their child is still alive after being thought dead for over four years by reading about it in a newspaper or watching the news. More importantly, due to the severity of the crimes in this case, we need to make sure all involved are incapable of getting to any witnesses before all the evidence and their testimony are a matter of record.

"We have now accounted for seven of the original twelve children, and they are now or will be in Seattle by Saturday. We have the remaining five couples under surveillance, and we'll collect them and fly out of Westchester with them this Friday.

"The more pressing problem will be locating the original parents who left Colorado after losing their children. Three of them left forwarding addresses and are still at those addresses: Barry and Emily Jonas, Chuck and Margie Harriman, and Scott and Diana Block. The other two couples, Evan and Donna Wells and Jonathan and Debra Stark, left no forwarding addresses. The Starks were divorced in 2011. Evan and Donna Wells filed for divorce three months ago. Both sold their homes in Colorado. We've got two days to find them and get them to Aspen. Who knows what you will run into? One parent might not want to come. There could be psychological problems. Doesn't matter. We want all four of them in Aspen on Sunday. I suggest you tell them that there is evidence of wrongdoing as far as the accident is concerned, and a grand jury is requesting all parties be in attendance. That's all of it. Good luck, and see you in Seattle."

Chapter 72

They located Debbie Stark's parents in Ardmore, Pennsylvania. After the supposed death of her son Jonathan, she went into a serious depression. For six months, her husband took her to a psychiatrist on a regular basis, but she was not showing any improvement. He brought her to her parents' house, and after exhausting all possible treatments, they had her committed to an institution. Sometime after that, Gary Stark filed for divorce and eventually moved back to New Jersey where he owned a furniture business.

They informed Mr. Stark of the FBI meeting in Colorado and that they would be escorting him to Colorado Saturday afternoon for that Sunday meeting. They would not require his ex-wife to be present.

Evan and Donna Wells sold their home in Michigan. He was in the brokerage business and relocated to San Diego. His wife, Donna, was presently living with her parents and their daughter, Gabrielle, in Palm Beach Florida. Arrangements had been made to have both of them escorted separately Saturday afternoon for the Sunday meeting.

"Hello, Sam, Dan Schulman here."

"Hi, Dan. How did you make out?"

"We're good to go, Sam. I'll see you in Aspen."

"Nice work, Dan. See you on Sunday."

Chapter 73

Wednesday, October 5, 2014, Mason, Colorado

Alicia sat in the park with Hope, her daughter, Karen Barnum, and Amy Fisher. Every Wednesday and Friday afternoon for the past four years or so, the three of them carried their easels to the park and painted. At first, it was strictly therapy, but over time, Karen and Amy started to show promise. The first year, all Alicia could do was not to laugh, but the painting improved, as did the emotional stability of her friends.

Hope insisted that she have her own easel like her mom, so next to Alicia were a miniature easel and a small chair. Hope was usually good for five or ten minutes of dots and circles before running to the playground to join Sam and Tammy.

Alicia became adept at dividing her concentration between her work and her friends. She would be in the middle of a project and sense a change of mood. Karen was usually the one to go first. The first indication would be a change in posture, the shoulders would slump slightly, next the hand with the brush would slowly descend to her lap, and then a sigh would break the silence.

Alicia's remedy was normally a suggestion as to her technique. "I think you need a little more color in that skyline, Kar. What do you think?"

Karen was onto her game, but it was easier to add a little blue to the skyline than to get into another discussion on looking ahead and keeping her chin up.

Amy was a little better at blocking out. Maybe she was a little more pragmatic than Karen or maybe losing twin boys was a little tougher. Who knows? They both handled it in their own way. It was strange that Karen went from two boys to a girl and Amy from a girl to a boy. This allowed the two of them to share the knowledge that raising the opposite sex brings to the table.

The truth was that the only reason none of them was under a doctor's care or sitting in a padded room is because they had an incredible support system. Their friends and family made it possible to function on those rainy Sunday mornings when all they saw was their child screaming frantically in an SUV that seemed to fall down the mountain forever before exploding. How many times had they played that exact scene over in their minds and then sat frozen, suspended in time, hearing and seeing nothing until their husband or wife or friend put an arm around them and hugged them back into the present?

Regardless of how nice and peaceful it all looked—the panoramic view, friends and their kids painting landscapes by the playground, and the people skiing down the mountains and vacationing in the town—life for those on Mason mountain was always only a moment away from an emotional breakdown. It was usually the domino effect. They'd all be at someone's house for a barbecue and be in the middle of a conversation about movies or politics or sports, there'd be a lull in the conversation, followed by one seemingly meaningless remark about family, and they would all look hesitantly at each other. If any one of them caught their breath or wiped their eyes or sniffled, it usually took about thirty seconds before all of them were crying hysterically. It only lasted a minute or so, and then they would laugh at themselves and continue on with the evening. It was life, but it was also a group session for friends who at one time in their lives had lost everything.

The girls were just finishing up their painting for the afternoon when Winnie came out of her house and walked over.

"I just had the strangest call," she said. "It was from the FBI."

"I told Nate if he kept filling all those shoeboxes with cash, he was going to get in trouble," Amy said, putting on one of her funny faces.

"I'm serious," Winnie replied. "The call was from an agent named Sam Pierce, who will be calling all of you today. We are being asked to be at the Aspen Hotel Sunday at 1:00 p.m. along with our husbands for a meeting pertaining to the accident. Something about irregularities."

"We're being asked to go to this meeting?" said Karen.

"That's how the conversation started," Winnie replied, "but when I was hanging up, I said we'd try to be there, and he said, 'I probably didn't make myself clear. This is not a request. We will send an agent out to pick you up if necessary.'"

Amy got up and walked over to Winnie. "This makes absolutely no sense. Let's meet at Sammy's after dinner tonight and discuss it."

"Good idea," responded Alicia.

Chapter 74

By the time they met at Sammy's, they had all received their phone calls from Agent Pierce.

"Well, I'll tell you what Michael and I think," said Marie. "This is one of the worst accidents ever, and we think the FBI is simply closing the file and wants to get everything in order. I mean they're not going to do anything about it now. I don't think any of us are looking to sue the automobile manufacturer if they say there was a defect in their braking system or sue Mason if they inserted those guardrails incorrectly. None of this is going to bring our kids back, so I don't see why they're making us go through this. No, I'm sorry, why they're demanding we go through this?"

"From a legal standpoint," said Amy, "it makes senses. This Agent Pierce mentioned certain irregularities. The FBI reveals everything they have and closes the book. That's the way they operate. It removes them from future financial repercussions. The FBI says, 'We gave them everything we had. They chose not to litigate. We can't be held responsible.'"

Nate, who had been sitting very quietly, stood up and walked to the front of the group. "I'm sorry, but you are all way off base. The Federal Bureau of Investigation does not assemble all the parents of children killed in an accident four years later to tell them why it happened or who in their opinion is responsible, assuming that's their reason for this meeting on Sunday. You're confusing the FBI with the cast of 20/20. This has to have a lot more weight."

"Hypothetically, you are the FBI and you have to get all of us together, but you don't want to tell us the real reason. If this was the case, I think I would say there are irregularities that need clearing up. After they tell us what these irregularities are, what do they expect us to do? It makes no sense. Unless, and please I'm just guessing here, it wasn't an accident. What if there was some lunatic that over the last four, five, ten years has been killing people and making it look like an accident?"

"Okay, Winnie is giving me that 'shut up immediately' look. Forget that example, but you get the idea. Something way out like that would require the FBI to let you know what's going on but also to keep it on the QT. All I'm saying is that on Sunday, we will find out that something else is going on here besides irregularities."

"I think Nate's right," said Paul. "Look at this logically. We've been told not to mention one word of this to anyone before Sunday, but after Sunday, this will all be public knowledge. Think about the headline in Monday's paper. 'The FBI this coming Sunday brought together all the families of the children killed in the October 2010 accident in Colorado to tell them that they've determined it's dangerous to go down a mountain in an SUV.' Seriously, they'd be crucified by the press. Can any of you recall the FBI ever doing anything that stupid?"

"Put your hand down, Tracy. I'm referring to the period after J Edgar Hoover."

"All I'm saying is that the FBI would not do this without a good reason. We have to go anyway. In a few days, we'll know what they want, and that will be that."

Everyone went home, trying to figure out what this could possibly be about, but the only certainty was that tonight everyone would be thinking about October 9, 2010.

Chapter 75

They put Dominic in the wing at Washington State Prison, also known as Walla Walla State Prison or the Walls or Concrete Mama reserved for lifers and those awaiting execution.

Dominic was impressed. This wasn't Rahway, New Jersey. They didn't fuck around out here. Since 1849, they had executed 110 people at Walla Walla: 3 by lethal injection and 107 by hanging. The one Dominic read about was this dude Westley Allen Dodd. He was hung at midnight on January 5, 1993, for molesting and stabbing to death ten-year-old William Neer and his eleven-year-old brother in 1989. He also confessed to strangling and raping four-year-old Lee Isli of Portland Oregon. The part that stuck in Dominic's head was his diary. He documented over fifty accounts of child molestation and was finally arrested while kidnapping a six-year-old boy from a movie theatre in Camas, Washington. He dropped his appeals and asked to be hanged. He was interviewed when he was first arrested in 1989, and when asked if there was a way to stop sex offenders such as himself, he said there was not. The week before his execution, they asked him again, and he said he was wrong. He said he found hope and peace in Jesus Christ.

The Neer and Isli families watched him hang and were certain he was on his way to someplace considerably warmer than Walla Walla.

There were nine cells presently occupied on death row—all singles, no cellmates. All nine inmates were allowed one hour of fresh air in the yard at 3:00 p.m. every day—always segregated from the rest of the prisoners, no visitors, no phone calls, permanent solitary confinement with the scum of the earth.

Dominic spent the days exercising. They weren't allowed any weights or machines, so it was strictly sit-ups and push-ups. During his hour outside, he tried to move as much as possible. He knew from experience that if you stopped moving, your muscles would atrophy, the pain would set in, and life in a cell would become intolerable.

Dominic's neighbors were the average for a psycho ward, maybe a tad more extreme. The fact that they were sentenced to life, or in some cases death, had no relevance. Most of them had stopped thinking and feeling long ago.

None of the other inmates had any interest in staying in shape. Who cared what you looked like when they tossed you in the box and shoveled dirt on your face?

Three of those seven couldn't talk anyway. Two of them had raped and killed girls under ten. Dominic didn't know how many girls they'd raped and killed and didn't care.

One of the inmates never blinked and simply stared straight ahead without ever speaking. Another was as crazy as a bedbug and never shut up. He talked day and night, much too loudly, and never seemed to put enough words together for Dominic to make sense out of his gibberish.

The last inmate made no attempt to befriend anyone. His two fifteen-year-old daughters were raped by a pair of country boys and dumped on the side of the road outside of Salt Lake City. After picking up the girls and his wife and dropping them off at the hospital, he drove to the farm where the boys lived with their stepfather and broke the necks of all three with his bare hands. He then drove to the police station and turned himself in. Tyson was 345 pounds, six foot five inches tall, all muscle, and Barbados black.

There was no trial, not much of one anyway. I mean, there was a jury. They were sworn in at 9:00 a.m. The case was brought to the court, and Tyson was found guilty and sentenced to death by lethal injection at 10:30 a.m.

He accepted his sentence. He did what he had to do. His only regret was that there was practically nothing for his family to live on. His girls would have to quit school and get jobs, but at least they would never have to set eyes on those animals again. He had five months left before his appointment with the hangman.

So much for the other cellmates; Dominic knew they would never let him out again. They set him up with that Cindy bitch, which means they must have known about at least some of the others. Trudy was definitely away somewhere, and that would probably lead them to the lawyers. Who knows how deep they went? It didn't matter now. It was a great run. He should have gotten out a year ago—easy to say now. They had probably confiscated his bank accounts and his house at the lake, but none of that mattered anyway. He wasn't planning on willing it to anyone. That made him laugh. No, the only thing he would do until they stuck that needle in his arm was look for an opening and try to get the hell out of this insane asylum.

Dominic had a court appointed attorney who told him he would do whatever he could, but Dominic wasn't sure whether he preferred a quick needle in the arm to thirty plus years in this box he called home.

Chapter 76

October 8, 10:00 p.m., Seattle, Washington

Agent Orzo had spent the entire evening in his hotel room. His was a simple task. He was flying to Aspen, Colorado, at 8:00 a.m. in the morning on a government transport. He was bringing eleven children and twenty of the adoptive parents along with him. The only parents not coming were Edna and her husband and Rob and Laura Foster. They would get into Aspen at approximately 11:00 a.m. and get to the hotel between 11:45 a.m. and 12:00 p.m.

Now came the tough part, separating the children and their parents. He would explain that they would all see each other in a few hours, but he didn't feel great saying that, as he wasn't sure what would happen in a few hours. Regardless, he would put all the parents together and put the children on their own floor with plenty of supervision. He might need extra agents for the Foster kid alone! That sounded doable, making sure they are on their own floor and completely separating them from the others.

At the same time, Agents Schulman and Giles would be at the Ramada Inn outside of town and wait until Agent Orzo called them to bring his nine parents to the hotel and their designated rooms. That should be completed by 12:45 p.m.

At that time, he would call Agent Pierce and have him escort the Mason families to the Aspen hotel and their designated rooms.

The Seattle group already knew everything that was going on and simply would have to wait until everything was finished. At that time, they would get to see their kids one more time and meet their parents. What happened from that point on was anybody's guess.

The big decision was how to break the news to the parents. Steve and Sam had discussed this twenty times already and could never come up with a method they both agreed on.

The director in Washington DC had told them it was not the jurisdiction of the FBI to involve itself in the feelings and future psychological problems of all these people. His suggestion was to bring all the biological parents into one room, explain to them what happened in 2010, deliver each child to his parents, and leave. The rest was none of their business.

They thanked the director for his suggestion, looked at each other after they hung up, and broke out laughing.

"That," said Sam, "is the man responsible for controlling the Federal Bureau of Investigation in this country."

"Scary isn't it?" said Steve. "At least anything we come up with will be a step up."

"Okay, let's try this again. I like your idea of breaking everyone down into four groups: the parents who adopted, the children, the parents who no longer live here, and your five families from Mason. Now how do we start?"

"The first thing is getting the parents who no longer live in Mason into their rooms at the Ramada Inn on Saturday. That's the easiest part—five rooms with no phones and three agents. Two vans should be enough for nine parents and three agents. We bring them to the Aspen Hotel at eleven o'clock. We've got four sets of parents and one single: Wells, Jonas, Harriman, Block, and Gary Stark."

"Our plane should land at about 11:00 a.m., and we should be at the hotel between 11:30 a.m. and 12:00 p.m. We arrive with eleven children and eighteen parents."

"How do we get to eighteen? I thought we were twenty?" Sam interjected.

"We started with twenty-two. Edna Collins and her husband were never invited, so that's twenty, and Rob Foster and his Wife will be in jail in Seattle until Monday, so that makes eighteen. Correct?"

"Forgot about Collins. You're right. Eighteen."

"Okay," Steve continued, "this entire group knows what's going on, so we can put them in the conference room with two agents to make sure no one disappears. We put all the children together in a few rooms until we're ready to bring them down to their parents."

"I was good until the kids," said Sam. "You can't put them together, except for Jill and Patricia, or Emma and Samantha. You know which girls I mean. The Foster's kid Teddy Foster, aka Charlie Byrnne is already one messed-up little kid. I don't think he's ready to mix with his peers. Do you? And let's not forget the Barnum twins. Melvin seems perfectly well adjusted and he's going to meet his twin for the first time, who will probably be in the corner with his head on the social worker's lap. That's going to be a tough one also, especially for Karen and Michael Barnum."

"That's a good point, Sam. Okay, so we can put the two girls together and put the other nine kids in separate rooms, all on the second floor. We have a woman from social services staying with Teddy Foster tonight. I'm going to have her stay with him on the plane and in the hotel. I want someone from children's protective services or one of our people with each kid at all times until they're reunited with their parents."

"Okay, Steve, now we have your friends. How do you want to handle them?"

"We put them in five rooms but not connected. The same goes for the five rooms with the rest of the original Mason parents. After going through all this, it would be a shame if one family was waiting and heard what was going on next door. Come to think of it. Let's make sure all the rooms of the original Mason parents are fairly well separated. I think we can expect at least a couple of hysterical screams.

"Okay," Steve continued, "now we have an agent sit down with each of our families and hand each parent a copy of our investigation. You and I will take one family each. The agents from New York and Seattle who have been involved will each take a family, and we will recruit a few agents and give them a quick briefing before sending them in.

"I've already notified the hotel that I want bottled water in each room along with alcohol in the refrigerators, if needed. I will have two medics and two nurses standing by if there's a problem. I've been in contact with the psychiatrist, Carly Stephens, who worked with the original families for the first year after the accident, and she will also be on call."

"So far so good," said Sam. "Continue."

"Where was I? Okay, so they read the file, allowing for screams and fainting and the hysteria that will no doubt occur. They will no doubt want to see their child as soon as they read Trudy's testimony. We will explain that all the children will be delivered at the same time so that their friends who may still be reading won't hear the screams and want to know what's happening. They will then have at least a dozen questions, which we will try to answer. We will give them some time to calm down so as not to frighten this child who will be meeting them, as far as he or she is concerned for the first time.

"While they are coming up for air and hopefully starting to breathe again, we will explain why all the foster parents are upstairs and that we wanted to give them a few minutes to think about the people who had raised their children these last four years—a time during which they had always assumed they were the legal parents of these children. And now, this weekend could be the last time they ever see them again. We wanted them to take these people into consideration before they are reunited with their children and before they meet these people later this afternoon. We wanted them to bear in mind that even though these children are theirs legally, as far as these children are concerned, they are being taken from their families and forced to live with strangers. It's something that has to be addressed immediately. To simply take these children away from the only family they know without so much as an explanation would not only be incredibly traumatic but criminal."

"Still with you. Go on," said Sam.

"We bring the children down at the same time and reunite them with their parents. At some point after the shock has been at least partially absorbed and the tears and hysteria are at a minimum, we bring down the adoptive parents and have them each spend some time with the biological parents and the child. At some point, they will have to leave, and I'm sure it will be quite a scene, but there's no way to avoid that.

"After all the adoption parents come downstairs, we will get them to the airport on a plane and back to wherever they live. Aside from some paperwork, I think at this point, we get to have a beer and go home to our families. At least you can do that. I will have to take some shit from my friends about knowing their children were alive and not telling them."

"Steve, one of the reasons they all have their children back is because the story never got out. I'm sure they'll see that."

"Eventually, I'm sure you're right," said Steve.

"Last of all, we have Ira and Helen Pierce under surveillance. An agent will introduce himself at 2:00 p.m. tomorrow and let them read the file. It's the least we can do. I don't really know them, but you have to feel for them. He was all they had. Four years ago, he was killed in a terrible accident, and tomorrow they will learn he was not killed in the accident but was killed by overdose while being kidnapped. How do you digest that in five minutes and then go on with your life?"

"Okay, Steve, I think it's the best we can do. We're all meeting in the lobby at 7:00 a.m. We'll have something for everyone to eat. I don't know, coffee, juice, doughnuts, bagels, whatever. They don't have stewardesses on government flights. We have a bus taking all of us to the airport. There will be four agents including us and one social worker each for Teddy Foster and Kenny Collins."

"Good luck for tomorrow. Don't be nervous. You're going to give your friends their children back. It's going to be a difficult day, but I'm betting next week you're going to be walking around with a shit-eating grin on your face!"

"Good night, Sam."

"Good night, Steve."

Chapter 77

The Grand Hyatt was total bedlam at 7:00 a.m. Normally Sundays at the Hyatt got busy around checkout time. This morning, twenty adults and eleven children with luggage were all trying to get breakfast and get their bags on the bus in twenty-five or thirty minutes. They could have planned breakfast at 6:30 a.m., but this day was going to be long enough for everyone without getting up at the crack of dawn.

"Did you think of any last-minute changes while you were sleeping, Steve?"

"As a matter of fact, I just called our agent at 6 Mason and told him as soon as everyone leaves for the hotel to pick up Alicia Langston and bring her to the lobby. We'll still have two agents on the mountain to keep an eye open for anything out of the ordinary. I will brief Alicia on what is about to happen and have her wait with the Barnum's while they are reading the file. With two strangers and two separate boys to deal with, not to mention one of them has been messed up pretty good by that psycho Edna Collins, I figure a little help from Alicia would be just the thing."

"Good thinking. Let's get this show on the road. We wouldn't want to be late for the party."

They boarded the families first. The parents were already getting very upset. This was the day they were going to lose their children. It was still hard to conceive how they had gotten to this point. They had all paid large sums of money to lawyers they assumed were first rate, and none of them could have conceived of the possibility that they were buying stolen kids, someone else's kids. That would have been far-fetched enough, but knowing they bought a child who was on that death ride off Mason Mountain was too much to grasp. They had purchased a child that was drugged and kidnapped and sold to a law firm and then sold to them. It was impossible to comprehend that they were involved in this.

Dina Roizin sat in the back of the plane with Michael and Elayne. Her parents, at least the only parents she could remember, had explained everything to her. She understood what had happened, but she couldn't make sense of what was happening now. She loved her family and her home and friends in Scottsdale. Her parents hadn't stopped crying since they left for Seattle. Now they were on their way to Aspen, Colorado, where they were going to give her back to the people who were her natural parents and go back to Scottsdale without her. How could they do that? How could they let this happen?

Teddy Foster sat with his chaperon. He didn't want to talk to these people. He had his Mac computer and was playing one of his favorite video games. Most of the other kids seemed sad. Many were crying. They obviously were coming from better situations than Teddy. He had spent the better part of four years with his housekeeper, Nicole. He did whatever he wanted and ate whatever food he wanted whenever he felt like eating. He had a large bedroom with a flat-screen TV, the latest stereo system, and DVD player, and his parents were away on vacations most of the time. He once asked Rob what the story was. He saw most kids spending time with their parents. He had never spent one afternoon with his.

Rob said, "I want you to know the truth, so you'll never be confused when you get older. Your mother thought it would be nice to have a kid, and she couldn't have one of her own. She's the same with shopping. She sees an outfit and buys it, and by the time she gets home, she can't remember why she liked it in the first place. So she tells me after three or four weeks that being a mother wasn't her thing. 'It's not a dress,' I say to her. 'You can't return it.' 'Then hire someone to take care of him because I can't do this every day,' she says. So we hired Nicole to look after you. Look at the bright side. You could have been adopted by a family that had very little. You will always have whatever you need. We will take care of everything. When you get older, it won't be as important to have your parents around, and then you'll see it wasn't so bad."

He was six-and-a-half years old, and the only thing in life that he knew for certain was that his mother was an idiot and his father was an asshole. They took them both into custody at the Grand Hyatt for obstruction of justice, which in simple terms means Rob could never keep his mouth shut. They were never planning to come to Colorado anyway. Rob took him aside when they got to Seattle and handed him a sealed envelope, labeled confidential and addressed to Paul and Tracy Byrnne. "Give this to your real parents. It's for your future, and it's important. Don't tell Laura!"

The only children who didn't have their heads down and a frown on their faces were Patricia and Jill. They were too well balanced to be traumatized by the recent turn of events. They had discussed it at length and both agreed that one way or another they would always maintain a relationship with the parents that had raised them until now. They were also best friends. The others were all going to this scary place alone while they already had each other. Their parents weren't taking it so well, but Patricia and Jill both knew that once these difficult days were behind them, their mothers would get themselves back on track.

CHAPTER 78

They landed at a private airstrip just outside of Aspen. A bus was waiting for them with several social workers and FBI agents waiting to escort them to the hotel. Agent Orzo had dropped the original plan to put the parents in the conference room and the children in their own rooms with an escort. He put himself in their shoes and realized it was going to be tough enough for them without waiting alone for the axe to fall. He would put each family in a room with their child; when it was time, an agent or someone from social services would collect them and deliver them to their natural parents. After forty-five minutes or an hour, when the natural parents felt comfortable, the agent would bring down the adoptive parents, and when everyone was ready or when 3:00 p.m. rolled around, whichever came first, everyone would go down to the lobby with their luggage and say their last good-byes. The biological parents, the adoptive parents, all the children, the social workers, friends who had made their way to the hotel, the psychiatrist, and the nursing station would all go home. The FBI would supply transportation, pick up the hotel bill, and get all their people back to their home offices. The two couples at 6 Mason Drive would hang around a week or two on the slight chance that someone attempted something stupid. Whatever else went down, it was not the concern of the FBI.

The Seattle contingent was settled in their rooms by 12:00 p.m. All the families were together except for Teddy Foster and Kenny Collins, who had social workers for company.

The Ramada Inn group arrived at 12:15 and were in their rooms on the first floor by 12:30 p.m.

The Mason families arrived a little before 1:00 p.m. and were divided and in their rooms by 1:15 p.m.

There were cold sandwiches and sodas in all the rooms, and everyone had lunch and waited.

Book IV

Chapter 79

October 9, 2014
Exactly four years since the accident

Everyone met in the cull-de-sac at 12:00 p.m. They had two babysitters watching all the kids as Agent Pierce had advised them it would be wiser to leave the children at home. Michael Corritore and Paul Byrnne both had arranged for someone to cover for them at work. Neither understood why. How long could this meeting take?

"I need to be at my restaurant by 5:00 p.m. Are you telling me this meeting could last longer than four hours?"

He was requested to make himself free for the entire day and to not be difficult.

They were getting into three cars to leave when the Aspen police chief pulled up in his patrol car. They all knew each other on a first name basis but were still surprised to see him.

"Odd time for a social call, Jim," Paul called over.

"Not exactly a social call. Paul. I've been instructed to escort you all to the hotel and make sure everyone is in attendance."

"As you can see, Jim," said Tracy, "we are all here and leaving on time."

"Could you all please take your own cars? I don't know why, but those are my orders. Maybe they plan to see some of you at different times and then the others. I really don't know."

"I can't wait to get this over with," said Marie. "If I was half crazy these past few years, this bull shit should take care of the other half."

They returned for their cars and dutifully followed the police chief into town.

Chapter 80

Alicia and William sat in the park with Hope. William sat on the stool with Hope on his lap as she made big red circles on the canvas with a very serious expression on her face.

Alice was painting a portrait of Hope painting a circle while sitting on William's lap. Today was especially quiet as the other children were all inside with babysitters. All her friends had left for this FBI conference, and no one was barbecuing. Alicia had a premonition all week that something was in the air. She only prayed that at the end of the day things were better, not worse.

"Mr. and Mrs. Langston, I hate to intrude on your afternoon, but may we speak with you?"

"Aren't you the couple that recently moved into 6 Mason Drive?" inquired Alicia.

"Yes and no," replied Agent Nelson.

"That's an interesting answer," said Alicia. "What can we do for you?"

"Well, your husband has already been very helpful by letting us use his house. We should be out by the end of the month. Thank you so much, Mr. Langston."

Alicia turned to William with a less-than-loving look on her face and said, "I had no idea you were so adept at keeping secrets, William. Do I get to hear the secret now or must I wait a little longer?"

"Mrs. Langston, your husband was asked by Agent Orzo if we could be placed here temporarily. The Federal government was asking the favor, and your husband knows absolutely nothing else except he was to tell absolutely no one. Now, Mrs. Langston, we are asking a favor of you. Your friend Agent Orzo thinks you could be of great service to your friends in their time of need. If you will accompany Agent Hobson and me, we would like you to come to the Aspen Hotel with us and have you help Karen and Michael Barnum through a very difficult afternoon. We must leave immediately, and as soon as you are in the car, Mrs. Langston, we will fill you in on exactly what is going on today.

"I'm sorry, Mr. Langston, but I don't have time to explain anything to you now. Your wife should be home by dinner time and believe me she will have quite a story to tell you."

As Alicia and William were looking at each other with their mouths still open, Agent Hobson pulled up with her car and Agent Nelson opened the door.

"If you don't mind, Mrs. Langston, we really have no time to waste."

Alicia turned to William with a questioning look in her eyes.

"Go with them, Alicia. If Steve thinks that Karen needs your help, it must be important. He wouldn't have two FBI agents make a special trip to get you if he didn't think you could make a difference. Go ahead. Call me if I can do anything. We'll see you later."

Chapter 81

Alicia got into the back seat. Agent Nelson hit the gas, and with a screech and a little rubber, the government car swung around and headed for Aspen.

"Are my friends in some kind of trouble?" Alicia asked.

"Mrs. Langston," Agent Hobson replied, "on the seat beside you is a file entitled adoption game. You have ten maybe fifteen minutes to read it before we get to the hotel. Please save any questions you might have until you're finished, and if we have time, I will try to answer them. Agent Orzo felt it would make more sense to give you everything from beginning to end. His only caveat being that before you open the file you understand that this story is seven years old and that the FBI entered this investigation last Sunday, October 1, 2014."

Agent Hobson turned around, and Alicia began to read. She read about Howard Rosenberg and Kenny Panzer and Patricia. She read about John Scully and Trudy Miller and the day that Jill Diamond realized she was in the same vehicle with Adam, Todd, and Patricia but missed the significance. She read Trudy's testimony, and when she came to the part of the story where the driver, Ben Webster, was murdered and the empty SUV was driven off the road, she murmured under her breath, almost hypnotically, "They're not dead." That was followed by the same words, screamed fifty times louder. "They're not dead! Oh my god, they're not dead!" Agent Nelson swerved and barely kept the car on the road before getting it back under control.

"Are they alive, Agent Hobson?"

"Finish the file, Mrs. Langston, and then I'll answer all your questions."

"I'm not reading another word until you tell me if my friends' children are alive," Alicia managed to get out between catching her breath and wiping the tears from her eyes.

"The Pierce boy, Arnold, was given too big a dose of whatever they used to sedate the children, and he didn't make it. The other eleven children are alive and are presently waiting at the Aspen Hotel. Now please finish reading the file, as you will be more help to your friend Karen if you are aware of the total picture."

"They're all alive—Adam and Todd, and Emma, and Samantha, and Gina, and Charlie. None of them were on the bus. I just can't believe it, after all these years. They've got to be six or seven years old. They were all around two years old. How much memory could they have of their parents at that time?"

"Almost none," responded Agent Hobson.

"Almost none," repeated Alicia. "Of course, that's why this is going to be so complicated. This is not a case of finding missing children. This is about taking children away from people they have come to believe are their parents and giving them back to people who are strangers to them."

"You're getting closer, ma'am. Please finish reading. We're almost there."

Agent Hopson called Agent Orzo and told him where they were and how far along Alicia had gotten in the file. He finished the call and turned back toward Alicia. "Take your time, ma'am. My instructions are to contact Agent Orzo from the parking lot when you have completed reading the file, and he will come out and get you."

Chapter 82

They sat in the parking lot for fifteen minutes until Alicia was finished reading and called Agent Orzo who came out immediately. It was almost 1:30 p.m., and Alicia was destroying his timetable. He opened the door for her and, with a quick glance at his watch, told her she was making mincemeat out of his schedule.

"Okay, Alicia, I'm going to tell you why I brought you here, and then we're going to pick up the pace and see if we can get you together with Karen and Michael and get back on schedule."

"No, I don't think so," Alicia responded, taking a seat in one of the couches in the lobby.

"What are you doing, Alicia? I don't have time for this now."

"I read your file, Steve. I understand everything that has happened up to a point. I follow what you are trying to accomplish by bringing everyone together at the same time. It's all very logical, and the fact that this was all done in one week is absolutely incredible."

"Thank you, Alicia, but I don't have time to discuss this with you right now."

"When you were putting this 'meeting in Aspen' together, did you have any help? I mean this is some undertaking for one FBI agent?"

"I had another agent whom I have been working with the entire week, although if I must say so, I more or less planned your meeting in Aspen by myself."

"Were there any women involved, Steve? Any psychologists, any psychiatrists, any representatives from the children's protective agency, any social workers?"

At this point Steve was beginning to get that uncomfortable feeling you get just before someone tells you how you messed up.

"I really did not have the time for a conference, Alicia. I did the best I could with the time and the tools I had."

"I appreciate that, Steve. Now, let me tell you and the rest of the FBI what we are going to do now."

Steve thought this would be a good time to breathe and swallow. Who knew when he'd get another chance?

"We are going to give each of these parents all the time that they need to read your file, ask their questions, and develop a complete understanding of what happened, why it happened, and where everything stands as of today. If any of them are not ready to meet their six-and-a half-year-old children, then we are going to give them some extra time. If they faint or experience some sort of mental breakdown, we are going to wait until they recuperate before we reunite them with their children.

"If after spending time with their children, they do not want to meet the people who have raised them these past four years or so, then we will have to postpone that meeting until this evening or tomorrow.

"Can you imagine if you lost Daniel and were certain he was gone forever and four years later, an FBI agent sat you down and told you not only was he never killed, but he had been raised these past four plus years by people from New York. He was presently upstairs with the couple he called Mom and Dad, and ready or not, they were coming over to meet you in twenty minutes. Surprise! How absurd!"

"Alicia, we have people here now from all over the country. We don't have the convenience of waiting until everyone is mentally prepared. We also didn't want one family to be finished and walk out of the room and have a family that hadn't read the file hear a second-hand version of what was going on."

"I understand everything, Steve. That being said, you cannot give these parents a time limit to absorb four-and-a-half years of a lie. They find out their children are alive. They look at their children and realize these children have no idea who they are. They watch them run into the arms of two strangers they call Mom and Dad. Then they meet these strangers and watch, as their children get hysterical because they have to stay with their biological parents and say good-bye to the people that have become their family.

"Ninety-nine percent of your work is done. Now, you are going to have to slow down and evaluate how these children and your original parents are dealing with the trauma that would make any sane person go off the deep end."

"Okay, Alicia, we'll try it your way. Karen and Michael are in room 104, waiting for you. When they have finished reading the file and you think they are ready to see their boys, tell the agent in the hall, and someone will bring them down. I'm going to try to bring all the children down at more or less the same time, so tell them not to be impatient if they don't come down immediately."

"I'll do my best."

"Good luck. I'll see you later." He gave her a few minutes before he started out for room 101, knowing she would need more time with Michael and Karen than he would with Nate and Winnie.

Chapter 83

Steve entered room 101 and said hello to the Whitcups, who were seated next to each other on the couch. Nate immediately jumped up with a shocked look on his face.

"What the hell are you doing here, Steve? I asked you on Wednesday if you knew what was going on, and you handed me some bullshit about knowing nothing and getting back to me."

"I'm sorry about that, but if you will sit down, I will try to make everything clear to you. By the time we leave here today, I think you will understand why certain things had to be done a certain way and that your best interests were always my principle concern."

"That's asking a lot, considering we have no idea what the hell you're talking about!"

"Nate," Winnie reprimanded, "please give Steve a chance to talk."

"Thanks, that's all I need," said Steve.

"The FBI was notified about this case last Sunday. I joined the investigation on Monday morning. I'm giving you the entire file to read together. After you're done reading, if you still feel I deserve your animosity, I'm not going anywhere. I suggest you don't get too far ahead of each other and if you want to stop and ask questions, there are no time restraints. All your other friends and the other parents whose children were in that SUV on October 9, 2010, are also reading this file in other rooms of this hotel as we speak."

The file began with Kenny and Carol Panzer's adoption process with Howard Rosenberg. It described how they took Patricia home and had to have her admitted into a hospital that first week. They read about Patricia and her nightmares and subsequent visits to her psychiatrist and how they worked with Harry Immerman to uncover Patricia's past. They read about the Saturday night when Jill Diamond called Patricia and told her she was on the bus with her and two twin boys named Adam and Todd.

Winnie who was holding the file in her lap while Nate read, leaning over shoulder, dropped the file on the floor as she gasped and put her hands over her mouth. She waved at Steve but couldn't make any sounds come out of her throat.

"What does this mean, Steve?" Nate asked in an uncertain shaky voice.

"It was an abduction, Nate, not an accident. They killed the driver, Ben Webster, and sent the SUV through the guardrail with no one inside."

"And Emma?" Winnie half asked, half cried out.

"Emma's alive," Steve responded, tears in his eyes as well. "Actually Emma is Jill Diamond. She was adopted through a lawyer in New York who worked with the law firm in Seattle. She's a pretty well-adjusted six-and-a-half-year-old girl who knows she was adopted at two and has a nightmare occasionally about being taken off a bus and drugged. Why don't you read the entire file and then we'll talk more."

Nate picked the file off the floor, and they sat back down on the couch and continued to read except now as Winnie read, she squeezed Nate's left hand so tightly his fingers were already turning red.

Steve had asked that two boxes of tissues and a wastepaper basket be placed by each couch, and he was already wondering whether two boxes were going to be enough. He had also forgotten to order a box for himself.

They read about Dominic and Trudy and how they were caught. The file described all the lawyers that were in custody and why they needed to take all of them down at once. They were moving along pretty well until they came to Trudy's testimony. Winnie must have said "Oh my god" a dozen times, starting with Ben being shot and continuing through the transfer of the children with chloroform and the Valium sedation; then she abruptly dropped the file back on the table.

"Arnold Pierce was killed?" Winnie questioned, looking at Steve.

Steve nodded.

"I thought you said the children were alive?"

"No, Winnie, I said Emma was alive."

"How many others did they kill?" Nate asked.

"Arnold Pierce was the only child in the SUV that died," replied Steve.

They caught their breath and continued to read the file.

After reading most of the file, Nate put his hand over the page they were reading and simply shook his head.

"What is it Nate?" Steve asked.

"How can these people look at themselves in the mirror? This Trudy Miller is a drug addict and her brain is fried, I get that, and this Scully lowlife is an animal, I get that too, but these lawyers are educated men. They've been stealing children and killing people to make money. What's going to happen to them? Are any of them still practicing law? Could any of them get off?"

Steve could see it in Nate's eyes. He wanted to get his hands on one of them and exact his revenge. He wanted some sense of justice. In cases like these, the victims can never get even. At best, they are comforted by the knowledge that these people can never do this to anyone else, ever. Sometimes they don't even get that.

"We have them all, Nate. Our cases are airtight. One or more of them will be executed, and the others will be incarcerated for a long time if not for the rest of their lives. We'll talk about that aspect another time. You still have a lot to do today."

Nate nodded, and he and Winnie continued with the file. They finished and placed it back on the table.

"So you knew about all this on Monday?" Nate asked.

Steve knew exactly where this was going and had been waiting for Nate to put it together.

"My friend Steve," Nate continued with a caustic edge to his voice, "knew that Emma was alive on Monday and never said a word." Nate turned his back on Steve and leaned his forehead against Winnie's.

"I got your little girl back," Steve replied, standing up. "Does that entitle me to sixty seconds with eye contact?"

"You bet your ass it does," said Winnie, turning Nate around on the couch.

"This past week has been excruciating for me, knowing that all six of my friends' children were alive, and not being able to tell them. It was the first thing I said to the agent I was working with. He explained that if we didn't bring in Scully and Miller and all the lawyers involved in addition to getting all the testimony, if one of them heard we were onto them, there was a good chance that people and evidence would start disappearing.

"We achieved that goal yesterday. I still couldn't let my friends know as there were parents like yourself who would find out today at the same time. Can you imagine hearing from Gary Stark that his child and probably yours might be alive?

"Right now, there is an agent at the home of Ira and Helena Pierce, explaining to them that their son wasn't killed in a crash but was abducted and drugged to death. Would you have liked them to hear that information on the eleven o'clock news? Believe me, both of you, it killed me not to tell you, but if I had to come and tell you that two days after I spoke with you, someone blew up Bob Diamond's car, killing him, his wife, their son, and your daughter, I would have felt a hell of a lot worse!"

Winnie looked Nate in the eyes, and they both walked over and did a three-way hug. Steve then walked over to the door and signaled the agent in the hall that they were ready.

Chapter 84

Alicia had a much tougher assignment than Steve. Her file had also included a psychological evaluation of Todd. She couldn't wait to tell Michael and Karen their twins were still alive, but she wasn't looking forward to seeing how devastated they would be when their children looked at them and had no idea who they were, and then she would have to explain that for the past four-and-a-half years, one of their sons had been led around like a doll and was going to need a lot of therapy. She had already made up her mind that helping to straighten Todd out was going to be one of her daily missions; you needed a positive attitude, and she had enough for her and Karen.

Alicia opened the door to 104 and stepped in.
"Alicia? What are you doing here?" Karen asked.
"Hi, Karen. Hi, Michael. I guess you're surprised to see me."
"It sort of fits into the week we've had so far, but, yes, we are. I believe we left you and William at the park about an hour ago."
"Two minutes after you left," Alicia replied, "the couple that just moved into 6 Mason Drive walked up to William and me and asked for my help. I got into their car and was given a copy of this file that I am giving you both to read. When you have finished reading it, you will understand what this is about. This was all Steve's idea. He thought I could be of help."
"Could we back up a second, Alicia?" Michael asked. "Why would the people who just moved in be asking you for help and what does Steve Orzo have to do with any of this? Didn't Nate call him Thursday night and ask him if he knew what was going on and get no response?"
"I'm sorry, but until you read the file, you will never understand a thing I'm saying. Steve Orzo is one of the agents in charge of this FBI investigation. The People at 6 Mason Drive are both FBI agents and were placed here last week to make sure none of you were hurt between then and now."
"Why would someone hurt us?" Karen asked.
"Please start reading the file, Karen. If you have questions at any time, you can stop, and I'll try to answer them."
"Let's read the file, Michael. It certainly can't make things any more confusing than they already are."

Alicia sat nervously and watched their faces. Jill Diamond's reference to being on the bus with Adam and Todd was on page four; she figured that gave her four or five minutes to relax before all hell broke loose. Michael was having a little trouble, reading over Karen's shoulder, so she actually had seven minutes before Karen stopped reading and started shaking. Michael was ten seconds behind her. He looked at Karen and said quietly, "Are you okay?" After she nodded, he turned to Alicia and waited.

"They're both alive," she said.

Karen and Michael held each other and cried for ten minutes or so until Alicia walked over and knelt in front of them.

"There's a lot more to read and a lot to get done. I know this is more than any one can be expected to accept after four years, but I want you to know everything before you start thinking about what this means. I know your minds are not functioning on a high level right now, but try to absorb everything you're about to read so we can talk about it and decide what's the best thing to do next. That's why I'm here, to make sure that you don't make a mistake in the heat of the moment."

Karen and Michael both nodded and slid the file back onto Karen's lap.

They read about Adam first, growing up in New York with the Kents, and nodded to each other as they were presented with a short but positive picture of his upbringing. That was followed by Todd's life in Seattle with Edna Collins and the psychiatric report that followed.

Karen was sobbing uncontrollably at this point, and Michael was about to blow a blood vessel. If he had an address of Edna Collins in Seattle, there was a good chance he would already be flying down the highway.

Alicia took the file from Karen and sat next to her on the couch. She put her arm around her and let her cry on her shoulder.

She looked over at Michael, who was staring straight ahead and smoldering.

"Michael," she said sharply, "do you want to continue thinking about strangling this Collins woman or do you want to take care of your wife?"

Michael snapped out of his trance and pulled Karen back into his arms. "Thanks, Alicia, I've got her now."

"Take ten minutes. I'll be right back." She took a walk outside and got some fresh air.

When she returned to the room, Karen and Michael were still holding each other but were obviously much calmer.

"Okay, guys, can we continue?"

"Is Todd the only one who was mistreated, Alicia?" asked Michael.

"Charlie Byrnne ended up with two people who decided they didn't want children and had a governess bring him up, and as you will read soon, Arnold Pierce died of an overdose the day he was taken, and of course, all the children now have parents they are attached to and will be separated from them this afternoon, Adam being one of them."

"That's so tragic," Karen replied. "All the original parents are going to find out this afternoon that their children are still alive, and the Pierce family is going to find out their son was never killed in the crash but died being abducted. Are the Pierces here, Alicia?"

"No, Karen, that would be too cruel. An FBI agent is at their home right now, showing them the file."

"She's right, Michael. Neither of our sons will know who we are. They will hate us for taking them away from their parents."

"One thing at a time, Karen. Let's read the rest of this file and then we'll figure out how to deal with our boys. It won't be easy, and Todd will probably take a long time to get back to us, but Karen, our little boys are alive. Think about that for a second. Adam and Todd are alive, and we can give them everything they need to get well and be a part of our family again."

At first, the frown on Karen's face was frozen, but as her head made slight assent motions, a small smirk appeared on her mouth, which turned into a small smile.

"Your right, Michael, none of this matters. The only important thing is that our sons are home. We can make all the rest of it right."

"You're going to need a lot of help," chimed in Alicia. "Hope will be a teenager in ten years or so, and I will be very busy helping her through that difficult time, so I can only promise to help you get through this for the next ten years. After that, you guys are on your own."

They all held hands for a while, and then Alicia put the file back on Karen's lap.

"Finish the file." She wanted them to know about the lawyers and the trials and most importantly the schedule for the rest of the day.

Chapter 85

Agent Giles entered room 112 and introduced himself to Michael and Marie Corritore.

"I know you have your work to do," said Michael, "but I have a business to run, and I can't see why you find it necessary to keep us here for the entire afternoon?"

"Mr. Corritore, may I address you as Michael and Marie? It's so much easier."

They both nodded.

"Good. I am going to give you an FBI file that covers the years 2008 through today. Once you have read it, I believe almost all your questions will be answered. We are not in a rush to finish this, so if you need a break or if you want to stop and ask a question, feel free. You should know that while we are covering an eight-year period in this file, the FBI was brought into this case last Sunday, October 2. There is water and tissues on the table next to you if you require them. There is also liquor in the refrigerator if you should need a drink. Here then is the file we have named adoption game."

"This file is not that thick, Michael. If we read quickly, we could be out of here by three, pick Lynn up, and get to Sammy's by four."

They began reading quickly and turned the first page in thirty seconds or so. The second page was considerably slower; by the third page and Patricia's nightmares, they had slumped down into the couch, their expressions had turned deadly serious, and they were reading each sentence with total concentration. By the time Jill remembered Adam and Todd being on the bus, Marie had the tissue box next to her and was having trouble reading.

Michael put the file down on the coffee table. He turned to Marie and asked her if she was okay.

Marie nodded, but Michael could see her eyes weren't focusing.

"Is there any red wine in that refrigerator, Agent Giles?"

"I think there's a small bottle of red."

Michael went to the bar and opened the wine. He poured Marie a glass and handed it to her.

Marie sipped on the wine slowly.

Michael turned to Agent Giles. "Red wine fixes everything in our house."

"Can I ask a question before I continue reading?"

"Certainly," replied Agent Giles.

"If Jill was on that bus with Adam and Todd and if she has been living in New York for the past four years, then you are telling us that all the kids that supposedly died in that crash were never in that SUV?"

There was a five-second delay before Agent Giles responded that seemed like at least an hour to Marie, who had been unconscientiously holding her breath for the past thirty seconds.

"Arnold Pierce was given too much Valium and overdosed. The others made it."

"Our daughter, Gina, was not killed in that crash in 2010 and she is . . . ?"

"Alive, Michael, yes. Gina has been living with a family in Austin, Texas, for the past four years. She is a pretty six-year-old girl with jet-black hair and green eyes just like her mother."

Michael bent over and put his head in his hands and sobbed. Marie could not speak. She was trying to compose herself and failing miserably.

"Why don't the two of you take ten minutes and let it all out? We'll continue when I come back." Agent Giles went out into the hall and took a deep breath. He didn't mind locking up crooked lawyers, but he wished they'd brought in a social worker for this job. It was too emotional for him.

He returned to the room and found Marie in pretty much the same shape she was in before.

"She can't accept the fact that Gina was alive all these years, and she could never get to her. She thinks she should have known she was alive. She's blaming herself."

"Marie," Agent Giles knelt in front of her on the couch, "they pronounced all those children dead at the scene of the accident in 2010. I read the police reports. No survivors. No possibility of survivors. There was no way any one could have guessed what had happened. This was done by a depraved individual who planned a very unusual crime and then got ridiculously lucky by having an SUV fall over an eight of a mile and land in an oil drum. The odds are off the charts. You can't hold yourself responsible in any way. Are you listening to me?"

Marie nodded.

Giles grabbed the phone and called the lobby, "Get me a doctor. This is Agent Giles. I'm in 112. Let's be on the safe side."

Michael held onto Marie and nodded. "I think that's a good idea."

The doctor gave Marie a 10 mg Xanax and had her lie down for thirty minutes.

While Marie rested, Michael continued reading the file.

My god, Michael thought, *this Scully was an animal.* "He killed people and took their kids. He blew up that woman's home in Montana and took both her kids and killed another one just like Arnold Pierce. Where are they now, Agent Giles?"

"All of them are locked up and awaiting trial, Michael."

"We're okay, Agent Giles. Give Marie another fifteen minutes or so, and then we would love to see our little girl."

"Okay, Michael. I'll be back in a little while."

CHAPTER 86

Scott and Amy fisher proved the easiest to deal with—two lawyers, by far the least emotional and most analytical. They were overjoyed at the news and processed everything that had happened immediately. They were both glad to hear that their daughter was one of the children responsible for starting the investigation and satisfied that the FBI had done a wonderful job and had finished this investigation in the only way possible. They knew this was going to be a difficult and emotional period for all of them and were prepared to deal with whatever came their way.

The agent who spoke with them was back in the lobby in fifteen minutes, waiting for the second phase.

Chapter 87

Paul and Tracy Byrnne were somewhat more difficult. Agent Pierce had elected to talk with the Byrnne family. After reading the first five pages and Jill Diamond's story, Paul had thrown the file down on the table and began pacing the room.

"Explain it to me again," Paul said, a little louder than was necessary. "Steve Orzo is one of the two agents in charge of this investigation, and he along with the rest of the FBI has known my son was alive a week ago. The two of you made the decision not to tell my wife and me that our son was alive? What right did any of you have to withhold that information from us?"

"Mr. Byrnne. Try to understand. At the time we knew your son was alive, we only had six of the eleven children. We did not have all the biological parents, and we did not have all the lawyers and felons locked up and unable to communicate. Until they were all accounted for and until all the evidence was processed and all the witnesses had given their statements, all of you would have been at risk."

"And you think that gives you the right to withhold the fact that my child is alive?"

"Calm down, Mr. Byrnne."

"Don't tell me to calm down. How would you feel if it were your son and someone was keeping information like this from you?"

"Try to understand this, Mr. Byrnne. The people we have indicted are being charged with murder and kidnapping among other charges. Some of these people will go to the gas chamber and others will be imprisoned for the rest of their lives. They have nothing to lose by eliminating witnesses. We already know they have no reservations about killing children. We arrested them all at the same time. We put them in solitary confinement until we were able to get all the witnesses and their testimony and their affidavits admitted as evidence. We built airtight cases against them within forty-eight hours and were able to show them that they were too late to do anything to anyone assuming they had those connections.

"We couldn't tell five of you that your children were safe because on Wednesday we only knew the whereabouts of four children, and by the way, Charlie was not one of them. Through the testimony we received from Edna Collins, whom you will read about in that file when you decide to read it, we were able to locate the remainder of the children. We found Charlie on Thursday and brought him to Seattle on Friday.

"All of you are being told this story at the same time. That includes the Pierce family whose son Arnold was given too much Valium when they grabbed him and died of an overdose. His Parents are also being told now at their home.

"If you have no other questions, I would suggest you start reading the file, Mr. and Mrs. Byrnne, as there are things that you should understand, and it would be easier for you if you had some knowledge of the entire investigation. If you have any questions or need anything, I will be right here."

"Agent Pierce, I would like to apologize for my husband and myself. We have no right to take this out on you."

"Please, Mrs. Byrnne, you don't owe me an apology. You've just found out that your son is alive after four years. No one can be prepared for a day like this. There's still a lot more to come. Read the file and then we'll talk."

Paul and Tracy settled onto the couch and began to read.

"Oh my god, Paul, Charlie was kidnapped! Paul, are you listening to me? Paul!" she shouted at him.

Sam walked over and shook him. He looked at his eyes and picked up the phone.

"Get a doctor to room 128. I've got a man in shock."

He laid Paul down on the couch and put a few pillows under his feet and a cold compress on his forehead.

"Don't worry, Mrs. Byrnne, I've seen this a dozen times. He'll be fine in a few minutes."

The doctor showed up immediately and administered ammonium carbonate to Paul, which produced fumes beneath his nose, which revived him instantly. His breathing immediately slowed down and the color began to return to his face. He was given a bottle of water to drink slowly, and a few moments later, he sat up, rubbing his neck.

"What just happened?" Paul asked. "One minute all I could think of was killing that son of a bitch and then I was lying on the couch, sweating like a son of a bitch."

"You went into shock, Paul," Sam replied. "It's not abnormal. You get filled up with all kinds of emotions: rage, revenge, hate, and so on, and your body can't handle it. You'll be all right now. Just take things slow and stay calm. Easy for me to say."

"Thank you, Agent Pierce. Sorry, I lost it before."

"No problem. Relax for a while and when you feel ready, we'll pick up where we left off."

"As long as we're on break, let me ask you a question," asked Tracy. "How did my friend Steve get involved in this investigation? He's a treasury agent. This doesn't have anything to do with his department, does it?"

"No, it doesn't, Tracy. This whole investigation broke in Seattle. The Diamond girl you just read about remembered the names of Adam and Todd, the twins, and realized she was on the bus that Patricia had mentioned in her Internet chats. That brought in the FBI, and Monday morning we circulated the file we named adoption game to all our offices in the United States. Steve read the first two pages of the report and realized we were talking about his friends on the mountain. He called me and put the whole story together, and he and I continued from there. Needless to say, if it hadn't been for Steve recognizing the names of his friends' children, we would never have put this together so quickly, if at all."

"That's far out," said Paul. "I think I'm okay now. Can we continue with the file?"

"Sure thing," Sam replied and laid the file back on the table.

They read all about the abduction and the kids being drugged and taken back to the lake. They read about four of the kids being dropped off at the law office of Peter Gold and the rest taken to New York, without knowing which group Charlie was in. They read through all the interrogations from Trudy through Edna Collins and still weren't sure what happened to their son.

"Agent Pierce," said Tracy, "would you mind if we go by first names from now on? I'm having trouble calling you agent."

"It's Sam, and I don't mind at all."

"Well, Sam, I can't wait until I finish the file. Can you give me a heads-up and tell me where my son went?"

"Of course, he was adopted by Robert and Laura Foster of Leander, Texas. He was one of the four children dropped off at the office of Peter Gold. I think you should read about his story yourself. You're almost there."

"I get the feeling you're holding something back, Sam."

"Listen, guys, I know this entire story by heart and could probably recite it to you, but we put this file together in the most comprehensive way possible. Please finish reading, and then we can discuss anything you like."

"Okay, Tracy," said Paul, "let's continue reading."

They read through the interrogations of Miller, Rosenberg, Flakowitz, and Levin. They followed Scully's arrest and incarceration at Walla Walla State Penitentiary. They read about the FBI effort to find all the children and both sets of parents, new and old; and they read about Agents Pierce and Orzo's interviews with Michael and Elayne Roizin and Robert and Laura Foster. Tracy began crying from the minute she read about the Fosters' declaration that after bringing Charlie home, they realized they didn't want to be parents, and when they both read about both parents asking if they could simply hand their child over to the FBI, not bother flying to Seattle, they were beside themselves.

"They had no feelings for him at all," Tracy said, half to herself. "He was like a piece of furniture they purchased and decided not to use."

"How did you talk to these people as if they were anything more than pond scum? They took a two-year-old boy and stuck him in a room and had a servant watch over him. They were only concerned that they would be prosecuted and didn't give a damn about handing over their son to strangers after four years. How can you be in the same room with morons like these and not want to grab them by their throats and shake some sense into them! When this is over, Robert Foster and his wife Laura will simply walk away as if the lease was up on their four-year-old Pontiac."

"Actually, Paul, the entire time we spent in the presence of the Fosters, we were revolted. I tried my best to be professional. Steve actually told them he couldn't stand to look at them for another minute and walked outside. They were so obnoxious in Seattle that we charged them with obstruction of justice and had them locked up. They won't be released until tomorrow. They were never planning on coming to Colorado anyway. On that basis, count yourselves lucky. There is no way, if they had come here, that you would have been able to hold back and not beat the stuffing out of the idiot. There was no legal adoption, and you will never have to see either of them ever again.

"Let me give you a different perspective, Paul. The Pierces have lost their son Arnold. Your friends the Barnums are getting back one of their sons, Todd, with severe emotional problems due to four years with a woman who dragged him around like a pet. Your son has gone through four years without any affection, caring, or love. He's had every toy and convenience that money can buy and he's spoiled rotten, but he's completely healthy. He may be obnoxious and spoiled rotten, but he's only six.

"Steve told me all about the two of you, and there is no doubt in my mind that in a shorter time than anyone thinks possible, you will straighten Charlie out and make these past four years a nonevent. You've got your son back. Underneath that tough, apathetic exterior is the same boy you gave birth to. He's in there, and I have no doubt you'll find him and bring him back out. Why don't you guys relax? I'll be back with Charlie in a little while."

Sam got up to leave and was almost to the door when Paul put a hand on his shoulder.

"We owe you and Steve a debt we can never repay. What you did in these last few days was incredible. You took the time to go through this with us and get us through an impossible day. We will always be grateful." Paul grabbed Sam's hand as Tracy came over and threw her arms around his neck. She hadn't stopped crying since she read about the Fosters, but she found a small smile for Sam.

Chapter 88

The first child brought down was Jonathan Stark, for the last four years, Harry Marx. He was the adopted son of Peter and Beverly Marx and their only child. Their story was a carbon copy of the others. They had tried to have children for five years and, after seeing a series of doctors, had tried to adopt a newborn. The lines were interminable, and after two years, they were no closer. One of their friends knew Larry Levin, and three months and $150,000 later, they were parents.

They picked up Harry at Levin's office and immediately knew there were problems. Harry was having trouble breathing, and he was burning up. They took him to the emergency room, and after some quick tests, the doctors told them he had traces of Valium in his blood. They kept him for two days, and from that point on, he was more than they ever imagined. He was sweet and affectionate and had a laugh that was so infectious that after ten seconds everyone around him was also laughing.

The past four years had been all that the Marx's could have hoped for. After the FBI informed them of what had transpired, they seriously considered going to court. Harry was their whole life. They both knew they were going to lose him, and they were inconsolable. They spoke with three separate lawyers and were told by each lawyer that they had two chances—slim and none. You cannot take a child from his natural parents, no way, no how.

So Peter and Beverly Marx waited upstairs for a chance to meet Harry's real parents and in all likelihood say a final good-bye to their son.

Harry was brought into the room by a social worker and sat on a chair opposite Gary Stark.

"Hi, Jonathan, I'm your father, Gary."

"I'm sorry. I don't remember you. My name is Harry, and my father's name is Peter."

"Okay, I'll call you Harry for now. Do you understand everything that's happened to you?"

"Well, they told us we were in a big car that everyone thought fell down a mountain, but we weren't really in it, and then some bad people stole us and sold us to lawyers, and then my parents found me, and everything was okay after that."

Gary didn't miss the reference to his being okay with his parents but continued, "I want to explain why your mother is not here with me. I don't want you to think she didn't love you or care enough to come see you. She was so upset when she thought you were killed that she had a nervous breakdown. Do you know what that is?"

"Is it when her mind doesn't work anymore?"

"Something like that. Anyway, she has been in a hospital for the past several years and has never gotten well enough to come home. We don't live together anymore."

Harry thought about that for a while, *I thought my first parents were coming here to take me away from my family today.*

Gary turned to the social worker sitting by the door.

"Will you please ask the Marxs to come down now?"

"Certainly, Mr. Stark."

She returned five minutes later with Peter and Beverly Marx.

Harry immediately ran into Beverly's arms.

"I'm sorry, Mr. Stark," Beverly said, caressing the side of Harry's head, "I'm not intentionally trying to make this more difficult for you."

"You don't have to explain, Mrs. Marx. I understand."

"I know this is asking a lot. You haven't seen your son in four years, and now strangers are asking favors of you, but if you would let us visit him a few times a year, maybe if you and your wife go on a vacation, Harry, sorry, Jonathan could stay with us for a few days. Whatever you'll allow us, we would be so grateful to at least be a small part of his life. Please don't cut him out of our lives completely. We couldn't handle that!"

Gary handed her the box of tissues and waited for her to regain her composure. Harry in the meantime had gone over to Peter and was holding onto his sleeve.

"Beverly," Gary said solemnly, "my wife was admitted into a mental institution six months after the accident in 2010. We were divorced a year-and-a half later. I own a furniture business in New Jersey, and I travel frequently. I can't bring up a child on my own, and it looks to me like he couldn't be in a better place with better people. If you'll have your lawyers draw up the papers, I think the best thing I can do for Harry is to let him stay where he is."

Beverly tried to keep a straight face and said nothing, regardless of the fact that she wanted to do cartwheels around the room while singing the hallelujah chorus.

"Is that okay with you, Harry?" Gary asked.

"That would be great."

Gary walked over and shook hands with Peter and Beverly Marx and gave Harry a kiss on the top of his head.

"Have a great life, kid," he said and walked out the door.

Chapter 89

Evan and Donna Wells had taken Steven's death out on each other. She had taken their daughter and gone to live with her parents in Florida, while he had relocated to San Diego. This was the first time they had seen each other in over three months. They sat on opposite sides of the couch with Agent Schulman sitting next to Donna in a club chair.

"Okay, folks, here's the story. The FBI has been working on a case that concludes today. We have two copies of that investigation sitting in front of each of you. If you would be so kind as to pick up the files and start reading, you will understand within minutes why we have brought you here."

"There's nothing in your files that holds any interest for me," Evan Wells responded.

"Then why are you here, Mr. Wells?"

"I'm here because an agent came to my apartment and asked me to be ready to accompany him to the airport in thirty minutes or he would physically assist me."

"Our agents are very determined. Aren't they? Listen, Mr. Wells, we brought you to Colorado along with all the parents whose children were involved in that accident in 2010 because we have become involved in a recent investigation, which profoundly affects you. I would rather let you read this file, which is very comprehensive. If you refuse, I will try to brief you myself, but I would strongly advise the former."

"Do whatever you want, Agent Schulman. My wife and I were forced to appear here and we have. We have no desire to be a part of this charade, and we will stay here until the FBI allows us to leave."

"Tell me, Mr. Wells, do people realize what an asshole you are as soon as they meet you or does it normally take a while?"

"Mr. Schulman," said Donna, "it's amazing how quickly you've gotten to know my husband."

Evan got up and started for the door. "I don't have to listen to this crap. I'm out of here."

"Sit down, Mr. Wells. I'll tell you when you can leave."

Evan dropped back into his chair, disgusted and red in the face.

"Okay, if this is the way you want it, this is the way you'll get it."

211

"On October 9, 2010, an SUV went off the road, driving down Mason mountain and fell into a gasoline drum. The SUV was completely incinerated, as was everything inside. We now know that aside from the driver who was killed on the road before the SUV went off the road, there was no one else inside. All the children were transferred to another vehicle and driven to a lake house outside of Seattle. One of the children, Arnold Pierce, was given too much Valium and died of a drug overdose. Four of the remaining children were delivered to Howard Rosenberg at the law offices of Peter Gold. The remaining seven were driven to New York and delivered to the law offices of Larry Levin. Steven Wells was one of these children. Later that afternoon, he was adopted by a George and Hali Liss of Rye, New York."

"Stop right there," Donna cried. "My son Steven is alive?"

"In this hotel. You'll be seeing him shortly."

Donna sat back on the couch and put her head in her hands. Evan sat down next to her and put his arm on her shoulder.

"We would like to read the file now," Evan said meekly, "if that's okay."

"Absolutely," said Agent Schulman. "I'll be here if you have any questions."

Mr. Wells simply nodded.

It took about thirty minutes for them to finish reading the file.

"So all the lawyers are in jail, awaiting trial. Trudy Miller and John Scully are also locked up somewhere, and Edna Collins gave everyone up and was allowed to walk. Have I got that right?"

"You do," agreed Agent Schulman.

"Could we have a few minutes alone before you bring in our son?" continued Evan.

"I'll take care of it," Agent Schulman replied as he walked out.

As soon as the door closed, Evan turned to Donna and said, "We both know that after we lost Steven, everything was a mess. Even after Gabbi came into our lives, we still had that loss hanging on our necks. Maybe this is a sign."

"There's no question," Donna offered, "that getting back a six-year-old boy who doesn't remember us is going to be a large undertaking even for two people. Let's take it one day at a time and see how it goes."

Chapter 90

The first of Steve's friends to see their children were Paul and Tracy. Charlie Byrnne entered the room like he was out for a stroll.

"Hey," he said, "what's up?"

"Hi," said Paul, "do you know who we are?"

"My father and mother?"

"That's right, Charlie," said Tracy.

"My name is Teddy."

"Actually," Tracy responded, "I carried you inside me for nine months, and when I gave birth to you at the hospital here in Aspen, Paul and I named you Charlie. You don't know any people here, so they won't be confused if we call you Charlie. From what I've heard about the people you've been living with, even though we haven't seen you in four years, we already love you a great deal more than they do. Any argument there?"

Charlie simply shook his head in agreement.

"We live fifteen minutes from here in Mason, on top of a hill. I think you'll like it. It's very pretty, and you will have your own room," Tracy offered.

"Does it have a flat-screen TV and a stereo system?" Charlie asked.

"No, but you can watch TV and listen to music in the family room until bedtime."

"I don't have a bedtime. I go to sleep when I want to."

"Okay," Paul said, "let me try to explain a few things to you. We know that you're at a disadvantage in that the people who have been taking care of you didn't care. People who don't care will let you do anything you want because it doesn't matter to them if you are overtired or don't do well in school or get sick and have to stay home. The good news for you is that we always cared and will continue to care. The bad news is that this will require an effort from all of us. Your mom and I aren't asking you to change overnight, only that you give it a try. Can you do that, Charlie?"

"I'll try."

"That's all we ask," said Paul, "and by the way, you have a younger sister."

Tracy let out a laugh as she watched Charlie's eyes open wide in shock.

"I think you guys will be just fine," said Sam, "and by the way, you can take him home whenever you're ready. Good Luck."

"Thanks for everything, Sam."

Chapter 91

Gina Corritore was the next to come down. Upstairs with her parents Michael and Elayne Roizin, her emotions had been spinning out of control. Her mother and father were crazy about her, and she thought they were the best. How can you take your six-year-old daughter to Colorado and leave her with strangers? She would never forgive them. She would never talk to them again or write them or see them. She was so mad!

And then an FBI agent came into the room and asked if she would come with him. That's when she began to cry and couldn't stop. She looked back at her parents, who were both sobbing hysterically as the agent led her out of the room.

They entered room 212, and she saw Michael and Marie sitting on the couch. The first thing she noticed was that they were younger than her parents. The second was that the woman looked a lot like her—dark black hair and green eyes and the same nose and mouth. She was definitely her mother. And the third thing she noticed was that the woman had definitely been crying and seemed to be shaking.

Michael was the first to break the silence.

"Hi, Gina. My name is Michael, and this is Marie. We are your mother and father."

"My name is Dina, and my parents are upstairs, waiting for me to come back. They love me very much, and they are not going to give me away."

That turned the floodgates on again, and Marie went to the other side of the room and tried to breathe between sobs.

"I'm sorry," said Gina, "I didn't mean to upset her."

"Okay, Dina, here's the story. I met your mother, Marie, here in Aspen seven years ago and fell in love immediately. We were married in less than a year. She was pregnant within a few months and gave birth to you the following year.

"You were seventeen months old when we moved into our first real home on top of the mountain, and we were incredibly happy. You had a lot of friends your age, and we had a lot of friends also. Everything was perfect until a few weeks later when that SUV went off the road and we were told that you and all our friends were gone. It was the worst day of our lives. Every day was torture. We cried as often as we talked. It was one and the same. Two years after you were taken from us, we had another child, and that helped bring my wife back, but make no mistake, she has never been the same since you were taken from us.

"I'm glad that the people who took you in were good people and that you had four years with a loving family, but you are our daughter. We made you. Marie gave birth to you. You were adopted illegally. It's not their fault, but they can't keep you. You're our daughter."

Marie walked over, knelt down on the floor, and looked into her eyes. "Gina, losing you was the worst time of my entire life. I cried every night for a year. I don't know how I've gotten you back, but I'm never going to lose you again. Give us a chance, please."

"What's going to happen to my parents? Will I ever see them again?"

Marie looked over at Michael and could see the understanding in his eyes. "How about we go home now and spend a little time getting reacquainted and tonight we invite the Roizins to our house for dinner and all get to know one another? Does that sound like a plan?"

Gina reached out and placed her hands on both sides of Marie's face and looked into her eyes.

"Thank you. That sounds like a good plan," Gina responded.

Marie took a piece of stationery from the drawer and wrote down her name and address with an invitation to their house for dinner at 7:00 p.m.

"Excuse me," she said to the FBI Agent at the door, "but would you make sure this gets to the Roizin family upstairs?"

"No problem, ma'am," he replied.

Chapter 92

Scott and Amy Fisher, as expected, once again had the smoothest transition. Patricia Panzer entered the room full of fight and immediately announced, "Hi, my name is Patricia Panzer." She then took one look at her mother, realized she looked exactly like her, and forgot her entire argument.

Fortunately, Amy had her covered.

"First of all, your name is not Patricia. It's Samantha. If you want to be called Patricia, we can discuss it, but it's not your legal name. Secondly, I have read the entire file on the people who thought they adopted you, Kenny and Carol Panzer. They are wonderful people, and I will never be able to thank them enough. Aside from bringing you back to me, they cared enough about you to risk losing you, and that says it all. So I don't want you to be concerned about losing them. Scott and I will have them over for dinner tonight and formally adopt them into our family. You will, however, have to get used to calling her Carol as I am going to insist on being called Mom. You have a three-year-old brother named Sam, and now, if it's okay with you, I would like to hug you for at least ten minutes," and that was exactly what she did.

Chapter 93

And then came Emma Whitcup. Having rehearsed their entrances together, Jill entered In the same fashion as Patricia Panzer.

"Hi," she said, "my name is Jill Diamond."

"Hi, Jill," said Winnie. "My name is Whitney Whitcup, and this is my husband Nathaniel. My friends call me Winnie."

"And my friends call me Nate."

"We read the file," said Winnie, "and it seems that you are the person that set this investigation in motion?"

"It was really Patricia. We've become good friends."

"I read that you remembered being in the bus with Adam and Todd, and that's what set off the bells and whistles. Do you remember anything else about your life here in Colorado?"

"No, I don't. I'm sorry."

"There's nothing for you to be sorry about, Jill. Tell me about the Diamonds."

"They're so nice. I knew that I was adopted, but I didn't remember anything before the Diamonds, so it never really bothered me too much. I have a lot of friends, and I have a twelve-year-old brother named Jason, who's great, and he plays basketball."

A few tears trickled down Winnie's face, and she wasn't able to continue, so Nate squeezed in next to her.

"You seem like a very bright girl, Jill," Nate continued, "so I'm going to talk about our situation and be honest with you. Okay?"

"Okay," Jill replied.

"Good. Here's my life in sixty seconds."

"Three generations of Whitcups have been business tycoons. I was the fourth generation. I did all the proper schooling and traveling. My path was set. I took over the business that my father and his father before him had always dedicated their lives to, no, their souls to. There was no salvation for me. I was the CEO of Whitcup, Whitcup, and Whitcup, and at the age of twenty, I was already working eighteen-hour days.

"I had no time for a social life or friends. There was only the company. I ate, drank, and dreamed work. There was nothing else. That was my destiny, and I accepted it.

"In May 2006, my mother of all people interrupted me at work and told me she had arranged for me to take a friend's daughter to dinner. I was furious at the interruption, but I could not embarrass my mother, and so I took your mother out to dinner.

"I was so rude in the beginning of the evening that Whitney asked to be taken home, and in a moment of clarity, I knew that if I let her go, it would be my ruination. So I apologized and begged her for another chance.

"She rescued me and changed my entire value system. I was happy for the first time in my life. More than happy actually. I was head over heels in love.

"We were married in February 2007. Winnie became pregnant with you in October 2007 and gave birth to you on July 4, 2008. It was such a glorious day that people all across the country had firework displays and shot Roman candles into the sky. They might have been celebrating the holiday. I'm not sure.

"What I'm getting at is, this is the most wonderful person I have ever met. I went from a business nerd to a loving husband and father. We moved onto the mountain in the summer of 2010. I think it was July, and you were just two, Emma."

Jill heard the name change but just nodded that she was following the story.

"If love and marriage and having a family could be perfect, then we were perfect. I loved my wife, my daughter, and my life in that order. At the time of the accident, Winnie was six weeks pregnant, and in 2011, we had a son Mark, your brother.

"During the afternoons that last summer, you and your friend Patricia or Samantha, and Adam and Todd would play up on the mountain together while your mother and her friends painted with their friend Alicia who's a very talented artist. It was like a fairy tale, and when the snow came to Aspen, we would take you skiing on the beginner slopes. You had a friend Charlie whose father Paul was a ski instructor. We were having the best life until one morning it all fell apart.

"We know that the Diamonds love you. How could they not? We know it's going to be difficult not to be living in their home with your friends and your brother, Jason, but we will do whatever is necessary to make you happy here. We have no intention of shutting out the Diamonds. They have become a part of your life and, therefore, will become a part of ours. We both live in nice places to visit, Colorado and New York, and they will have an open invitation here."

Nate noticed as he was talking that Emma had assumed her old position when confronted or was upset. Her hands were on her hips, and her head was tilted to the side with that "you're not fooling me!" expression.

"We want our daughter back, and we will make any sacrifices necessary to make you a part of our family again."

Jill walked into Nate's open arms and got a big hug, followed by the same from Winnie.

"We're going to go home now and get you settled in. Tonight we will have dinner at our house with the Diamonds and get to know one another. How's that sound?"

"It sounds like you guys are really terrific."

"As are you, Emma Whitcup, as are you."

Chapter 94

Last of the friends to be united with their children and certainly the most difficult were the Barnums. Karen and Michael were a combination of intensely excited and excruciatingly nervous.

They brought down Adam first, figuring one at a time would be better and it would be easier to get to know the well-adjusted son before all three of them met the child with the problems.

Adam walked in and introduced himself, "Hello, Mr. and Mrs. Barnum, my name is Melvin Kent." Melvin was very tall for his age, and as soon as his parents got up and walked over to greet him, he knew why. Damn, his mother must be six feet tall and his father was about six-and-a-half.

"You are really tall," Melvin said. "Did you ever play any basketball?"

"Actually, I played two years with USC and two years with the University of Rhoda Island, where I met your mother."

Melvin looked at Karen. "Did you play basketball also?"

"No, Melvin, I'm just tall. I find it very difficult to call you Melvin, even though I know that's been your name for as long as you can remember. Would you mind if I called you Adam? I know it may take some getting used to, but it is your real name."

"Karen," Michael cut in, "he's been Melvin for four years. Let's give him some time to get adjusted before we ask him to make those changes."

"Are you guys kidding?" Melvin replied. "Do you know any six-year-old who wants to be called Melvin? If it's okay with you guys, I'll be Adam from now on."

"Well," said Michael, "looks like we made everyone happy with that move. We read about the Kents, and they seem like very nice people. We're thankful that they found you and took such good care of you. We want you to know that they can be as much a part of your life as you'd like. So don't worry about not seeing them or becoming distant. That's not going to happen. As for the immediate change, I think you will find it exciting. Bob tells me you are really into sports, and we have all that here, plus spring skiing."

"Don't they have spring skiing in New York?" asked Adam.

"They do occasionally, but it's very cold. You can ski in 70-degree weather in a short-sleeved shirt and shorts in Aspen, where the snow is like powder instead of ice. When you look at people who have skied their whole lives in New York and then start skiing on powder, you can see their faces light up. You'll love it!"

"Sounds great."

"Now let's discuss something that's not so great. Are you aware that you are a twin?"

"My father, sorry, Bob told me last night, but I never saw him yesterday. He was kept in a separate room. This morning, he sat in the back of the plane and never walked near us or raised his head. Is he retarded?"

"No, he was fine when he was two, before you both disappeared. He was taken by a woman who treated him like a doll instead of a boy. He's had no schooling. No one's taught him how to read. He's never had any friends. This woman led him everywhere like a pet on a leash. He has no social skills. Fortunately, he's only six, and now he has Karen and me and you to make him well again."

Michael nodded to the FBI agent at the door, and he walked down the hall and brought back Todd. The social worker accompanied him into the room, and they both sat on the couch.

Karen got up and sat on the other side of Todd. "Hi, Todd, we're so happy you've come back to us. My name is Karen, and I'm your mother. This is Michael, and he's your father, and this boy next to you, the one that looks exactly like you, is your twin brother. His name is Adam."

"Adam, why don't you come over and let Todd see how much you look alike?"

Adam walked up to Todd and stuck his face right in front of his. "Hi, Todd, we're twins."

Todd put his finger on his brother's nose and laughed.

Karen couldn't keep a few tears from streaming down her face, but for the most part, she held up pretty well.

"You're right, Michael," she said. "This is not going to be an easy job, but I think the three of us can handle it."

Adam, standing between his parents, put one arm around each of their necks and said, "You bet we can."

Karen could feel her heart swelling.

Michael stood up and called the agent over. "Please ask the Kent family if they would join us for dinner at our home at 7:00 p.m."

"I think we're done here. Let's go home."

Chapter 95

The five Mason families left with their children and drove back to their homes. There was no fanfare, no commotion, and no FBI. There were just the five families, looking for a little privacy and a chance to bring their families back together.

Steve and Sam sat in the lobby and watched them walk to their cars.

"What do you think, Steve?"

"I think we did the best we could with the time constraints, and I think it went pretty well, as well as it could have. I see only better days ahead. How about you, Sam?"

"I'd like to give it a few days before I make any predictions."

"Well, I'm really happy with the way we dealt with the families. It looks like all the natural parents have made a commitment to include the adoptive parents, and even those children who were adamant about staying with their new parents seem to have found the middle road."

"I will admit, Sam, that I was surprised that the Byrnne family made such a quick adjustment. I know they're wonderful people, but they still surprised me."

"And how about the shit-eating grin on the faces of the Marx family. They thought they were attending a funeral and found out it was a wedding. It makes sense, you know. Stark had left that life and his wife years ago and couldn't even relate to becoming a single father, but nevertheless it was still a shock."

"By the way, Sam, Alicia and Howard Langston invited us to dinner tonight at their house. All the other families will be attending dinner parties with their children's parents. It wouldn't be a bad idea to be around just in case. I'd also like you to meet Laura before you leave."

"It sounds like a good idea. Count me in. By the way, who was that woman who was talking to all your friends as they were leaving before?"

"That was Carly Stephens. She's the psychiatrist that worked with the parents when the accident occurred in 2010. They had a connection with her, and I thought a few of them might be able to use her services now."

"You know, Steve, for a treasury guy, you're not so dumb."

"Easy with the compliments. You'll give me a swelled head. And come up a little early so I can show you the mountain before it gets dark."

"Will do, Steve."

Chapter 96

The rides back to Mason were uneventful for all the families with the exception of the Byrnne family. Halfway home, Charlie leaned over between Paul and Tracy and said, "Listen, you guys know all about me from that file of yours, but I think there's one thing you missed."

Tracy and Paul both held their breath and awaited what could only be another heartbreaker.

Paul thought, *One or both of them must have molested him. I may have to find these animals and kill them.*

Tracy thought, *Maybe he wants to leave? He's been on his own for four years and now he has to listen to strangers tell him what time he has to go to bed. Maybe he wants to go back to Texas and his housekeeper.*

"Hey," Charlie laughed, "are you guys still here?"

"Sorry, Charlie," Paul replied, "but every time someone says here's something I haven't told you, it sends shivers up and down my spine."

"Sorry about that. This is nothing bad. In Seattle, Rob, the guy who played my father, handed me an envelope and told me to give it you guys. He said it would take care of my future and that it was the least he could do. So here it is," and he passed over an envelope to Tracy.

Paul looked at Tracy and said, "You might as well open it. It won't bite."

Tracy ripped open the envelope and pulled out a check made out to Paul and Tracy Byrnne, in trust for Charlie Byrnne. "Well, I have to admit I wasn't expecting this!"

"What does the letter say?" Paul asked, as he turned up Mason Drive.

"It's not a letter, Paul. It's a check made out to us in trust for Charlie, for the sum of one million dollars."

"You're kidding!"

"Not even a little."

"Wow," said Charlie, "a million dollars! Am I rich?"

"You will be when you're older, but right now, you're still a six-year-old with an allowance. It means that your college education is guaranteed as well as any postgraduate education you might pursue. We will invest that money today, and it will also provide you with a significant amount of money that will become available to you when you reach the age of twenty-five or thirty."

"That's cool!"

"No surprise there," said Tracy. "Paul and I have always been cool."

"That's a fact, Jack. Hot stuff, in the groove, the main man and big mama!"

"Stop already. You guys are making me nauseous!"

That broke Tracy up, and by the time they reached the guardhouse, they were all doubled over laughing.

Chapter 97

Helena Pierce answered her doorbell at 2:00 p.m. The FBI agent on the stoop asked if he could speak with both Helena and her husband Ira at the same time.

He sat down in their living room, and a few minutes later, Ira Pierce came down from his study.

"I was notified a few days ago that I should expect someone to come by today and to make sure my wife and I were home. Maybe you can explain what this is all about and why all this cloak and dagger stuff is necessary."

"If you want me to explain it to you, I would be glad to, Mr. Pierce. If, on the other hand, you would read this file first, I think you will get a far better explanation than I could ever give you."

"Before I sit down and read what looks to be at least 100 pages of an FBI file, would it be possible to give me some inkling of what this is all about?"

"Certainly. In 2010, your son Arnold was killed in an SUV on Mason Mountain."

"We are well aware of that fact, Agent!"

"Please, Mr. Pierce, allow me thirty seconds before responding."

"Yes, of course, continue."

"Your son was not killed crashing into an Exxon storage facility. He was never in that SUV that fell off the mountain. All the children in that SUV were abducted and transferred into a different vehicle after the driver was shot and before their SUV was driven off the mountain and into the gasoline tank.

"Your son was at first chloroformed and then given Valium sedation through an IV. Sometime between his abduction in Mason and his arrival at a lake house in Seattle, Arnold overdosed and died. We believe the people responsible took him out into the middle of a lake along with Ben Webster, the driver, weighted them down and pushed them over the side."

"And this story comes from what source?" asked Ira Pierce, trying to stay calm.

"Mr. and Mrs. Pierce, the file in front of you is a comprehensive investigation that began last Sunday. It's all there—the people who performed these nefarious acts, the lawyers who abducted children from all over the country and sold them to families who thought they were adopting them, and all the people that were murdered during these years. It describes in detail all the court cases that are ongoing and the reason the FBI acted as it did so that as many children could be found and returned to their parents as possible."

"How many of the other children were found?" asked Helena Pierce.

"All of them."

"Our son was the only one that died?"

"I'm sorry, ma'am, but, yes, he was the only one. We don't need anything else from you and your husband. We arranged to tell you at this exact time because all the felons and lawyers have been indicted and will no longer be able to make an attempt at eliminating evidence. In your case, we didn't want you to hear about this investigation on the news or from a neighbor.

"Please read the file when you get a chance. I'm sure it will be a great deal more comprehensive than my narration. I am truly sorry that we could not have made things easier for you this week, but this was the only way we could accomplish all our goals without possibly causing problems for the people involved, including the children. Please forgive the intrusion. I hope this is the last time you are inconvenienced. Good-bye."

Chapter 98

Five families returned to Mason: Barnums, Fishers, Whitcups, Corritores, and Byrnnes. In addition, Alicia and Carly Stephens had been driven back earlier.

The first sight the families observed upon returning was a banner set up in the memorial lot that read The Arnold Pierce Memorial Playground. William had removed all the previous miniature tombstones.

It was 4:30 p.m. Everyone, except the Byrnne family, was expecting dinner guest at 7:00 p.m. Alicia and Carly greeted each family as they drove in and asked that a member of each family walk over to the park at 5:00 p.m. for a fifteen-minute meeting. They proceeded to their homes with their children who hadn't been there in over four years and got them comfortable. Each of the women then walked over to the playground.

Alicia stood next to Carly, and when all the women had arrived, she said, "If you've got this covered, that's fine. Carly and I have had an hour or so to discuss what you're going through today, and it occurred to us that you might need a little guidance. We'll tell you our thoughts, and then you can all make your own decisions with your husbands. If any of you object to this, if you think this is an intrusion and you don't need one right now, then please go home. You will not hurt our feelings. If, after we talk, you disagree with our ideas, then please ignore them. We know it's hard for you to think rationally right now, and we're just trying to offer you suggestions.

"Okay, here goes. Let's start with you, Karen. In my mind, you have the most difficult situation to deal with. Not only do you have to bring Adam into your family and make some sort of accommodation with the Kent family, but you have Todd to deal with, and that's a project in itself. Carly, why don't you take over? This is your area of expertise."

"Okay, thanks, Alicia. Here's what I think, Karen. I spoke to Adam before and after you saw him today. The Kents did a wonderful job raising him. He's a nice, confident boy with a big heart. I don't think anything could be as important to Todd as his relationship with Adam. My suggestion would be to explain to the Kents that for these next few years at least, you will not let Adam be separated from his brother. With that in mind if they would like to come to Colorado and visit, they will always be welcome. I've spoken with the Kents, and I believe they will be very understanding about your problem.

"Another thing that none of you are aware of," continued Alicia, "is that the owners of the Aspen Hotel Chain are allowing one free week's lodging at the hotel available for the next five years for any of the children's visiting parents."

"These are the nicest people," Marie said. "First they help us with housing and now this. I think we should write them a letter and tell them what it means to know that they care this much."

All the girls nodded in agreement.

"Now let's take Tracy," Carly continued. "There's four years of a miserable upbringing to get out of Charlie's system. I like your chances. Charlie's been spoiled rotten, but more importantly, he's healthy and he's smart. You also have the added benefit of no interference whatsoever. Charlie already understands that the Fosters were terrible role models, and I think you will be amazed that as soon as he understands he's six years old and has parents now that he can look up to, he'll be fine.

"Amy, Winnie, and Marie, you have your work cut out for you. I've met the Panzers, the Diamonds, and the Roizins. They are three of the nicest couples I've ever met. The Roizins are so devastated at losing their daughter that I am seriously worried about their mental health going forward. If you read the initial interviews that they had with the FBI, you know that through their tears, they understood immediately that their daughter belonged to her natural parents and were appreciative of the fact that Agents Orzo and Pierce were making an effort not to exclude them completely.

"The Panzers were instrumental in the discovery of this abduction. As soon as Jill contacted their daughter, they knew that continuing the investigation and bringing in the FBI could result in the loss of their daughter. The Diamond family was also aware that they could lose their child, and yet they both acted in the best interests of the girls, not themselves.

"My first reaction was that these couples should be rewarded. You should bend over backward to make sure they are not hurt any more than they already have been. It took me one minute of reflection to realize that wasn't possible. The people you must consider first and foremost are your daughters.

"Alicia and I have been discussing this for the past two hours and think we have come up with the best scenario available. You cannot share children. Eventually, your girls will be your girls again and their parents from two-year-old until six-year-old will become somewhere between good friends and great relatives. These next few years though, nothing could be more harmful to these girls than being forced into severing ties with the only family they remember. More than anything else, you must impress upon your daughters that their real parents would never do anything to cause them pain.

"My suggestion, and it's just a suggestion, is to let your girls visit their foster parents and the friends they left behind for two weeks this coming summer, that's eight months from now. I would also allow the foster parents a one—week visit here in Colorado sometime between then and now. I would do that for the next two years and then revisit the situation and see how everyone has progressed.

"Additionally, and I know how hard this is going to be for you, I would make sure your girls have an open line of communication with their previous families, whether it be by phone or on the Internet. Emma, in particular, has a brother in New York that she adores. I would wager right now that they will always be close. Over this next year and the next few months in particular, your children should always be permitted to contact their former families and never feel that it's wrong to miss them.

"I will be going home now, but before I leave, I want all of you to know that this week has been like a wonderful dream. I still have trouble believing that all my friends have their children back. I love you all, and if you need me for anything, you have my number." Carly and Alicia gave bear hugs to all their friends and sent them home to get dinner ready.

Chapter 99

Seattle, Washington
December 15, 2014

On the first day of trials in the Washington Supreme Court, both Trudy Miller and Ed Flakowitz were convicted of second degree murder, kidnapping, and child abduction and were sentenced in accordance with their plea bargains to twenty years and fifteen years, respectively.

The trial of Dominic Merano lasted a week, and after deliberating for less than thirty minutes, the jury returned a guilty verdict with a recommendation for the death penalty. The judge upheld the recommendation and gave February 10, 2015, as the date of execution.

The trials of Larry Levin, Howard Rosenberg, and Peter Gold began on January 3, 2015. The evidence against the three was so overwhelming that everyone involved was extremely confident. The only thing in question was the degree of punishment. Guilty was a given.

The defense team representing Gold, Rosenberg, and Flakowitz had no misconceptions. There was a pile of evidence against their clients and a long line of witnesses ready to testify, but they weren't the top criminal defense lawyers in the country for no reason.

Somewhere during the third week of the trial, Margo finished producing evidence and witnesses and rested her case. She smiled at Sam, who was sitting a few rows behind the prosecution's table with a look of total confidence. She had presented an excellent case.

All the Mason families had testified in addition to many of the families that had tried to adopt. After they gave their testimony, all of them returned home with the exception of Ira Pierce, who sat in the same seat in the back of the courtroom every day and listened intently to every witness and all the testimony.

It was during the fourth week of the trial that the defense made its argument. The lead attorney for the defense was a silver-haired gentleman named Walter Higgins. Higgins was possibly the most successful and expensive defense attorney in the country and for good reason. He was a miracle worker. The evidence became irrelevant if Higgins was defending you. If you could afford him, there was an excellent possibility that you would get off.

Ira Pierce was well aware of who Walter Higgins was, and for that reason, he sat expressionless every day, watching the trial and trying to make an objective assessment as to how he would be leaning if he was on the jury.

On the fifth week, Higgins began taking the prosecution's case apart. He began with Peter Gold.

"Ladies and Gentlemen of the jury, Peter Gold has been an upstanding lawyer in Seattle for four decades. All the witnesses who have testified as to their adoption process have named several lawyers they interacted with. Not one, I repeat, not one has mentioned Peter Gold. The only witness to connect Peter Gold with these abductions is his old secretary Edna Collins. This is an unbalanced woman who has been categorized by her husband as a few cards short of a full deck. This is a woman who in 2010 took an abducted child home and kept him for four years. She did not adopt him. She did not provide a temporary foster home for him. She simply took him. Over the next four years, she never enrolled him in school. She never homeschooled him. She simply used him for company. All the testimony she provided was given after agreeing to a plea bargain with the district attorney. In exchange for putting away Peter Gold, the district attorney agreed to drop all charges. If I were Edna Collins, I would have gone after Peter Gold myself. Her husband testified that his wife brought home a two-year-old four years ago and claimed she adopted him. He further acknowledged that she treated him like a pet and took him out with her every day. The only other people to implicate Peter Gold in these proceedings are one drug addict who received a plea bargain and two lawyers who received lighter sentences in exchange for their testimony.

"As it's Friday, Your Honor, I would like to stop here and continue on Monday. At that time, I will show how the prosecution has put a case together against my clients by accumulating circumstantial evidence combined with a series of plea bargaining deals with a drug addict and a psychotic woman with absolutely no sense of morality."

Sam glanced over at Margo. Her confident look had been replaced by a slight frown. His attention was diverted by the sound of the courtroom door closing. He glanced left and found the now empty seat of Ira Pierce.

Steve, Sam, and Margo met at the Highstrike Grill to discuss the case.

Steve began the first toast with a glass of merlot. "To a great team. I've got to admit I never thought we could put it all together in one week, but I think you presented a great case. I'm still on a high. You were incredible, Margo."

Margo was next to lift her glass. "Thank you for the compliment, but it's far from over. I don't know if you were watching the jurors, but I saw a lot of nods while Higgins was making his case. I'm starting to think we bit off too much. Maybe we should have gone after the big two and not gotten greedy. In any case,

I couldn't have nailed any of these monsters if you two hadn't run around like Batman and Robin and gotten me everything I needed to put this group away."

"Which one of us is Batman? Seriously, Steve, I want to be Batman."

"You are such an idiot, Sam!"

"I'm sorry, but I always thought Robin was the meaningless part of the duo."

"Okay, Sam, you can be Batman. Either way, I haven't spent two days in a row with my wife since we started this investigation. I'm on a plane to Colorado this afternoon."

"I don't care if you're Batman or Robin, Sam," replied Margo, "as long as you hang around here this week and make good on all those promises you've been making to me long distance."

"I think that's my cue to leave. Good luck to both of you, and on the serious side, thank you both. This case meant a lot to me personally, and I'm just thankful it turned out the way it did."

"So are we, Steve," said Sam, "so are we." They all touched glasses.

Chapter 100

October 16, 2014

Winnie and Nate made a barbecue for 7 Mason. The Orzos were honorary members. They were definitely a larger group, but they were all back together.

There were no more hysterical scenes, although it was hard not to get emotional watching Michael teaching the basics of basketball to Adam and Scott or Charlie eating a hot dog and laughing at a private joke with his sister, Charlotte.

Alicia and William sat with Steve and Laura and watched their friends enjoying each other.

Steve lifted his bottle of Budweiser, looked out at all his friends, and lifted his glass. "Here's to the only miracle I've ever seen with my own eyes. My friends are whole again. Their children are reborn. Here we sit as if nothing ever happened, looking at what has to be one of the most beautiful vistas on the planet."

"I'll drink to that," said Charlie Byrnne, tilting a bottle of Bud to his lips.

"One sip of that passes your lips," yelled Tracy, "and you'll wish you were back in Texas!"

William held Alicia's hand and breathed in the beauty that surrounded them. "You know, my love, this place is starting to look good to me again."

Chapter 101

Sunday February 8, 2015

At 9:00 a.m. in the breakfast hall at the Pine Lodge Correctional Center for Women just outside of Spokane, Washington, Mary Evans Dressler sat calmly eating her scrambled eggs and oatmeal. She had served ten years of a thirty—year sentence for stabbing her cheating husband thirty-one times in the chest. She had two daughters that moved in with her mother that she had not seen once since she was convicted.

Mary was an ideal prisoner. She was soft-spoken. She liked to read, stayed to herself, and never gave any of the guards a problem. They more or less ignored her.

Mary finished her breakfast, turned to Trudy Miller, who was having breakfast on her left, and plunged her butter knife through Trudy's right eye until it wouldn't go in any further. She then took Trudy's butter knife and stuck it in Trudy's heart. She then calmly finished her coffee and was dumping her tray in the garbage bin when they grabbed her arms and took her away.

Coincidentally, at approximately the same time at Walla Walla State Penitentiary, a racial conflict arose between the Surenos and the Nortenos. These outbreaks happened occasionally, and normally the person or persons involved were taught a lesson, and the fight petered out. This fight continued for over forty minutes and left three dead and two injured. What was unusual about this mini-riot was that the three dead men were all gringos: Larry Levin, Howard Rosenberg, and Peter Gold.

At 3:00 p.m., Dominic took his one hour in the yard. He was about to go in when he noticed that Tyson, who never moved unless he was eating and never looked anyone in the eye, was smiling at him. This was interesting, and months could go by without anything being interesting. Tyson walked over to where Dominic was standing against the wall. He was standing over him, and it was as if a building was in his face.

"What are you so happy about, Tyson?"

"I don't have to worry about my girls no more." He slowly extended his right arm and locked his hand around Dominic's throat. He lifted him off the ground until he was looking directly into his eyes and squeezed his throat until he was seconds away from suffocating. "I got to say this exactly. Arnold Pierce sends his condolences." Dominic's eyes blinked his understanding, at which point Tyson squeezed his right hand and broke every bone in Dominic's throat, killing him instantly!

Chapter 102

That afternoon, Steve and Laura were sitting at the playground with Daniel when Steve's cell phone rang.

"Hey, Sam. It's Sunday. Don't you ever rest?"

"I guess you haven't heard the latest news up there on the mountain?"

"No, I haven't heard anything. What happened?"

At nine o'clock this morning in a women's prison outside of Spokane, Trudy Miller was stabbed to death by a fellow inmate. At about the same time at Walla Walla, there was a gang fight between two Mexican groups, which amazing enough resulted in the deaths of Larry Levin, Howard Rosenberg, and Peter Gold, and about an hour ago, Dominic Merano had his throat crushed by a fellow inmate and died instantly.

"You know it can't be a coincidence," Sam continued. "Two Mexican gangs have a war and three white lawyers get killed. On the same day, a prisoner who has never said a harsh word to anyone except her husband kills Trudy Miller, and then Merano gets knocked off. The list of potentials is extremely small, Steve."

"Smaller than you can imagine, Sam."

"Why do you say that, Steve?"

"Today is February 8, isn't it?"

"Yeah, so?"

"Today is Arnold Pierce's birthday."

"Holy shit! What are we going to do?"

"I don't know about you, Sam, but I am a strong believer in coincidence. I'm going to throw a few burgers on the barbecue and enjoy the evening with my family. I think you should buy Margo some flowers, take her out for a romantic dinner, and try your best to keep a smile off your face, the same way I'm going to try to keep a smile off mine. Good-bye, Sam."